Lord Harrow's Heart

Susan M. Baganz

Contact Information: titleadmin@pelicanbookgroup.com

Scripture quotations, unless otherwise indicated are taken from the King James translation, public domain.

Cover Art by *Nicola Martinez*

Prism is a division of Pelican Ventures, LLC
www.pelicanbookgroup.com
PO Box 1738 *Aztec, NM * 87410

Publishing History
Prism Edition, 2018
Electronic Edition ISBN 978-1-5223-9792-2
Paperback Edition ISBN 978-1-5223-9794-6
Published in the United States of America

BOOKS BY SUSAN M. BAGANZ

Black Diamond Regency Romantic Suspense
The Baron's Blunder (Prequel) novella
The Virtuous Viscount (Book 1)
Lord Phillip's Folly (Book 2)
Sir Michael's Mayhem (Book 3)
Lord Harrow's Heart (Book 4)
The Captain's Conquest (coming soon)

Orchard Hill Contemporary Romances
Pesto & Potholes
Salsa & Speed Bumps
Feta & Freeways
Root Beer & Roadblocks
Bratwurst & Bridges
Donuts & Detours
and others coming soon!

Historical Christmas Novella
Fragile Blessings
Gabriel's Gift

Short Story Compilation
Little Bits O' Love

Dedication

To Heidi B. who has been a sweet friend, a listening ear, and a coach as we both navigate this tumultious journey through life. Thank you for being there for chai and chat, and everything in between.

Author's Note

During the tempestuous years between 1800-1820 or the more specific "Regency" years of 1811 to 1820, it was common for the upper classes, especially the men, to drink various forms of alcohol as part of their daily life. A glass of port wine was often savored by the men after the evening meal. French brandy was considered superior and highly coveted even though England was at war with France. In these stories my characters do at times drink, and sometimes even to excess with serious consequences for their overindulgence. This is not in any way a recommendation on the part of the author or Pelican Book Group to advocate the drinking of alcohol or to abuse any substance. Laudanum is an opiate that was often prescribed medicinally (although many did become addicted to the drug). The use of these in the story are merely an attempt to use this period in history and its notorious excesses as a backdrop where appropriate.

Lord, I don't know where to go or who to trust.
Please keep my son and me safe from the evil that surrounds us.
Lady Valeria St. John

Heart
Καϱδία kardia kar-dee'-ah the heart, i.e. (figuratively) the thoughts or feelings (mind), also (by analogy) the middle; - +(broken)heart(ed)

But as it is written, eye hath not seen, nor ear heard,
neither have entered into the heart of man,
the things which God hath prepared
for them that love him.
1 Corinthians 2:9 (KJV)

Prologue

The Duke of Diamonte, also known as the elusive Black Diamond, stewed as he paced the expensive Turkish carpet in his study. His staff had been wisely avoiding him since he'd returned to the estate.

He'd killed the wife and unborn child of Sir Michael Tidley, his by-blow from a liaison designed to ruin Tidley's grandfather. Michael had proven a worthy adversary, but he'd have to deal with him at some other time. For now, his focus turned to his grandson, Dartanian. Since his only legitimate son, Damon, had died, the Duke had been stalking his daughter-in-law, Valeria. The emotional games he played with her were nothing compared to what he would do when he found her again.

Valeria had done well in covering her tracks. He grew frustrated with the fruitless efforts of his minions in searching for her and his grandson. When he found them, he had plans to torture her further. He'd never hurt the boy. At least not yet. Too many grand dreams were tied up in that lad whether or not his mother cooperated. He had no qualms about punishing Valeria. She had cost him precious time. She would pay dearly for her betrayal in leaving. He knew just how to draw her back into his lair.

"Bellen!" he called for his butler.

The weak-kneed man was slow in responding. "Yes, my lord?"

"Have my horse saddled and a bag packed. I depart for London within the hour."

The man bowed and backed out of the room, shaking in fear.

The Duke stood and stared into the fire. “Soon, sweet Valeria. Soon you will wish you had never crossed me and rue the day I rescued you. I may have a use for you yet. A spare son is always an asset.” He clenched his teeth. She would never leave here again and once he had a second son to replace Damon, not even her precious Dartanian would be safe. Such was the fate of those who crossed him.

Once he found his grandson…he could move forward with his plans.

1

London 1812

The perfectly matched black horses pranced down Rotten Row in Hyde Park. The sun shimmered on their muscular flanks as the high-steppers moved along pulling the open carriage.

"What do you think, Phillip?" Lord Theodore Harrow asked as he loosely held the reigns.

"They are a sight to behold, Theo, but why are you even considering buying this pair? You own enough horseflesh already. I realize you possess the money to spend, but as beautiful as these horses are, they appear high-strung to me."

"I don't have your dashing good looks, Phillip. If I want to attract a bride, I need to be noticed."

Phillip shook his head and laughed. "Theo, all you need to do is show up at a dance and propose to any young debutante there. They would trip over themselves to get your ring on their finger."

"All for a title and my money."

"What's wrong with that? It is the way many marriages in the *ton* are made." Phillip's eyebrows went up as he folded his arms. "It's not worth them loving you for the horses in your stable."

"You have all managed to make love matches. I want a woman who will love me. *Me*. Not my title or wealth. I want what you, Marcus, and Michael have."

"Are you willing to go through what we went through to get there, Theo? I don't regret anything when it comes to my dearest Beth. I would prefer to have done it without the kidnapping and attempted murder of both her, me, and our unborn child."

Theo waved a hand at this friend. "You came out all right in the end."

Phillip sighed, and Theo could sense his gaze on him. How could he get his friend to understand? His friends and their wives adored each other. For once Theo wanted a woman to gaze at him like Elizabeth looked at Phillip. Or Josie at Marcus. Or Katrina at Michael. He was left behind in the game of love. He wanted someone to love him for who he was inside. He decided to drop the conversation for the moment. He'd hoped Phillip would understand.

"What about God, Theo? Have you considered your relationship with Him?"

"Pardon?" Theo almost dropped the reins in surprise. "Why would you bring that up?"

"You want love. The basis of love that we all have with our wives is Jesus Christ. I realize that for Michael and me, it didn't start out that way, but now I cannot imagine any way I could be happily married to anyone without having God as part of the equation."

Theo clenched his teeth. "I don't want to talk about religion on a beautiful morning like this." The clip clop of the horses' hooves kept time to the symphony of bird sounds from the trees around them.

His friend let the subject drop for now but it would probably be raised again. While Marcus never preached at him, Phillip and Michael had been exerting more pressure on him to explore Christ and a "relationship" with him. Absurd.

As if God would care to have a relationship with him. Most women weren't interested except for his title and wealth and beyond that, he possessed little else to offer to God. He shook his head and focused on the beautiful horses pulling his new carriage.

The park was sparse this morning in the way of human traffic. There were a few governesses or nurses with their young charges, taking the air. The elite, fashionable crowd was still sleeping off the previous night's excesses.

Theo yawned. He would go home and back to bed when he was done here. There were no other plans.

A horse jolted, and the reins were almost pulled out of Theo's hands as the other one reared. With a jerk the carriage moved forward at greater speed.

"What?" Theo yelled, "Whoa!" He pulled back on the reins, but the horses plunged forward anyway.

"Get them under control, Theo."

"What did you think I was doing? Waltzing with them?" Really, Phillip could be quite irritating at times. He would have asked Michael to join him today, but he was still in the country.

The horses careened off the road and by sheer force of will, Theo urged them back on.

A small child ran into their path and stopped to stare as they bore down on him. As the nightmarish consequences raced through his brain, Theo pulled back on the reins with all his might. "Pull the brake, Phillip!"

The horses reared and pawed in the air. Theo feared the child would be killed underneath their sharp hooves.

A woman dressed in black rushed forward and pushed the child out of the way as the horses' hooves came crashing back to the ground.

Phillip gasped out loud. The horses went only a little beyond the accident and finally slowed, foam forming on their heaving sides. Theo threw the reins to Phillip and jumped down to run back to the prone figure lying in the grass. His heart beat fast and sweat beaded on his forehead. He reached the individual, her face and form faced away from him. He moved around her and knelt. Blonde hair escaped its pins and the cap she'd worn was laying close by. "Ma'am?"

He reached out to brush the hair off her face and checked her pulse. She was alive. Theo sighed in relief. He moved to roll her to her back and uncovered the little boy tucked underneath her.

The young man stood up, red-faced. He kicked the ribs of the woman who'd saved his life. She didn't make a sound. "How dare you? My mama is going to be told about this and you will be fired!" The little boy's face was scrunched up and his bottom lip stuck out.

Theo grabbed the young man's arms and turned him so he could glare in his stubborn face. "You, young man, are fortunate to be alive. What were you thinking running away from your nanny? You could have been killed!"

The boy folded his arms across his chest and began tapping his feet and yawned. "How dare you talk to me that way? Don't you realize who I am?"

"You are a spoiled little boy with more sass than sense," Theo proclaimed, but he did release his arms from the boy.

"I am Master Reginald Fishbottom."

Theo snorted at the proclamation. Fishbottom was a name associated with trade. He'd met a couple who must be this brat's parents at one event. Social climbers trying to use money to buy title and status and doomed to fail because of their puffed-up arrogance.

"Well, Master Fishbottom. Lord Theodore, Marquess of Harrow at your service. What is your governess's name? I will attempt to rouse her and escort you both back to your home in my barouche."

The boy's eyes lit up as he glanced over at the shiny carriage and the now calm and docile horses grazing with Phillip by their side.

"Can I go by the horses?" The boy's eyes were bright now, his face smudged and dirty.

"Her name first, if you please."

The boy glanced at his caretaker with eyes narrowed and a scowl. "Mrs. Wilson," he spat out. He raised his eyebrows at Theo expectantly.

"Lord Westcombe is with the horses. You may go wait by him."

The young man's scorn was replaced by a grin and he ran over to the carriage.

Theo turned his focus to the woman lying in the road in front of him. Her face was dirty and a cut on her cheekbone showed where she'd been grazed. "Mrs. Wilson?" He touched her shoulder and shook her gently.

She moaned in pain and her brown eyes opened to look up at him.

Theo's heart skipped a beat as he gazed at her. Bruised and dirty she still took his breath away. "Mrs. Wilson?" He asked more gently and her eyes narrowed.

"Do I know you? What happened?" She looked around and spied the horses and carriage as well as her charge off in the distance. "Reginald!" If she was trying to yell, she failed miserably. She struggled to rise and quickly fell back to the ground in pain. Her left hand touched her right shoulder.

"Mrs. Wilson. I am Lord Harrow. I'm terribly sorry about the accident. May I assist you? I will take you to your home and fetch a doctor for you."

She grimaced in pain. "The accident would not have happened if *L'Enfant terrible* had not tried to run away from me. It was not your fault."

Theo picked up on her French accent. "You are too generous, *Mademoiselle*. Does your shoulder hurt?"

Her hand moved to the base of her neck on the left side. "Yes. I fear I have injured my shoulder." Her eyes became watery.

"Let me assist you to stand and convey you home." He put his arm around her back from the other side and helped her. She was a tall woman who stood eye level to him. She wobbled so he pulled her closer to him. "I have you. Lean on me."

She shook her head and tried to pull away.

Theo held fast. "Allow me. Please?"

Mrs. Wilson's brows furrowed together but she nodded. He escorted her over to the carriage and helped her in. He picked up young Reginald and plopped him on the seat across from her. "Where do you live, young man?"

The boy gave an address only a few blocks out of the park.

Theo went to Phillip.

"How is she?" Phillip asked.

"Injured. Will you drive us to their home? I need to make sure she is well taken care of and that her employer understands what happened."

Phillip took the reins and jumped up to the driver's seat as Theo got into the back by Mrs. Wilson. With a jerk the carriage moved forward, and the young woman winced in pain.

Theo could not help but stare. Even bruised, she was stunning. Her hair fell around her shoulders. It was the color of butter and appeared soft as silk. His fingers twitched, longing to touch those tresses. Sitting near her he could smell orange blossoms and it took him back to his childhood, visiting his beloved Grandmother Bennett. She always had homemade treats and a sweetly scented hug for him, even up until her passing a few years ago.

The woman next to him possessed the bearing of the aristocracy though, not that of a servant, and he found himself intrigued. He would have never in the past sought to pursue someone in service but speculated that she was a noble woman who had fallen on hard times. She was not eying him as her next meal ticket, but with wary caution.

As they pulled up to the Fishbottom townhouse he knew only one thing for certain. He had found the woman he had been searching for. She wore widow weeds. He wondered how long it had been since she'd lost her husband.

~*~

Valeria ached all over. Even breathing hurt. It was such rotten timing for Reginald to enact such a scene at Hyde Park. She'd experienced terror when the wicked little boy ran away and right into the path of those horses. She'd watched her future being trampled under those hooves. She was under no illusion that her heroic act would have any bearing with her puffed up employers.

She let her breath out slowly. Her collarbone hurt like the dickens and she clenched her teeth so as not to whimper in pain with each bounce of the well-sprung barouche she found herself in. She glanced over at the handsome man by her side.

Lord Harrow was sturdy, and of a height to her, with darker, sandy blond hair, grey eyes, and a gentle demeanor. Such a man provided protection, as many she dwarfed with her own height. If she were seeking a husband, the benign man beside her would be who she would want. But she didn't want another husband. As much as she found herself physically attracted to this lord, she was in no position to strike up a romance.

The carriage pulled up to the townhouse.

Lord Harrow helped her out of the carriage and up the stairs to the front door. "Let me explain to your employer what happened this morning. I take full responsibility." The man appeared genuinely concerned.

"I would prefer you didn't, Lord Harrow. It would not matter. They will believe whatever yarn Reginald spins for them." Hurt flashed in his eyes. He was a man not used to being denied his wishes. She needed to avoid being beholden to him for his care of her. "Thank you for your kind assistance."

The door opened, and a starchy butler stepped aside as the boy preceded her into the house yelling for his parents.

She turned and walked away. The door closed as she bit back tears from pain and prepared to face the consequences of this morning's mis-adventure. She followed the sound of her charge's excited voice into the drawing room where Mr. and Mrs. Fishbottom sat.

"What is this my son is reporting to me? You pushed him to the ground? Look at his outfit. I will be deducting that from your salary." The plump woman stuffed a candy into her mouth and crunched down like a cow chewing its cud, as she spat out venomous words.

Valeria schooled her features to be blank. *Wages? What wages?* She functioned more as an *au pair,* only earning her room and board and not much else. The promised wages for the past few months failed to materialize. "I believe you were misinformed, ma'am."

The woman started to sputter and almost choked on her candy. "Are you accusing my son of lying? Dearest Mr. Fishbottom, did you hear her accuse our precious boy of telling an untruth?" The woman's beady eyes, practically swallowed up by her plump cheeks, spun toward her equally plump husband who lounged next to her.

"Yes, dear," he said wearily and appraised Valeria. "However, I would be interested in why she herself has such a disreputable appearance."

Valeria cringed as her employer looked her up and down, mentally undressing her. A wave of revulsion overtook her every time he did so.

Mrs. Fishbottom turned back to Valeria, oblivious to her husband's perusal of their servant. She sighed wearily. "Well, Mrs. Wilson, let us hear your little fib to cover your actions."

Valeria gritted her teeth and surveyed her charge who was also stuffing his face full of candy. "Reginald ran away from me and into the path of an oncoming carriage traveling at great speed. I did push him out of the way of the horses' hooves as they reared over him. He is fortunate to be alive."

Mrs. Fishbottom shook her head. "Tsk, tsk, tsk. I suppose this carriage was from some member of the *ton* and he graciously helped you and brought you home?"

"Lord Harrow and Lord Westcombe!" Reginald blurted out and quickly covered his mouth, realizing he had revealed his own lie and confirmed her statement as truth.

Mrs. Fishbottom's eyes grew wide at her son's statement. "Really? Lord Harrow is a Marquess and Lord Westcombe is a second son to an earl. Highly exalted indeed." She turned back to Valeria. "They brought you home?"

Reginald jumped into the conversation again. "They brought us in a spanking new barouche with a matched pair." Another piece of candy found its way to his mouth.

Mr. Fishbottom started at Valeria. "Is this true?"

Valeria nodded, keeping her eyes to the floor.

"Hrmph." Lord Fishbottom rose to his feet and even so fell several inches short of Valeria's height. "You disgraced us by your actions today, Mrs. Wilson. You may pack your bags and take your child and be out of this house by morning." He turned and waved to her in dismissal. "You will be given no references and no pay. Good day, Mrs. Wilson."

Reginald cheered. "Hooray! Can I get Mrs. Swenson again? She was really nice."

Valeria didn't stay to listen to any answer but climbed the stairs to the third-floor nursery and the room she shared with her six-year-old son, Dartanian. He was playing a card game with Susan, one of the maids who sometimes helped out in the nursery.

"*Maman*!" Dartanian dropped his cards as he jumped up and wrapped his arms around Valeria. She winced as she tried to wrap her left arm around his small body.

"Mrs. Wilson, are you injured?" Susan walked toward Valeria as Dartanian backed up and peered more closely at his mother.

"A little accident at the park." Valeria fought back the tears.

"Let me help you." Susan turned to Dartanian. "Could you go to the kitchen and get the basket of medical supplies there? And ask cook to send up some soup and willow bark tea for Mrs. Wilson."

"Yes, Susan. *Maman*?" Dartanian's eyebrows scrunched as he surveyed her torn dress and the cut on her cheek.

"I'll be fine, Dartanian. You go ahead." Valeria walked over to the bed and sat on the edge as Susan went to the wardrobe to find a clean dress.

"Hasn't it been well over six months since your husband died? Why are you still in blacks?" Susan asked as she brought another plain frock over to the bed and assisted in helping Valeria disrobe.

"No money for new clothing and I'm not seeking a new husband. The blacks keep men at bay." Valeria winced as she pulled her arm out of the sleeve.

"Or it makes you fair game. You realize what many widows do?" Susan set the torn dress aside and assisted getting the new on.

"I am not that kind of woman." Valeria tucked her injured arm to her body and closed her eyes against the tears from the pain the whole process induced.

"Is Mr. Fishbottom aware of this?" Susan asked with a snort.

"The closest he's come to propositioning me is with his eyes. I've been dismissed and will be out on the street tomorrow morning."

Susan gasped.

"At least I will not need to worry about Mr. Fishbottom anymore."

"They terminated you?"

Valeria nodded. "I humiliated them in front of the *ton* by rescuing their precious son from certain death."

"Abominable."

"I've endured worse." Valeria turned as her precious son entered. He appeared so like his father that it pained her. She wished he'd inherited her light-colored hair instead of Damon's dark coloring. She would have preferred to not have any reminders of the horrors of her marriage to the man, yet she adored her son. Of all the pain she'd endured in her marriage, he was the one blessing that resulted. And now she would do anything to keep him safe. Which meant trying to find new employment as soon as possible.

"*Maman*?" He came to the bed and handed the basket to Susan.

"Yes, *mon enfant*?" Valeria smiled at the face before her. He may appear like his father, but his temperament was totally his own and for that she was grateful.

"Are we leaving?"

Valeria nodded as she reached up with her left hand to ruffle his hair. "I'm afraid so, *mon petit*."

Susan fashioned a sling to help with Valeria's painful collarbone. "You need a doctor." She cleaned and applied salve to the cut on her right cheek.

"I possess no funds for such. I am denied my wages as well."

"And no references?"

"*Naturellement,* but of course." Valeria shrugged and winced as she was reminded of her pain.

"He will proposition you."

"I will refuse."

"But where will you both go?" Susan packed up the supplies.

Valeria shook her head. *"Je ne sais pas."*

"Maman?" Dartanian came to sit beside her. "God knows where we are to go next. We can trust Him."

Valeria peered into her son's shining brown eyes and wrapped her good arm around him drawing him to her side. *"Oui, on peut.* Yes, we can." Her eyes met Susan's and she could not help the sinking stone of dread in the pit of her stomach. *What if He doesn't?*

2

Theo had a skip in his step the rest of the day. He had summoned his physician to attend to Mrs. Wilson at the Fishbottom residence and felt good about being able to do something nice for her. How else would he court a woman like her? She was obviously quality. He wondered what her history was. French blood from what he could tell, but that didn't bother him. She obviously chose to live in England.

A note came around a few hours later from the doctor stating that he was denied access to Mrs. Wilson but had looked after a young man who was in good health.

Theo crumpled the note in frustration. Why would the Fishbottoms deny a servant medical care? Especially when they didn't have to pay for it? Tomorrow he would find out.

~*~

Theo cheerfully made the rounds to the requisite balls he had been invited to. He danced with wallflowers while inwardly dreaming of the day when he would be able to dance with Mrs. Wilson. He wondered what her first name was. He was lost in his daydreaming when Phillip found him and handed him a lukewarm glass of lemonade.

"I never liked these events. Beth isn't all that fond of them either, yet here we are." Phillip sipped his drink and grimaced before setting it down on a nearby table.

"It is a tolerable evening. I am enjoying myself." Theo scanned the ballroom. "Where is your lovely bride?"

Phillip pointed to the dance floor.

Theo spied the graceful redhead going through the motions of the minuet. "Does it ever bother you when other men dance with her?" Theo wondered aloud.

"It used to until I realized that I was the fortunate one to be able to take her home. They may share her on the dance floor, but when it comes to the bedroom, she's all mine." Phillip grinned and gave a wink to Theo. "That's one of the perks of marriage." He paused and frowned. "What was your decision on those horses?"

"I returned them. No sale. I could not in good conscience risk anything like this morning ever happening again."

"Whatever happened with that young woman from this morning? Is she well?"

Theo shrugged. "I suspect a broken bone, but when I sent Dr. Morton to look in on her, the Fishbottoms refused to allow him access. I plan to visit tomorrow to ensure that she is recovering."

"Let me know what you find out. I mentioned to Beth what happened this morning and she, of course, was concerned for the woman. If there are any problems with the Fishbottoms, Beth and I would gladly help out Mrs. Wilson." Phillip put an arm on Theo's shoulder and gave him a pat.

Theo nodded and grinned. "Thank you, Phillip."

With that the men separated to claim their partners for the next dance.

~*~

Theo woke the next morning eager to get to the Fishbottoms's residence. His breakfast was disturbed by his solicitor paying an unplanned for visit.

"Mr. Tanner, what brings you to my door this early in the morning?" Theo grinned. It irritated his solicitor that his wealthy clients often slept in until noon while solicitors began their work far earlier.

The elderly man turned red in the face, shoved his spectacles further up his nose, and disregarded the comment. "I want to discuss some changes in the market that affect your investments. I have some recommendations that would net you even more income."

"Have a seat and we shall discuss that." Theo motioned for the man to join him in his study and they spent the next hour in there negotiating the changes.

~*~

When Theo arrived at the Fishbottom residence it was much later in the day than he had anticipated. He knocked on the door and was met by the same starchy butler who'd opened it yesterday. He stepped into the door and handed the man his calling card. "Lord Harrow to see Mr. And Mrs. Fishbottom."

The man looked at Theo and at the card and back again but did not move.

Theo raised his eyebrows. "I suggest you go and announce me to your master." Theo removed his hat and set it on the table in the foyer.

The butler walked away and disappeared.

Theo waited a long time. Finally, he spied a maid

walking into the hallway. "Excuse me. Would you be able to help me?"

The young woman was startled. "Have you been announced?"

"I doubt it. I have been waiting here for quite some time."

"Who did you come to visit?"

"I requested an audience with Mr. Fishbottom. My real purpose in being here is to inquire as to the welfare of Mrs. Wilson."

The maid put her hand over her mouth. "Are you Lord Harrow?"

Theo grinned. "She mentioned me?"

She nodded.

"How does Mrs. Wilson fare? I sent a physician to check on her yesterday, but he was denied access." Theo scowled at this and the maid backed up a step. "I'm sorry. I am only concerned for her. She seemed to have some serious injuries."

The maid nodded some more.

"Would I perchance be able to see her?"

The maid shook her head.

"Why?"

"Because she was dismissed, my lord. She left early this morning."

"Dismissed? Why?"

"I was not privy to the conversation. I believe it had something to do with her embarrassing them among the aristocracy. They aspire to being one of you."

"Embarrassed? Mrs. Wilson only did a noble act that should be rewarded, not punished. Where did she go?"

"I do not know, my lord. I pray for her. She had no

family to turn to and they refused to pay her wages. I am worried about her in the city and injured at that."

"She still suffers from her injuries?"

The maid nodded, and the servant's eyes began to tear up.

"You were a good friend to her, I imagine."

She curtsied. "Thank you, my lord. Would you like me to go announce you to my master?"

Theo glanced down the hallway and picked up his hat. "There is no need to bother them. I may say something I would later regret. I appreciate your assistance." He put his hat on and let himself out the front door.

~*~

Valeria did not own much but with her injury and no place to go to, Susan agreed to hold on to her belongings until she found a place to stay. Valeria counted her savings but if they wanted to eat, they could not afford a hotel, unless she went to the meanest part of town. That would be a long walk and unsafe for her and Dartanian.

She opted to go to Hyde Park and sit beneath a tree so Dartanian could run around and play while she waited for God to reveal his next steps to her. A little like Hagar must have experienced when Sarai sent her away and she was in the desert with her son waiting to die. She laughed at her imagination.

They were not in a desert and due to cook's generosity and forethought they possessed food that could last them for a few days if they were careful. If the weather held, perhaps they could sleep outside, hiding in some bushes. She really couldn't figure out what other choice they would have.

She sat for a few hours there, watching the traffic and at times sitting with her son, reading from the Bible. Eventually he fell asleep with his head on her lap. Her legs were sore, but she was loathe to move with him finally resting. Her collarbone ached, and she still wore the makeshift sling. She leaned back against the tree she'd sat under for hours and closed her eyes for a moment.

~*~

"Mrs. Wilson? Is that you?" A male voice was close by and she fluttered her eyes open. She must have fallen asleep, the pain, exhaustion, and anxiety finally having taken hold of her body. She glanced up to see the tall, blond aristocrat from yesterday. Lord Harrow's companion.

"Lord Westcombe, is it?" She gazed up at him and the woman by his side.

"I'm surprised you remember. This is my lovely bride, Lady Elizabeth Westcombe." He turned to his wife. "Beth, this is Mrs. Wilson, the hero from yesterday."

"Oh, I heard about your daring rescue. Is this the young man you saved from death?" She motioned to Dartanian, still sleeping.

"No. This is *mon enfant,* Dartanian. He was not with us at the time."

"Did you gain the day off? It has turned out to be a fine day for a picnic." Elizabeth smiled down at her. The woman's red hair shimmered in the sunlight.

"In a manner of speaking." Valeria kept her gaze averted. She hated lying but this was more of a distraction from the truth.

Lord Westcombe frowned as he took in the travel case sitting by her side. "You were dismissed?"

Mrs. Westcombe grabbed his arm. "No! That could not be. Phillip, no one would dismiss a servant who saved their child's life."

Lord Westcombe didn't say anything, but Valeria could sense his penetrating gaze and finally looked up to meet his cool blue eyes. She sighed. "Apparently the Fishbottoms had no need to keep on an injured governess." Valeria turned her gaze down to her son and gently touched his hair as he slept.

"You will come and work for us," Lady Westcombe announced.

"*Pardon*?" Valeria startled at this pronouncement. "You do not know me. I possess no references and I have a child I need to keep with me."

"None of that is a problem, is it, my lord?" She glanced up at her husband and gave him a brilliant smile. "After all, our child could use someone else to help provide care when I cannot, and it would be wonderful for him to grow up with a friend."

"You are serious?" Valeria couldn't believe this.

"We are. Let me go get my coach that is parked over by the gate. We will come and transport you to our home immediately." Lord Westcombe gave his wife's hand a squeeze before he walked back the way they'd come.

"After we get you settled in, we will call a physician to check out your injury." Lady Westcombe smiled down at her. "I am thrilled I get to meet you, Mrs. Wilson. After Phillip and Theo told me the tale I realized you were a woman after my own heart. I am so pleased that we had the good fortune to come upon you before someone else obtained your services."

Valeria couldn't wrap her mind around this sudden change in her circumstances. Maybe God was watching over them after all.

~*~

Theo returned home from visiting the Fishbottoms and sat in his office filled with rage. Thoughts of revenge consumed him. Socially they were on the fringes and he could easily ensure they were shunned by society. He debated his options. *Forget it, Theo, focus. Where could she be? How will you ever find her again?* After a few hours of unproductive contemplation, he sought his club and ran into Phillip there.

"What brings you out tonight? No balls to escort your wife to?" Theo asked as he sipped a glass of wine.

"We canceled tonight's activities as my bride has a new project she is working on. I am, as a result, on my own for a few hours."

"Her loss, my gain." Theo ran his forefinger round the rim of the glass, listened to it sing, and frowned.

"You appear blue-deviled. What is amiss?" Phillip sipped his own wine, leaned back in his chair, crossed his legs, and awaited an answer.

"I lost her."

"Who did you lose?"

"The woman I fell in love with."

Phillip's eyebrows rose. "You are in love? That is wonderful news, Theo."

"Not so wonderful. She disappeared." He drank deeply and set the glass down so firmly the remaining wine splashed.

"Who is the fortunate lady? Am I acquainted with

her?"

"You met her yesterday." Theo crossed his arms and leaned his head back.

"I did? Who is she? Remind me, please." Phillip leaned forward with his elbows on his knees.

"Mrs. Wilson."

"Mrs. Wilson?"

"Is that not what I said?" Theo frowned at his friend.

"And you are in love with her."

"Yes."

"You want to marry this woman?"

"Yes."

"But you know nothing about her."

"You knew nothing about Elizabeth when you married her."

"I wasn't in love with her either. It is a heavy expectation to put on a marriage."

Theo leaned forward, getting closer to Phillip. "Are you saying it's not possible?"

Phillip's hands went up in surrender. "I did not say that. But you don't even know where she is so that would be a major obstacle."

Theo leaned back, and his eyes closed. "I realize that. I have mulled this over for hours and short of hiring a Bow Street Runner, I can come up with no other way to discover her whereabouts."

"I wonder if Mr. Neville is still in that line of work."

"No. He is now working for Whitehall. Remember?"

Phillip nodded. "Perhaps I can help?"

"How?"

"What would you say if I told you I knew where

she was?"

"I would say you are lying, and that alone would surprise me. Why would you torture me like that?"

Phillip grinned. "Because it's rare for anyone to be able to get a rise out of you, Theo. Besides, I speak the truth."

"Where is she?"

"My wife hired her."

Theo fought the urge to spar with Phillip right there at White's but swallowed it. He would have expected this kind of behavior from Michael. "You do realize I'll be haunting your house now."

"I suspected that might be case." Phillip set the wine glass down, and quirked an eyebrow at Theo. "However, tonight will not be the night to be stopping by."

"Why?" Theo contemplated picking up his hat and doing just that.

"I told you that Beth has a 'project'. That project happens to be Mrs. Wilson. The doctor has seen her and you were correct. Her collarbone is broken. It appears a fellow servant assisted her in stabilizing it, but she has been ordered to rest, and another servant called upon to assist with her son until she is up and able to take care of ours."

"Tell me about the child. I assume she is a widow?"

"You are a fool, Theo, if you think you can step in and sweep her off her feet. How would you know it's not your title and wealth that would be drawing her, any more than the debutantes you escorted to the dance floor last night?" Phillip sighed and shook his head with a frown at his friend. "The young man is about six-years-old. She was widowed six months or more hence. She should be in half mourning but dresses in blacks and does not want to discuss her husband." Phillip leaned forward. "I suspect she is keeping some secrets and she is not all she pretends to be."

"You only met her and already disparage her? Why have you taken her in?" Theo scowled. How dare he?

"I do not disparage her, my good man. I am only making an observation. I'm not saying her secrets are nefarious, only that she has some."

Theo leaned back to sip his wine and think about this. "Do you think she could come to like me?"

"I thought you were searching for love?" Phillip grinned.

Theo sat quietly for a few moments. Was it love that he experienced for Mrs. Wilson? He'd only met her for less than half an hour and yet desired her instantly. Was that love? Touching her face and her hand produced sensations in him that no other woman had stirred before. Was that love or lust? He never considered bedding her. Well, to be honest, it crossed his mind. He was a man, after all, but he refused to entertain those thoughts as worthy of the woman he wished to make his wife.

He could envision her entering a grand ballroom on his arm, in a flowing cerulean gown, with her golden locks piled high but spilling forth with tantalizing ringlets. Every man would be staring at her and envying him. He would waltz with her and keep her close to his side. In time, he would allow other men to dance with her, but he doubted he could do so with as much equanimity as Phillip did.

"Theo?" Phillip's voice was almost a whisper.

Startled out of his reverie, Theo turned towards his friend. "What?"

Phillip laughed. "You have the worst case of calf love I've ever witnessed."

Theo growled.

Phillip put up a hand and laughed. "Realize that love requires sacrifice. Don't go around telling yourself that she'll fall at your feet in gratitude and you will be able to whisk her off to your estate outside of St. Neots without having to do some work to get there."

"You didn't need to work to get Beth." Theo pouted.

"Ah, but Marcus sacrificed for Josie, and what Michael and Katrina went through I would not wish on any person. No, I did not sacrifice much to marry my wife, but to love and keep her was brutal." Phillip leaned back again lost in memories, a sadness shadowed his eyes. "I would've given my life to keep her safe, Theo, but those deeper affections did not develop overnight. God certainly blessed us as we leaned on Him in our trials."

"God again?"

"It always comes back to Him, Theo. He was before time began and He is the One who determines your eternal destiny. Earthly love and joy are temporary but for all that, a blessing beyond description."

"Since when did you wax poetical?"

Phillip grinned. "Probably since our son has stolen any hope of a full night's sleep. Delirium, my dear friend, but worth the price."

Theo rose to his feet. "I am headed for home. Thank you for keeping a lonely man company. May I stop by on the morrow to check on Mrs. Wilson?"

"You may, but Beth is protective of her. Do not be surprised if you are denied an audience with your heart's desire." Phillip stood, claimed his own hat, and the two men walked out together before parting ways.

~*~

Theo arrived early the next morning at the Westcombe residence.

"Lord Harrow has arrived, my lady," the butler intoned as Theo followed him into the breakfast room.

"Theo. I was expecting you. Break your fast with me. Sit. Share the *on dits*." Lady Elizabeth Westcombe was a lithe beauty with red hair and a winning smile. The haunted look in her eyes when they'd first met disappeared after she married Phillip. They overcame many challenges, including the loss of her father, Lord Follett, due to the machinations of Lord Wolton, who was presumed dead.

Theo'd initially been jealous of Phillip and his good fortune to find such a lovely wife who had softened the edges on his orderly friend. Over time he came to realize what a good match they both made. He helped himself to some food and sat across the table from a woman he now thought of almost as a sister.

"You are gracious as always, Beth." He waited for the footman to fill his cup with coffee and added sugar to it. The servant departed, closing the door behind him. Theo sipped the coffee and burnt his tongue. He set the cup down and considered the woman across from him.

She was nibbling her toast with one eyebrow raised, much like her husband was wont to do, as she awaited his request.

"I came to inquire of your most recent employee, Mrs. Wilson."

Beth took a sip of her tea. "I expected you. Phillip alluded to the fact that you are intrigued with the young widow. I am not surprised. Her elegance and regal bearing speak of someone who was not born to the servant class."

"How does she fare?" Theo dug into his eggs with relish. The Westcombe's cook was one of the best, and he never ate a bad meal when at their table.

"In a month or so she should be much better. She will need to be careful and we will allow her to recuperate fully before expecting her to assume any duties as a nanny. She has already met our dear Andrew and Dartanian has already taken over supervising his play in the nursery. Andrew cannot help but toddle along after him everywhere. It is a blessing to see him so happily occupied."

Theo grinned. He had not seen the red-headed little boy in several weeks since they'd celebrated his one-year birthday. It had been difficult for him watching his friends with their wives and children and him being alone. They included him in everything like a favorite uncle, but it didn't fulfill that inner longing in his heart for a family of his own.

He chuckled to himself that several years ago, if someone told him he would be pining for a wife and children of his own he would have ascribed it to insanity. Now, he wondered if he was the one going insane. "I am eager to visit Drew again and meet Dartanian. Will I perchance get to see Mrs. Wilson to check on how she fares?"

Beth pursed her lips as if trying to restrain a smile. "I will ask if she is feeling up for visitors but I suspect,

Theo, that you may need to wait a few days. She has been instructed to rest in her room and she is quite proper. I doubt she would care for you to see her in *deshabille.*"

Theo's face grew warm at the thought of the woman of his dreams dressed in her nightrail. "I shall wait, if that is what you deem best, my lady."

Beth nodded. "If it would be more tolerable for you, I could send you a message in a few days when she has recovered enough to leave her room."

Theo nodded as he cleared his plate and was finally able to drink his coffee. "I would appreciate that." He rose and bowed to Beth. "Thank you for the meal. It was a pleasure seeing you again."

He left to return to his own home, trying to figure out how he would wait all these days before viewing the beautiful blonde who held his heart hostage.

~*~

Valeria rested in bed which went against everything she wanted. She could hear her son playing with the toddler that would soon be her charge. She was being cared for with great consideration by the servants and given personal attention by Lady Westcombe herself. She was uncomfortable. Her life was totally beyond her control.

Lord Harrow had come to visit her and had been denied for the time being as she recovered. Did she want to see the handsome aristocrat again? She'd never experienced the physical reaction that came over her when the handsome lord touched her. Remembering his tenderness sent shivers up her spine, not from fear but from some form of strange delight. No man ever before evoked desire and safety in her and she distrusted those emotions. The heart was deceitful if she remembered the Scripture correctly. It had certainly been when her husband and his family wooed her.

Darkly handsome, Damon had managed to whisk her away with dreams and promises that turned into horrible nightmares. She had not mourned his passing.

For the first time in her life, once Damon had been buried, she experienced freedom. That was, until her father-in-law visited. He assumed that she would continue as chatelaine of the estate and that he would step in to replace his son. Disgust and a new conviction of the danger of her situation compelled her to take drastic action.

Months later and she was living with the consequences of her decision. She and her son were safe. Even leaving the Fishbottoms' was an answer to an unspoken prayer of her heart. Mr. Fishbottom had begun to stalk her in the upstairs hallway and make indecent proposals. She lacked any desire to ever be touched by a man in *that* way, ever again.

The only blessing from her marriage was Dartanian. She fled in the middle of the night with her son, hoping to disappear, but wondered now if that was going to be possible. As safe as she was at the moment in the bosom of this family, it was only a matter of time before she was exposed, and the danger would be greater than ever. If the Fishbottoms had been part of that exposure she wouldn't have cared, but the Westcombes were a different story. Out of necessity she would take advantage of their hospitality until she was recovered enough to escape once more.

Where would she go? France was not a viable

option. Her family no longer existed there. All had lost their lives in the Revolution and she held no affection for the Little Emperor, Napoleon Bonaparte. The Americas were a possibility, although the thought of a voyage across the ocean nauseated her. She remembered the brief time on board ship when she was brought here by her father-in-law to marry his son so his heirs would inherit noble French blood. But a sea voyage was the lesser evil to being discovered by those who sought her and her son.

She possessed little money and would need to earn more before she could make such a trip. The treachery of the Fishbottoms's deceit with regards to her wages set her back by several months from achieving her goal.

What else could she do to keep her son safe until they could depart?

3

A week later, Valeria sat in the nursery watching the antics of her son and little Andrew as they pretended they were ponies. Before she realized they had visitors, she heard a gasp come from the doorway.

A petite young woman with brown hair and big eyes halted in the entranc. Her hand covered her mouth and she appeared about to faint.

Lady Westcombe stood behind her.

Valeria stood. "Let her have my chair."

Lady Westcombe brought her friend to sit in the rocking chair.

"What is wrong?" Valeria asked.

The woman's gaze was fixed firmly on Dartanian. The lady's mouth tried to move but no sound came out.

"Katrina, what is it? What has you so shaken?" Lady Westcome asked while rubbing the woman's back.

"Michael," Katrina whispered.

"Do you want me to get Michael?" Lady Westcombe inquired.

Katrina shook her head and cried.

Lady Westcombe motioned for Valeria and the nursery helper to remove the children from the room.

"Dartanian, Andrew," Valeria called to the boys, who had stopped playing to stare at the woman sobbing in the chair. "Time for a nap."

"*Maman*?" Dartanian asked.

Valeria glanced at him. "Please go. Lie down or

read and stay with Andrew for right now. I will come to get you in a little while."

Once the children left the room the woman in the chair peered up at Valeria.

Valeria stepped forward. "I'm Mrs. Wilson, the new governess for the Westcombes. Is there anything I can do?"

Katrina's eyes were filled with pain and swollen with tears. She shook her head. "I'm sorry for being such a watering pot. I am *enceinte*. Your son…"

Valeria grew concerned. "What about my son?"

Lady Westcombe spoke at the same time. "Congratulations, Katrina! How wonderful!"

Katrina seemed unsure who to answer first. She was saved from doing so by the entrance of the men into the room.

Valeria was shocked. The man who entered alongside Lord Westcombe was *identiques* to her deceased husband. Before Valeria was aware of it the room went dark.

She awakened in the arms of the man who caused her to faint. "Impossible. You are dead." She struggled to free herself from the man's grasp.

Lord Westcombe reached out and helped her rise to her feet.

The twin of her deceased husband went over to where Katrina sat.

"I suspect introductions are in order. Mrs. Wilson, may I present to you some of our dearest friends, Sir Michael Tidley and his wife, Katrina."

"Michael?" Valeria asked.

"Michael. How could you?" Katrina rose and punched her husband in the stomach.

"What have I done now?" the knight answered.

He was only a little taller than his wife and not to Valeria's height. His dark hair and eyes were furrowed as he gazed at his bride and protected his stomach from another blow.

"You. And her?" Katrina spat out.

"I have never met her before this moment. What are you insinuating?"

At that moment, Dartanian ran to his mom's side and wrapped his arms around her legs. "*Maman*?" The little boy stared at Sir Tidley. "*Maman*?" He started to cry and hid behind her, gripping a handful of her skirt.

Lord Westcombe shook his head. "What is going on here? Katrina, would you care to start?"

Katrina nodded and pointed. "That little boy."

"What of him?" asked Valeria.

"He appears just as Michael did when he was younger. There is the painting your mother had done of you at that age." She folded her arms across her chest and turned her back on her husband, as much as she could while sitting in a chair.

Valeria pointed at Michael. "He is my husband come back to life!"

Michael retorted. "I've never seen you before in my life, Mrs. Wilson. I do not understand what game you are playing at, but I do not appreciate you casting aspersions on my character." He tried to reach out to his wife who stood and took steps away from him.

Lady Westcombe stepped between the two sparing spouses. "I believe there is some kind of misunderstanding here that can be easily resolved."

"Maman?" Dartanian whined as he peeked his head out. "Will *Papa* hurt me?"

"He would need to get through me first." Valeria experienced fear and rage at the threat the man before her presented. She crossed her arms and mentally prepared herself for battle.

Michael raised his arms as if in surrender. "I am unclear as to what is going on here. Young man, I have no desire to harm you or your mother." He turned to his wife. "Believe me. I have never seen this woman before. While I will not deny that my past life was not pristine by any means, I have never, to my knowledge, fathered any children in the process. I would never want to do to a child what had been done to me."

"I can vouch for Michael. If he says he is not the father, then he is not." Lord Westcombe turned to Mrs. Wilson. "You acted as though you saw a ghost when Sir Tidley entered the room. Who exactly was Mr. Wilson? Who was your boy's father?"

Valeria shook her head. No. She could not share the truth of her past with these people. There was too much at stake. Sir Tidley, Michael, glared at her and she shivered in response. She knelt down by her son and drew him to herself with her good arm. "Dartanian," she whispered in his ear, "*Espère en Dieu,* hope in God, *mon petit.*"

"Oui, Maman," Dartanian whispered back to her.

"Go back to Andrew. I will come for you in *un instant.*" She shoved Dartanian toward the door. He gazed longingly back at her as he went. Her heart broke at the bleakness she witnessed in his eyes.

She forced her attention back to the adults in the room. She felt like a spy about to be interrogated. Her only recourse would be to leave. "*Je suis désolée,* I did not mean to cause *la difficulté.* Dartanian and I will leave." She lowered her eyes and moved toward the door her son exited from.

"I do not think that will be necessary, Mrs.

Wilson," Lady Westcombe spoke up and moved over to Valeria. She placed her hands gently on each of Valeria's arms. Warmth and compassion emanated from the woman who had extended so much kindness already.

"I have caused you much trouble." Valeria tried to communicate her need to go to the woman holding her captive with her warm gaze and gentle touch.

"No trouble. You need a place to heal and be safe. *Est-ce la vérité?"*

"Yes, my lady, 'tis true." Valeria let her gaze drop.

"Well then. We shall leave you to rest. Perhaps we will discuss this later." Lady Westcombe glared at her husband and the Tidleys, who were still not physically close.

Katrina looked doubtfully at her husband.

Lord Phillip was grimacing that his inquisition was thwarted by his wife.

No one gainsaid her. Lady Westcombe left the room and the rest followed, leaving Valeria standing there alone. What was she to do now?

~*~

Theodore appeared daily at the Westcombe residence and had been denied access to Mrs. Wilson every time. He was in the foyer when Phillip and Beth, along with Michael and Katrina, came down the stairs.

Michael's brow was furrowed as he scowled. His hands were fisted by his side.

Katrina's arms were folded across her chest.

Phillip's jaw was clenched tight and a muscle moved on the side of his face.

Only Beth appeared genuinely happy when she

glanced up and noticed him at the bottom of the staircase. “Theo! How good of you to come and visit us again.”

“I would be jealous if I didn’t understand it was not my wife who drew you to our door.” Phillip riposted.

Elizabeth giggled and slapped her husband on the arm. “You doubt my ability to gather a cicisbeo about me?”

“None would dare, given the way Phillip guards you, Beth.” Theo joked.

“My goal is to make sure you have no desire for any beaux dancing attendance upon you.” Phillip reached out to draw his wife into the shelter of his arm and planted a kiss on her loosely twisted chignon.

Beth looked up at him with a smile.

As a group, they moved into the drawing room.

Michael closed the door shut behind them. His face remained stoic.

“Is something amiss?” Theo asked.

Silence met his question as the various parties chose their places in the room. Beth sat down with Katrina across from her. Phillip stood behind his wife. Michael wandered to the fireplace, leaned his back against it and crossed one booted leg over the other. One hand was rubbing his chin.

Theo sat in a chair and leaned back to wait. They would divulge their secrets when they were ready.

The fire crackled and finally Katrina spoke. “Michael, do you swear you never met her before today?” Her hands were squeezed together in her lap.

Michael met his wife’s gaze. “I swear that I have never seen her before today. The child is not mine.”

Katrina finally nodded. “I will choose to believe

you."

Michael's shoulders drooped, and he moved over to kneel before his wife. "I would never do anything like that to you. After all we've endured, I would never want to do anything to jeopardize what we have found together."

Katrina gazed down at him and ran one hand through his hair.

Phillip cleared his throat.

The two lovebirds grinned. Michael rose to sit next to his wife on the settee, holding her hands tight in his.

~*~

"Will someone tell me what happened?" Theo asked.

Phillip spoke up. "There was a misunderstanding upstairs. Mrs. Wilson's deceased husband is a twin to Michael, and her son looks like our friend did when he was a child."

Theo looked at Michael.

"It wasn't me. She's really not my type. I've never really gone for women who were taller than me." He reached for Katrina's hand.

"Is Mrs. Wilson well?" Theodore was jealous that they'd been able to see her, and he had been denied that pleasure for a week.

"She was distraught, Theo. It obviously shook her to see her husband come back from the dead. Even her son was terrified. I get the impression he was not of the same temperament as our Michael here."

"That alone should be proof that it was not I," Michael said.

Katrina leaned away from him. "I remember a

time when you were pretty nasty to me."

"I lost my memory and was a fool. I eventually came to my senses." Michael grinned, showing a dimple in one cheek.

Katrina leaned over and kissed it. "So, you did."

"She's hiding something," Phillip asserted.

"What if she is? She has a right to keep her past private." Michael spoke in defense of the woman who caused a temporary rift in his marriage.

"She's too refined to be a nanny or governess," Phillip said.

"Are there any Wilsons in DeBrett's?" Beth asked.

"We can check. Great idea." Phillip walked over to a bookshelf where the volume was situated and pulled it down. He sat in a chair near his wife and began to search.

"Is it possible for me to see her today?" Theo asked.

"See who?" Katrina inquired.

"Mrs. Wilson, of course."

"How are you associated with her?" Michael asked.

Phillip piped up as he continued to peruse the pages of the book in his lap. "He ran her over with that silly matched pair he was thinking of purchasing."

Katrina gasped. "That's how she came by her injuries?"

"Unfortunately, it is true. She rescued a boy in her care who ran into our path. The boy survived unscathed. She and the horses' hooves unfortunately met." Theo frowned.

"Theo likes her," Phillip stated.

"Really?" Katrina asked. "She is a striking woman."

Theo grinned. "That she is."

The women exchanged glances.

Theo disregarded them.

"Not here. No Wilson listed."

"We could investigate her if it would make you feel better, Phillip," Michael offered. "I still have contacts at Whitehall."

"Perhaps she is in danger?" Katrina offered.

"If she is, could she be endangering us or Andrew by being here?" Phillip asked.

Beth put a hand up to halt the conversation. "I do not think we should pry into her past. She has been wounded. I believe she has a previous connection to the Black Diamond."

Everyone's attention snapped to Beth.

"How would you possibly know that?" Michael asked.

Beth's voice softened. "She has a diamond shaped tattoo on her right shoulder blade."

Katrina gasped.

Michael wrapped an arm around her shoulder and she buried her head into his broad chest.

Phillip placed his hands on his bride and squeezed her shoulders.

Theo swallowed.

The Black Diamond had been a nemesis of their band of friends for years when a minion of his terrorized Josie, now Viscountess Remington. Elizabeth had been attacked and the shape of a rhombus carved into her right shoulder. And then, the worst of all, was Katrina, who had been branded with the same shape. To uncover another woman who had been thus marked was unsettling. And to realize this was a woman he had his heart set on shook him deep inside.

They were interrupted by a knock on the door.

"Come in," Phillip called.

A servant entered and curtsied.

"Yes, Margaret?" Beth asked.

"I thought you would want to know that Mrs. Wilson and her son are packing their bags."

"She's leaving?" Theo asked.

The maid nodded and departed, shutting the door behind her.

Phillip headed to the door with Elizabeth at his heals, followed closely by Theodore. They quickly took the stairs to the third floor. Phillip knocked on Mrs. Wilson's bedroom door.

It was opened by the woman herself. "Yes?" Mrs. Wilson asked innocently. Her gaze took in Theo and rested on him for a time before focusing to the left of Phillip's shoulder.

"Are you leaving?" Beth asked.

Mrs. Wilson nodded. "I am grateful for your assistance and hospitality, but I cannot stay here."

"Where would you go?" Phillip inquired, his voice firm but soft.

"That is not your concern." Mrs. Wilson maintained her posture and no emotion was evident on her face.

Theo longed for her to look at him.

"I could offer you shelter." The words were out of Theo's mouth before he realized it.

She finally glanced at him. "That is most kind, Lord Harrow, but I do not think you need an injured governess who causes trouble amongst your friends." She stepped back to close the door.

Phillip put his foot in and shoved his weight against it. "Not so fast."

"Yes, Lord Westcombe?"

"I think you owe us a month of service for the medical care we are providing for you. You are not fit for travel or service elsewhere with your injury. You can continue to recover here for the remaining five weeks you need to have your arm in a sling. Then you owe us another six weeks before you can depart. We will compensate you fairly and give you a letter of recommendation if you can fulfill those terms."

"Please stay. We only want to help you," Beth implored, reaching out a hand to grasp Mrs. Wilson's.

Theo willed her to stay as she looked over to him. Fear and uncertainty were reflected in her wide eyes. He longed for the time when he could offer her comfort such as his friends had to their wives. His arms itched to hold her. His nose desired to bury itself in the scent of orange blossoms and his fingers itched to touch the silken tresses that hung down around her shoulders. His body…he mentally slapped himself for letting his mind wander to territory he had no right to venture into.

"*Oui*. I stay for now." She bowed her head and Phillip allowed her to close the door on them.

The three of them went down the stairs.

Phillip protectively held his hand over Beth's as she rested her arm on his.

Once again, Theo was left out of the best life had to offer.

When they came to the bottom floor, Michael and Katrina were gathering their wraps. "Katrina needs to rest. We will leave you now," Michael stated.

"Mrs. Wilson is staying for the time being," Beth announced.

Katrina nodded her understanding.

"Take care of that little one, Michael. Congratulations." Beth smiled broadly as Katrina blushed.

"Little one?" Phillip asked. His face lit up as the truth dawned on him. He walked around to pat his friend on the back. "Congratulations, Michael. Fatherhood suits you."

"I am not sure about that, but Katrina suits me perfectly." He held out his elbow.

Katrina hooked hers around it and placed her hand on his forearm. "Theo, it was good to see you again."

"Yes. Congratulations, Michael," Theo said softly. Michael and Katrina were having a second child. He hadn't even managed to have a conversation with the woman he desired for his wife. He felt alone—terribly alone. "I believe I will depart as well." Theo grabbed for his hat and placed it on his head.

"Will you visit on the morrow?" Beth asked and gave him a wink.

He nodded and departed.

Walking home he mulled over all he had seen and heard today. Somehow the woman he desired had at one time fallen into the clutches of the Black Diamond. She was a widow with a child. Was that child the Diamond's spawn? The thought repulsed him. He'd never heard the full details of Katrina's or Beth's interactions with the Black Diamond's minions. He understood Katrina had even been face to face with him, masked though it was. They still had no clue to his identity.

And now Mrs. Wilson was also a victim of this power-hungry traitor to the Crown. But how? Why? Something inside of him believed she had been unwilling, but he had no proof of that. The Black Diamond needed to be discovered and stopped. Theo had been around to help his friends in their battles, but now—it was personal.

~*~

Valeria sank to the edge of her bed after Lord and Lady Westcombe left. Lord Harrow still made her heart beat faster and it was shocking to see him there although she was aware he had been inquiring after her daily.

What was she to do? She'd agreed to stay almost another three months. Dartanian would become attached. If she saved enough money she could afford to purchase fare to the Americas. She needed to leave the country. It was the only way she would ever be safe. Could she hold on that long without being discovered?

Valeria was summoned late the next morning to the drawing room. Upon entering she found Lord Harrow standing there. Elizabeth invited her to sit with them for tea. Valeria sat down across from Lord Harrow. She had a hard time focusing on the conversation he was having with Lady Westcombe.

"How are you recovering from your injuries, Mrs. Wilson?" Theo asked, his gaze fully attentive to her. He'd glanced at her appearance when she'd entered the room, but he had not mentally undressed her as Mr. Fishbottom and others had done. Statuesque, was how her father had described her. Unfortunately, nude statues appeared to be all that men thought of when she entered a room. But not Lord Harrow.

"I have some discomfort but am much improved

from the day we first met." She sipped her tea. How long had it been since she had the luxury of something as simple as a cup of tea in a drawing room? Too long.

"I am glad. I was wondering if you would accompany me on a ride in my barouche tomorrow."

"I am a *gouvernante,* my lord."

"Theodore, or Theo, if you please."

Valeria shook her head. She could not afford familiarity.

"It would be acceptable to me. As your mistress, I can give you freedom to do this. And I would also prefer if you would call me Elizabeth or Beth." Lady Westcombe set her cup down and smiled at Valeria.

Valeria did not know what to do. She needed the money that the Westcombes could provide for travel to the Americas, but she could not afford to be seen by the wrong people. She swallowed hard. She prayed that God kept watch over them but still sometimes doubted it after all she and Dartanian had endured. "My name is Valeria. What time would you like me to be ready for you, Lord Harrow?" As much as she longed to use his first name, she couldn't do it. It would lead to dreams she'd no right to entertain.

The time was established, and conversation turned to other things. Valeria did not contribute.

The door opened and Dartanian and Andrew came running into the room followed by a frazzled maid.

"Dartanian! *Ce n'est pas correct."*

"J'en suis désolé. I am so sorry, *Maman*. See what we have? A *chaton*! May I keep her?"

Valeria peered into her son's eager face and glanced over at Beth.

"I have no prohibition against a kitten in the

nursery if it is acceptable to you, Valeria." Beth grinned at the young man as she lifted her son up onto her lap.

"Uncle Theo is here!" little Andrew yelled. He jumped off his mother's lap and launched himself on to Theo's.

Valeria smiled at the little one's antics. She turned her gaze back to her son who was older than his years in so many ways. What could a kitten hurt? "What would you name him, *mon petite*?"

"Mittens. He has little mittens on his feet. See?" Dartanian held up the white kitten with black paws.

Valeria held out her hand and he placed the kitten in them. She ran her hand gently over the soft fur and Mittens purred loudly. "It appears we own a cat, Dartanian. You will need to take care of her."

Her son's eyes sparkled with excitement. "*Je te remercie, Maman*! Thank you, Lady Westcombe!" Dartanian scooped up the kitten and snuggled it close. "Come on, Andrew. We need to make a bed for Mittens."

With that the maid escorted the children out of the room and up to the nursery.

"You were gracious in allowing him this pet, Elizabeth." Valeria grew overwhelmed at the generosity of this woman.

"It is nothing, Valeria. A little boy needs a pet. When Andrew is older perhaps he will have a cat or a dog of his own. It will be good to learn from your son how to care for an animal. So, it is purely for selfish reasons." Beth nodded with a half-grin at Valeria and sipped more of her tea.

4

The next morning Valeria went to her closet to find that her black gowns had been replaced by dresses in various shades of lavender, and in the latest styles. She was not sure how that happened, but she understood a conversation needed to be had with her employer. She slipped on one of the dresses and found it fit perfectly, accentuating her figure. The shade complimented her complexion.

She struggled to do something with her hair and grew frustrated. It would not do to be seen in public with her hair down. Even with a hat on it would be obvious. It was almost as uncomfortable a thought as being seen in her corset and drawers.

Angel was in the nursery with the boys.

"I cannot do my hair with one arm. Angel, would you be able to do something with this mane?"

Angel nodded. "You look a picture, Mrs. Wilson. I am certain I can do something."

Valeria sat down in front of the mirror with the boys playing nearby as Angel worked magic on Valeria's golden tresses. Soon they were up and off her neck in a tidy bun.

Valeria did not recognize the woman staring back at her in the mirror. The cut to her cheek was healing well. She appeared rested, and the hat, along with the cut of the gown, flattered her square jaw line. The dress was far nicer than anything she had ever owned in her previous life. Matching shoes were also in the closet and fit. She managed to be ready by the time she was informed that Lord Harrow awaited her.

Valeria arrived in the foyer.

Lord Harrow's gaze held admiration. He had a slight smile and his gray eyes appeared almost green as she approached. He stepped forward and held out his hand to help her down the last stair. "You look lovely in lavender, Mrs. Wilson."

"Thank you, Lord Harrow," Valeria spied Lady Westcombe peeking out from a room nearby, so she raised her voice a little louder. "My usual wardrobe seems to have been stolen and replaced with half-mourning."

Theo's lips turned up at the corners.

She liked how they were of similar height. She could not help but smile in return. Lord Harrow was probably the first man she ever felt safe and comfortable with. His demeanor toward her did funny things to her heart and alarm bells went off in her brain. She could not afford a dalliance, no matter how charming the temptation might be. A life amongst the *beau monde* was not for such as her.

~*~

Theo couldn't help but look at the lovely woman by his side in the barouche as his groom drove them through the park. She held such mystery to him and he was not sure how to broach it. How had she recovered after the conflict with Michael and Katrina the other day? How did she come to have a rhombus tattooed on her shoulder? No, he could not ask about that no matter how curious he was. Too personal. She would realize that he and his friends discussed her. Guilt plagued him. He sensed that the woman beside him was still cloaked in sadness that went beyond mourning a deceased spouse. "How is Mittens doing?" A poor conversational gambit, but it was at least innocuous.

Mrs. Wilson's somber expression dissolve into a soft smile. "He is doing well. The boys delight in playing with him and he has only climbed the draperies in the nursery once. Dartanian sleeps with him next to his head on his pillow."

"You are a wonderful mother." Theo admired her for her care of her son. He remembered his own mother treating him with affection when he watched Mrs. Wilson with the dark-haired boy. His heart warmed at the sight. She was exactly the kind of woman he wanted as the mother of his own children.

Children? His heart was set on marriage and now he was already anticipating children. He grinned at the thought of what that entailed.

She glanced at him with eyes narrowed and her head tilted to one side. "What was that grin for?"

Theo startled, and his face heated under her scrutiny. "We all have secrets we like to keep."

The mention of secrets erected an immediate barrier between them. She stiffened her spine and moved ever so slightly away from him. He experienced the loss of her heat.

The conversation on the rest of the ride was sparse and stilted.

Theo escorted her inside the Westcombe townhouse when they returned. "I am sorry if I said anything to offend you. I admire you, Mrs. Wilson." Theo held his hat in his hand nervously moving the brim through his fingers so that the hat appeared to be spinning in a circle.

"It is awkward being in public with you. I'm only a governess."

"You are much more than a governess."

"You are gracious, Lord Harrow."

"Theo or Theodore."

She took a step back—eyes wide.

"It would please me to hear my name on your lips."

"It would not be proper, my lord." She turned to go but paused and looked back at him. "Thank you for the outing."

Theo watched as she took the stairs in a stately manner. Measured steps and her back straight, even with the sling holding her right arm. He admired the view. Everything about this woman he found intriguing and praiseworthy. But how could he make her see she was far more than a governess to him?

~*~

Valeria enjoyed the antics of Dartanian and his kitten as Andrew napped. She loved her son and chafed at the imposed wait for them to depart to distant shores. For the moment, she figured they were safe enough hidden away in the Westcombe townhouse.

She fingered another lavender dress that she'd donned that morning. She loved the design and her heart ached at being so dependent on the goodwill of Lady Westcombe. Beth, as her husband so affectionately called her.

She was wary around Lord Phillip Westcombe. His gaze searched hers as if expecting her to spout horns at some point. The Westcombes encouraged her to take her meals with the family in the evenings and she found the experience trying. She was not a part of that world anymore. Not that she ever really was. Lord Harrow was a frequent visitor and having him gaze across the table each evening was unsettling. If life were different—if she were not hunted—he would be the kind of man to set her heart aflutter. Not that her heart didn't already respond. Her pulse rate would increase, her palms would sweat, and she felt like a gauche *ingenue* in his presence.

As sincere as his attentions were, however, there was only one position a man at his level of peerage would offer a widow of unknown origins. As tempting as an *affaire de coeur* would be, she did not believe she could be heartless enough to walk away when the time came.

She shook her head as the kitten chased after some yarn. Dartanian giggled. She needed to protect her son and that was her first priority. She could not risk any kind of entanglement that would interfere with her goal. As much as finding another position and staying in England tempted her, the dangers were too great.

Angel interrupted her reverie. "Mrs. Westcombe has requested that you join her in the blue drawing room."

Valeria nodded. "Andrew is asleep."

Angel took a seat.

Valeria went to place a kiss on the top of her son's head. "I will return later, Dartanian."

"*Oui, Maman.*" The little boy glanced up momentarily but quickly returned to entertaining his kitten.

Valeria entered the blue drawing room to find Beth sitting with Mrs. Katrina Tidley.

"Would you be so kind as to close the door behind you, Mrs. Wilson?" Beth asked.

Valeria did so and sat in a chair adjacent to both women. "You requested my presence, my lady?"

"Beth."

"Beth," Valeria repeated.

"And you may call me Katrina," Mrs. Tidley stated.

"You are kind to me. My name is Valeria."

"That sounds exotic. Valeria. You possess a French accent. Is that where you are originally from?" Katrina asked as she handed Valeria a cup of tea.

Valeria accepted the cup and stared down at it. Why this question? "My family was from France," she offered. It was true but she did not want to give away too much information. To do so could be deadly.

"Do you still have family there?" Beth asked.

Valeria frowned. "No. They are all gone now. I alone remain."

"I am sorry. I, too, have no immediate family remaining beyond my cousin Lord Remington." Katrina sniffed. "It is a hole in my heart that few understand."

Valeria nodded. It had been so long ago and so much had happened in the years since her parents were murdered. She shivered at the memory and willfully set it aside. "You wanted to see me for something?" She glanced at Beth.

"We did. Valeria, when I assisted the doctor last week, I noticed a distinct mark on your right shoulder blade."

Valeria's mouth dropped open and quickly covered it with her left hand, managing to keep the teacup stable on her knee with the fingers peeking out of the sling.

"Please do not be alarmed. This is a private conversation. Katrina and I have had interactions with a personage who refers to himself as the Black Diamond. Both Katrina and I have suffered and bear a branding similar to yours. While yours was tattooed, mine was cut out of my skin leaving a rhombus shaped indentation—a scar."

"Mine was received at the end of a branding iron," Katrina experienced an involuntary shiver as she set her teacup aside. "Valeria, we are concerned because the Black Diamond has been elusive and dangerous. He is the biological father of my husband, who appears identical to your husband."

"What do you want from me?" Valeria set the teacup back on the tray. Her hand shook and perspiration trickled down her back.

Beth exchanged glances with Katrina before answering. "We want the name of the Black Diamond. He needs to be captured and held accountable for his crimes."

The world went black.

She awoke to two anxious faces waving fans at her and the burn of smelling salts making her eyes water. They helped her to her feet and she settled back in her chair. She became aware of two more people present in the room—Lord Westcombe and Sir Tidley.

"Is this an inquisition?" she whispered.

"No. Far from it. We understand your fear, Valeria. We only want to help you and keep any other potential victims safe from his machinations. He is in league with Napoleon. If we could capture him it may save lives," Katrina said.

"Who would be given this information?" She was

only buying time, time she no longer had if she were discovered.

"Whitehall, Lord Remington and his wife, and Lord Harrow."

Her eyes grew large at the mention of Theodore's name. Even though she had not allowed herself to call him that to his face, it was how she thought of him. Her heart sank at the thought that her secret would become public knowledge. "I do not know that I can tell you. My son…"

"You may be in more danger if you do not tell us. We will provide protection for you and your son until we are certain we are all safe."

"May I think about this?"

The men glanced at each other. Michael finally spoke. "We only wish you the best, Mrs. Wilson. But I suspect that is not your real name and that you are more terrified of discovery than you let on. You know too much, and you are aware of what the Black Diamond is capable of. It would be to your benefit to tell us about it now, so we can act, rather than wait until the Black Diamond finds you or Dartanian and forces the issue."

Phillip's expression was stern and his gaze intense. "You may think about it, but please do not take too much more time. People die every day we do not have him in custody."

Valeria looked from one face to another. Could she trust them? She really didn't know. "May I be excused?"

Beth nodded.

The men parted before her as she walked between them to the door and sought the sanctuary of her room. Once there and the door locked, she collapsed onto her pillow and released the tears she'd held back for years.

~*~

Theo sat across from Michael as his friend shared what had happened at the Westcombes's townhouse that afternoon.

"The Black Diamond has terrorized Mrs. Wilson?"

"That is not her real name, Theo."

Theo bristled at the insinuation that the woman he adored would be deceiving them. "Why would she lie about her name?"

"Same reason I did when I worked for Whitehall and traveled around France. To preserve my life."

"Surely she realizes we would never harm her."

"She cannot know that. Theo, you have yet to meet my father." Michael snorted. "I've not viewed him without a mask and domino. He remains an enigma to me. I would recognize his voice but little else."

"So, she keeps a secret and is loath to share. Why pressure her, Michael?" Theo sipped his brandy and set the snifter down gently.

"Think about it, Theo. She believed I was her husband. Her *deceased* husband. Her son appears as if he could be mine. From what I understand from my mother, I bear much of my father's physical appearance."

Theo shrugged. "What are you insinuating, Michael? You already told Katrina that you had never known Mrs. Wilson in the past and Dartanian is not your child."

"Are you so dense? I'm suspecting that Dartanian is the rightful grandson of my father…I hope that means I *had* a half-brother. She insists she buried her husband. But if this is all true, that means Dartanian is my nephew and the heir to whatever estate the Black Diamond overseas. If she has him in hiding she must fear for his safety."

"She's a wise woman if she ran from the Black Diamond."

Michael's face bore no sense of his trademark humor. "Smart, but not safe. Theo, if all of this conjecture turns out to be true, Valeria is in grave danger, as is her son."

"Wait. If Dartanian is not your nephew, what would he be?"

"He would be my half-brother."

Theo jumped up and grabbed Michael's cravat. "You are saying that your father…"

"I'm saying I would not put it past him. He made it clear he would take Katrina, and if Fidget had not interfered…" Michael shivered.

Theo released him and sat down. His heart sank. All he wanted was a woman to love. Once again they had been thrown into political intrigue and deadly threats. He leaned back and closed his eyes. "What do we do, Michael? How can we keep her safe?" He opened his eyes and turned his head toward his friend.

"We need to find out who the Black Diamond is. Theo, I need you to woo her and get this information."

"You mean seduce her?" Theo sat up straight and frowned.

"Whatever it takes. I thought you were attracted to her?"

"I am. I want her to be the future Lady Harrow."

Michael sipped his wine with a slight upturn of his lips. "As with the rest of us, Theo, you will need to work hard to win her heart."

Theo laughed. "You never had to earn Katrina's heart. She's loved you forever."

"But I had broken it and needed to earn her trust and prove that my love was real. I was too thick-skulled to see it for too long. I wasted too much time. Don't make my mistake."

Both men picked up their drinks and made a toast: to love—and war.

~*~

Valeria held the note with shaking fingers.

I know where you are. I will have what is mine.

She crumpled it up and threw it into the fireplace. Her father-in-law could send his cohorts, but they would never take her or her son. He wanted both and it nauseated her. She needed to leave. But how? She had not saved up enough, possessed nothing left to sell, and was not healed from her injury. How would she take Dartanian away from here without breaking his heart? She was sure a kitten would be welcome on a ship. But he had also grown so attached to little Andrew. Did she dare confide in Beth and Katrina?

They included her daily in tea time and another woman, Viscountess Remington, joined them.

"Mrs. Wilson, I would like you to meet our dear friend, Lady Josephine Remington. We call her Josie. She is married to Marcus, who is Theo's, Phillip's and Michael's best friend. Marcus will join us for dinner tomorrow night." Beth made the introductions. "Josie, this is Mrs. Valeria Wilson."

Josie smiled. "It is a pleasure to meet the woman who seems to have Theo at sixes and sevens. I never thought to see the day when he would lose his heart."

Katrina giggled. "I think Theo feels left out now that everyone is married."

"Everyone but Jared, you mean?" Josie sipped her tea.

"Captain Jared Allendale is Marcus's younger brother. He serves with Wellesley but has also been at times associated with our men in their adventures," Elizabeth said.

Katrina nodded. "The Captain's an attractive man. I'm surprised no woman has brought him to the altar yet."

Josie winked. "God knows who He has for Jared. We only need to wait for Jared to figure it out."

The ladies tittered, and Valeria experienced the warmth and camaraderie threatening to encase her in its talons and wear down her defenses.

Elizabeth spoke up in between bites of her cucumber sandwich. "Josie, we shared with Valeria about our run ins with the Black Diamond. Why don't you share your connection?"

Josie frowned, exhaled, and set her cup and saucer on the table. "During my first season, a man by the name of Sir Bastion sought to make me his bride, by force if necessary. Marcus and Jared worked to uncover his treasonous activities and he was captured, but hung himself before he could be tried. We found out later he was associated with the Black Diamond in doing some illegal trading with France. I alone have never been branded, although I shudder to think that it would have happened if Bastion had succeeded." Josie shivered and held her arms, rubbing them with her hands as if to warm up.

Elizabeth rose to stir the fire into a warmer blaze.

The room suddenly grew colder to Valeria as well.

Katrina spoke up. "It was surprising to hear of Marcus going to a brothel to discover the information." She turned to Valeria. "My cousin, Marcus, has a reputation as the Virtuous Viscount. His actions that helped capture Sir Bastion, almost cost him his relationship with Josie."

Valeria raised an eyebrow.

"It seems so long ago now, but it was only a few years past." Josie smiled. "But all our men, your Theo included, fought valiantly to save me from a kidnapping by my uncle." Her face looked sad. "I almost lost Marcus. He was so seriously wounded in that fight. He still walks with a limp and he can tell now when bad weather is coming." Josie's eyes teared up. "I am blessed to be able to call him my husband. I could not imagine being married to anyone less worthy."

"Well, my Phillip has definitely proven himself worthy of my love," Beth inserted.

Valeria was intrigued.

"Phillip and Beth's relationship did not start out as a love match. They were married hardly even knowing each other and quickly thrown into a difficult situation with her father, Lord Follett, and his partner, Lord Wolton, whom we found out later had ties to the Black Diamond." Josie sipped her tea.

Beth shivered. "What a difficult time we experienced. I thought I was losing my mind and would have done anything to save Phillip from Lord Wolton. I was foolish, but God watched over us. Phillip was so brave, but he was furious with the risks I took with our unborn child." She gave a sad grin. "I was pregnant but had a miscarriage. I didn't realize at the time that I had conceived twins and one still lived within me." Her face brightened. "That would be Andrew. My father did not survive the fire that occurred the night that Wolton was defeated and buried under one of the underground smugglers' tunnels at Follett Hall in Ipswich." Beth wiped away a tear. "I'm glad to be done with the evil that he participated in."

Katrina patted her friend's knee. "Michael and I are the only ones to meet the Black Diamond face to face, but he wore a mask. He was evil incarnate. We discovered that Michael is his illegitimate son. The Black Diamond wanted Michael dead and expressed an interest in taking over as my lover. Michael and I were not even married yet."

"It took a solid knock to his head to bring him around to realizing he loved Katrina." Josie giggled.

"It took far more than that." Katrina placed a hand over her stomach. "Our daughter, Michaela, is four months old, and now we are hoping for a son."

Valeria took in the three unique women sitting around her. Three men, all friends, had found wives, but each had a tragic interaction with her father-in-law. It seemed ironic that the one single man in that band of brothers was now sniffing at her skirts. She shook her head and tried not to laugh at the thought of Lord Harrow as a puppy wagging his tail in an attempt to gain her favor. But in many ways his gray eyes held that kind of earnestness when he would gaze at her. An unspoken promise that he would never hurt her lured her heart into dangerous territory.

Josie set her tea down. "Mrs. Wilson…Valeria, you have been quiet as we have shared our misadventures with you. We want to help you in whatever way we can."

"We would be your friends if you would let us." Beth's eyes pleaded with her.

Valeria assessed the beautiful women around her. Lady Elizabeth Westcombe, Phillip's wife. Red hair, lithe figure, and winning smile who had compassion on her and given her a safe place to heal. Lady Josephine Remington, with dark wavy hair and warm smile. Valeria wondered what Lord Remington, Marcus, looked like as she had yet to meet him. Then there was Mrs. Tidley, Sir Michael's bride, petite with brown hair and big eyes that no longer held accusations but...friendship? Valeria set down her teacup and took a deep breath.

"You have all been gracious to me. I do not deserve your offer of friendship." She swallowed hard. "Yes, I am acquainted with the Black Diamond and I fear him." She stared at Beth. "Lord Wolton didn't die. He is still seeking vengeance. Please be careful."

Beth's right hand went to cover her heart and she became pale. "You cannot be serious?"

Valeria dropped her gaze to her hands. "I don't want to cause trouble here. If you wish to help me..."

"We do, Mrs. Wilson. We long to help you." Katrina reached over and clasped one of Valeria's hands.

The tears stung in Valeria's eyes. "I would like to sail to the Americas with Dartanian as soon as possible. I fear it is the only way I will be safe."

Silence fell among them.

Katrina released Valeria's hand.

Valeria waited. It was humbling to need this kind of help. She feared what may befall these lovely women and their families if she stayed.

"I do not think we can help you with that," Josie

spoke softly.

The first tear escaped.

"We want to help you, Mrs. Wilson, but running away will only leave the problem for someone else. We need you to stay and fight and help us defeat this evil."

"Do you understand just how wicked this man can be?" Valeria stood.

They all nodded.

Valeria paced. "He will rape and kill to get what he wants. No one can stand in his way. He has power—evil power—at his disposal. This is not a game."

Katrina walked over to her and placed a small hand on Valeria's forearm. "We understand. He desired to rape me. He tried to kill me and my husband, who is his own son." Katrina stepped back a moment and placed a hand over her mouth. "Oh, my. Valeria."

Valeria peered into Katrina's startled brown eyes, wide open with fear. "What?"

"He is your father-in-law, is he not? You were married to his son who would have been Michael's half-brother."

Valeria shifted her gaze. "Damon was as evil as his father, but not as powerful."

"I am so sorry, Valeria. I am not sure why I never guessed this before now."

"I hoped you never would. If you will excuse me." She walked to the door with as much decorum as she could manage.

~*~

Theo found Mrs. Wilson sitting in the garden. Her

shoulders were slumped as she stared into the distance. He followed her gaze and found only a dead bush amongst the shrubs. He approached, and she straightened up as he drew near.

"Lord Harrow."

"It would please me greatly if you would call me Theodore or Theo."

She gave him a wan smile and shook her head. "You are *obstiné*, are you not, my lord?"

"When it is important to me." He motioned to the bench she sat on. "May I?"

"I cannot stop you." Her words lacked bite as her eyebrows rose.

Theo longed to see a real smile on her face. One that would light up her dark eyes. Her hair shimmered gold with the sun shining on her. Her nose was slightly pink. She must have been sitting here for some time. Theo sat and followed her gaze back to the dead bush.

"I am like that bush," she stated.

"How so?" He folded his arms across his chest and saw a hitch in her breathing. He stifled a grin. She was not as immune to him as she would indicate. He let his legs stretch out in front and crossed one boot over the other.

"I am dead and stripped of all that would give me life."

"It does not need to stay that way."

"A dead bush is useless."

"I disagree." She glanced over at him and he experienced a jolt as her eyes met his. Such desolation in those dark brown depths.

"How so?"

"While the bush appears like this. it may be so for two reasons. One. It has lost its life to disease or lack of food and water."

"And two?"

"It is merely dormant, awaiting the nurture and care of someone to bring it back to life."

"And which one do you think I am?"

"While a dead bush is great for kindling and can help start a raging fire, that burns out and eventually dissolves to ashes."

"Ashes to ashes, dust to dust. We all share that fate."

"Eventually, perhaps. I think you are the second kind. Perhaps dormant and neglected, in need of love and attention you would bloom to greater beauty than those who surround you."

Valeria gave him a soft smile. "You wax poetical, Lord Harrow."

"Only when so inspired."

"And what inspires you today?"

"You do, Mrs. Wilson. You most certainly inspire many things in me." His words struck home and a blush rose prettily in her cheeks. He longed to do nothing more than kiss her, rub his thumb along her square jaw, and convince her somehow to be his to protect and care for.

She broke the gaze and rose to her full height. "Thank you, Lord Harrow for your lesson in the finer art of...gardening." With that she walked away.

Theo stayed. It may take time, but she would be his. She hadn't realized it yet. As much as he desired a drama-free romance, he was finding that he was inwardly enjoying the pursuit of the elusive Mrs. Wilson.

5

Theo entered the house and found Phillip in his study with Michael and Marcus.

"Theo, just the man we wanted to see." Phillip greeted his friend.

Marcus gave his friend a pat on the back. "I hear that a romance is in the making. Am I understanding Michael correctly?"

Heat rose in Theo's face. "I'm making the attempt."

"I have yet to meet this paragon who has so inspired you to leap into the matrimonial pool." Marcus grinned and sat back down.

Theo also found a chair.

"We have new information, Theo. Our wives have been trying to befriend Mrs. Wilson."

"Oh?" Theo was definitely interested.

"The Black Diamond is her father-in-law and his son, Damon, was her husband." Michael gave a smug grin.

"So, you were right about that." Theo rubbed his chin. "There's something more?"

Phillip nodded. "It seems that Lord Wolton survived the tunnel crash and Mrs. Wilson warned Beth to be careful."

Theo's brow went up at this. "Lord Wolton? But he was in league with…"

"The Black Diamond," Marcus said.

"It always comes back to him," Theo remarked.

"True. There's more." Phillip handed Theo a burnt

piece of foolscap. "A maid found this in the fireplace in Mrs. Wilson's room."

Theo looked at the slanted masculine script and a chill traveled up his spine. *"I know where you are. I will have what is mine."* He glanced at his friends. "He realizes she is here."

Phillip nodded. "That means none of our wives or children are safe, least of all Mrs. Wilson, and Dartanian."

"What can we do?" Theo was eager to do anything to protect Mrs. Wilson and her son.

"I have already called in favors and have set up extra guard around the perimeter," Michael stated.

"I suggest we all repair to Rose Hill. It will be easier to provide safety for all if we are in one location."

"The Black Diamond is aware of Rose Hill, Marcus. His thugs attacked my wife on your property," Phillip stated.

"Will Mrs. Wilson relent to this plan?" Theo asked.

"Has she any choice?" Marcus asked.

"If she would marry me I could protect her better," Theo suggested.

The three men stared at him, nonplussed.

Phillip finally broke the silence. "Marriage will not protect her, Theo. I was already wed when Beth was assaulted."

A knock at the door broke the silence.

"Come in," Phillip called.

The door opened, and a footman entered, out of breath. His coat was ripped, and his face stained with dirt and blood.

"Jem, what happened to you?"

Jem bent over, gasping for air. "They took him. I

tried ..."

"Who was taken?" Phillip asked in clipped tones as he strode towards the footman.

"Dartanian."

Theo jumped up. "Who took him?"

"A group of men. At the park."

"Andrew?" Phillip asked in a whisper.

"Your son is unscathed but crying. Angel took him to Lady Westcombe."

"Is Mrs. Wilson aware?" Theo asked.

"I only arrived."

"Did they say anything?" Phillip asked.

"No. But they left this." Jem handed over a crumpled-up envelope.

Phillip broke the seal. *"The boy is mine. Be warned, Valeria. I will be coming for you too. You will pay dearly for your betrayal."*

Phillip threw the paper to his desk and called for his butler. "Have Mrs. Wilson brought to me immediately." He turned to Jem. "You may go to the kitchen. Let Mrs. Miller tend your wounds and feed you. You served us well."

An anguished look appeared on the young man's face. "I failed you, Lord Westcombe."

Phillip placed a hand on the young man's shoulders. "It appears to me you fought valiantly to save Dartanian. You went beyond what was asked of you. Tell Mrs. Miller to send for the physician to make sure nothing is broken."

"You are too kind, my lord." Jem bowed and departed.

~*~

Valeria walked into the room filled with men. The grave expressions on their faces filled her with fear. Another inquisition?

Lord Harrow moved forward to clasp the elbow on her left arm, the one not in a sling. He drew her to the couch and sat beside her, holding her arm on top of his as it rested on his thigh. She found herself momentarily distracted by the warmth from his touch and the solid muscle revealed by the stretch of his trousers as he sat. She saw heat and sorrow in his eyes, those gray depths flecked with green. "What is it?"

Phillip handed her the note.

Valeria searched his steely blue eyes and her heart sank. Her hand left the comfort of Theo's arm to reach for the paper. But her heart knew.

Dartanian was gone.

She turned her face into Theo's shoulder and his arm wrapped around her. His strength surrounding her, and the smell of clean linen and man combined to break down the rest of her defenses. She sobbed. A handkerchief was pressed into her palm and she clasped it as she placed her hand on his solid thigh. The muscle contracted and all she longed for in that moment was his strength and safety.

When her sobs subsided, Phillip spoke. "Do you think you would be able to give us the information we need to help you find your son?"

Valeria sighed. She continued to lean on Lord Harrow and took comfort from his arm around her. She glanced at him and he solemnly nodded.

"Please, Mrs. Wilson. We only want to help."

Her body shuddered in the aftermath of her grief. She nodded. "What do you need to know?"

"We need the identity of the Black Diamond and

where his estate is."

She gulped. "Lord Harold St. John, the Duke of Diamonte. His estate is near…"

The men looked thunderstruck.

"Ashbourne, of course. Derbyshire," Michael finally stated.

She nodded.

"You are aware of this person, Michael?" Marcus asked.

"There was a St. John over at Cambridge. Nasty reputation. Never met him but sure heard of him. Remember?" Michael asked, glancing at Phillip.

"Yes, I remember his reputation but never met the man or his father," Phillip answered.

"How did you come to be married to his son, Damon?" Michael asked.

"Damon and I met while they were in France. My father was opposed to the match but for some reason Damon desired me and his father was willing to do what he could to acquire a French bride for his son. In one night my parents died and our estate was torched. I was left orphaned and homeless. I had no one else to turn to. We married in France and traveled back to Ashton."

"Did the Duke ever…?" Michael tilted his head and raised his eyebrows.

"Proposition me?"

Michael nodded.

Valeria's face grew warm. She stared down at her hands. Lord Harrow's much larger one engulfed hers and gave her a reassuring squeeze. "I could not stay in Ashbourne any longer. I did not want Dartanian to be raised to be like his father or grandfather."

~*~

Mrs. Wilson's eyes were bleak, and he sensed her despair and helplessness. He nodded. "I am sorry for what you have suffered. We will do everything we can to see you and Dartanian safe."

"I fear it is a trap to get me back into his power. He is evil. He will not hesitate to kill Dartanian if pushed too far." Terror for her son made her voice hitch and she struggled to bring her emotions under control.

"Dartanian is the sole heir?" Michael asked.

Valeria nodded, unable to speak.

"What is your real name?" Theo asked.

"Lady Valeria Barron St. John."

"Do you have any idea where they may have taken Dartanian?" Marcus asked in a take-charge manner.

"He most likely took him to Damon's principal estate near Newcastle-under-Lyme."

"We need to make a plan. Theo, you'll join us?" Marcus asked.

Theo looked at the woman next to him. She stiffened at Marcus's brusque tone. "I will personally accompany Lady St. John to Newastle-under-Lyme."

"She cannot come with us. She needs to remain safe here," Phillip said.

Theo stood, dragging Valeria to her feet. "She is Dartanian's mother. She needs to be there when he is rescued. He will need her." He squeezed her hand which he still held. "She is also the only one who knows that estate and could get us in. I would say she is an essential part of any plan you care to make."

Valeria leaned into him and he put an arm around her shoulder again, drawing her close. He thought he heard her whisper, "Thank you, Theodore."

It made his heart beat faster.

"There is a problem with this plan," Marcus said.

"What?" Valeria spoke now.

"You would need a chaperon," Marcus stated.

"I am a widow. I do not need a *compagnon.* As I will be traveling in the company of four men, it is unnecessary."

"If you are worried about proprieties, Marcus, I could marry her." The look on the faces of Theo's friends was priceless. He had left them dumbfounded.

Valeria's reaction was different. She pulled her hand from his and stepped away. "No. No. No." Her head was shaking.

Before he could grab it she fled the room. "Bad timing?" He glanced at his friends.

All three men nodded.

Theo sat down and covered his face. He most certainly had messed up. No wonder he was still unmarried. "I'm a buffleheaded idiot."

"Never fear, Theo. I'm sure she will begin to see that you are a lovable, buffleheaded idiot. Give her time." Michael grinned at him.

Theo could only shake his head in response. "I hope so."

Phillip patted him on the back. "Glad to see you finally join the club. Each of us have been idiots in one way or another."

"Speak for yourselves," Marcus chided. "That is one term that's never been applicable to me."

"True, Marcus, but the three of us never had a news sheet printed with a cartoon of us in a brothel." Phillip grinned.

Marcus laughed. "True, Phillip, but it was for a

noble cause."

"My cause is noble as well," Theo proclaimed.

~*~

The carriage was ready by mid-day. Theo opted to ride inside with Valeria who still would not speak with him. Michael was driving the carriage and Marcus and Phillip were on horseback, armed and prepared for any possible danger.

Josie, Elizabeth, and Katrina waved them off, promising to pray for Dartanian's safe recovery. The women were well guarded by armed footmen patrolling the Westcombe property where all the women and their children were staying together until the men and Lady St. John returned.

It took time for the carriage to leave the city. Theo leaned against the squabs by the door and stretched his feet out, making sure that he was not touching Lady St. John. The tension inside the carriage was high. "Lady St. John, we are to be closed up in this carriage for days. It would be far more comfortable if we could at least be friends. I am sorry for my inappropriate comment earlier. Should we decide to wed in the future, you are worthy of a far better and more private proposal than the one you received in Phillip's study," Theo said.

"Apology accepted."

"Could we be comfortable again? I would be your friend if you would let me."

"If you can't settle for being my husband you will be happy with the role of friend?" A gaze penetrated his deepest thoughts and emotions. She shook her head. "Men are never happy with less than what they ultimately desire."

"Perhaps I am proposing friendship in the hopes of you growing to love me someday." Theo turned to the window. Did he love her? How would he really be sure? All he was aware of was a growing desire to touch her. He respected her and admired her strength, even now, not knowing how her son fared, she was not helpless. Perhaps he only wanted her because she was the one woman who did not throw herself at him.

No, that could not be true. Josie never threw herself at him, but he realized she was meant for Marcus all along. He held no desire for her and viewed her like a sister. Beth was beautiful but married to Phillip before he ever really met her. Married women were always off-limits in his mind. Katrina? He'd grown up with her as an annoying little friend, more like a sister. Besides, she only ever had eyes for Michael. Just once he wanted someone of his own.

He'd finally found a woman who made his pulse race and his stomach perform funny flips. A woman who taunted him in his dreams and left him waking up disappointed that she was not by his side. A woman who didn't need or want his title or wealth, or even his help, if he was honest. He wanted her as he'd never wanted any woman and she'd rebuffed him at every turn. After she had soaked his waistcoat and cravat earlier with tears he hoped that perhaps she was beginning to view him in a different way. Then he'd opened his mouth and spoiled it all.

~*~

"I am not angry with you, Lord Harrow." Her voice was soft, and it soothed his spirit.

He said nothing.

She fiddled with the strings of her reticule. "After Damon died, I swore I would never marry again. It is nothing personal. I simply could not bear the thought of. . ."

"Not all men are beasts, Lady St. John."

"Tell my heart that."

Silence hung between them for many miles.

"Maybe someday I will exercise my rights as a widow and consider a dalliance. But marriage? I cannot conceive of ever wanting any part of that again."

"You deserve more than the life of a mistress, my lady."

"You would not be tempted?"

Theo gazed into her brown, almost black eyes and slowly scanned her figure with its tailored cut accentuating every delicious curve. He met her glance again. "I would be tempted but I would never be satisfied with access only to your body, lovely as it is."

Her eyebrows raised. "Why not?"

"Because I have witnessed the beauty of love in the lives of my friends and could settle for nothing less than what they have found. That goes far beyond what happens between the sheets." Theo averted his eyes and shook his head. Buffleheaded. Most certainly buffleheaded. Since when did his honor as a gentleman preclude him taking a gift willingly offered by a woman? He groaned and closed his eyes. They were startled open when a hand landed on his knee.

~*~

What man would turn down an offer like that? She

was coming to care for this gentle man sitting across from her. She had never experienced safety in any man's arms until Theo. But she had almost nothing to compare it with. The man sitting across from her appeared forlorn. They had days to spend together cooped up in this cozy carriage. It would be a shame to be at odds with each other. Why couldn't he accept that she could not entrust her future to another man? She placed her hand on his knee.

His muscle tightened and his eyes flashed open. Deep pools of green warmth penetrated hers. "Lady St. John?"

"Valeria. Call me Valeria."

"Valeria." He watched her closely.

She moved to sit beside him on the rear-facing seat. Valeria reached up and placed her left hand on his cheek. She ran her thumb over the stubble on his jaw. She moved up to massage away the worry lines on his forehead and between his eyes. His gaze never left her face. She smiled. He really was such a sweet man. Her forefinger ran down the bridge of his nose and played along the shape of his lips. "Do you seek to tease me, my lady?"

"Valeria."

"Valeria."

She placed her lips on his and experimented with how gently he responded. He only took as much as she was willing to give. All of a sudden, she longed to give him far more. She never knew sensations like this before. Kisses had always been forcefully taken.

His hand came up and pulled her jaw back to his and this time he initiated the kiss.

It was like a string of excitement started there and traveled from her head to her toes and everywhere in between. Desire overwhelmed her. It was a new and startling experience. She pulled back, suddenly afraid.

He let her go.

"Theodore."

He gazed at her and waited.

"I want you."

His eyes changed color from green to gray. He stared out the rear window and tensed up. "Valeria, get to the floor. Now!" Theo's voice was rough as he reached for his gun.

"What?"

"Riders coming from behind fast. They have weapons drawn. Down! Now." His voice was strong and angry.

Fear enveloped her, but she obeyed. She sank to the floor as a bullet pierced the rear window shattering the glass and putting a hole in the squabs where her head had just been.

Theo slid across the seat to the edge of the window and took aim with his pistol.

The report and the odor of gunpowder filled the carriage.

Valeria coughed.

Lord Harrow grumbled, reloaded, and fired again.

The returning report of a bullet sounded. Theo's gun fell and landed by her hands.

"Blast it!" Theo said as he curled his body back into the corner.

The carriage slowed and stopped. Sir Tidley peered in. "Are you well, Lady St. John?"

Valeria nodded, rose to her knees, and gazed at Theo in the corner. Blood oozed from a cut along the side of his forehead and his eyes were closed.

"Theodore!" Valeria scrambled to sit next to him.

Michael untied his cravat and handed it to her.

She tried to clean the blood with her handkerchief, but it was too dainty. She grabbed inside Theo's breast pocket for his and applied herself to putting pressure on the wound. She untied his cravat and wound it around Theo's head. He opened his eyes and gazed at her with a cheeky grin. "Shall we resume where we left off?"

Valeria shook her head. "I believe you are too injured for any kind of activity."

"Trust me, my lady. The most important parts are still intact." Theo exited the carriage and leaned against it to confer with the men.

No one else had been injured. It appeared that Lady St. John was the intended victim. The assailants did not survive the counter-attack and were unable to give information. Their horses were tethered behind the carriage, and one of the guards cleaned up the broken glass.

Marcus rode ahead to the next town to alert the magistrate to the dead bodies by the side of the road.

Valeria settled back into the carriage. She leaned over to Theo and gave him a kiss on the cheek.

"What was that for?" He gave her a sleepy grin.

Valeria tilted her head and considered him for a moment. "That was for a man who acts like a hero." Color rose in his cheeks. She reached over and smoothed back a bit of the soft, sandy brown hair that was still visible above the makeshift bandage. "Of course, right now you appear more like a pirate." She grinned at him and flicked at the ends of the cravat that hung down off the side of his head.

"A pirate?"

She nodded.

"Does that mean I can claim my treasure?"

"What treasure would that be?"

"A kiss from the pirate princess?"

"Hmmm. I am sure that could be arranged." Valeria leaned in to give him a kiss she hoped he would never forget.

~*~

By the next day, Theo removed the bandage and allowed the area where the bullet had grazed him to scab over. He was able to partially hide it under his hair if he did not comb it back. Valeria had been more subdued in the carriage. They'd been unable to replace the glass, so dust filtered in through the back window.

"Valeria."

"Yes, Theodore?" Her voice was soft. She sounded lost.

"You are quiet today."

"You are observant. I am anxious for Dartanian. I miss *mon enfant*." Her hands were clasped tightly together in her lap.

"Relax. They cannot be too far ahead of us. As my friends would say, trust God to take care of him."

Valeria's eyes flashed as she met his gaze. "You are a believer in Christ?"

Theo shrugged. "I believe He walked the earth. I am inclined to even think He is God. I have a harder time accepting that He cares anything about my life."

"How sad." Her hands relaxed. "I used to doubt too."

"But no longer?" This woman was a believer?

She sighed. "I still doubt, but I pray anyway and try to read my Bible. I find great comfort there. The more evil I saw the more I believed in the goodness of God."

"That makes no sense."

"A diamond is only made more brilliant against a black fabric. The stars shine more brightly against the darkest sky."

"So, if there is evil. If there is a devil. There must be a counterpart. God?"

She nodded and bit her lip.

"But you struggle to trust Him?"

Tears sprang to her eyes. "My faith in Him is *nouveau*. New. I am human. David in the Psalms had questions too. And I am a *maman*. My heart breaks for my little boy. I worry he is afraid or might be injured."

Theo moved to sit next to her and drew her close, wrapping an arm around her shoulder. It felt so right to hold her in his arms. He placed a kiss on her golden hair. She turned to look at him and her good arm reached up to touch his cheek.

"The last time we tried this I got shot at." Theo grinned at her.

"We shall not dally then, *oui*?"

"*Oui*."

Their lips met, and the the orange blossom scent Valeria wore filled his senses. She relaxed and leaned into him more, pressing her body against his. He thought he would burst for all the emotions that her touch evoked.

When the kiss broke, Theo was breathing as heavily as if he'd run several miles. He moved to sit back across from her where he could continue to keep vigil out the back window. Focusing on the potential danger was a good antidote to the urges that warred within him. His friends kept an eye on them as well which was sobering. He grinned. Caught compromising the lovely widow could result in their marriage. Marcus would insist. He did that to Phillip and Beth and it turned out to be a love-match.

Theo scolded himself. Valeria was worrying for her son. It was wrong for him to take advantage of her vulnerability and force himself on her. He would act the gentleman. *Wait a minute. She was the one who propositioned me!* Theo glanced over to her as she gazed out the window at the scenery. He was certain her mind was miles away.

How would he ever get her to consider uniting her life to his in marriage? For now that he'd tasted her lips, he could settle for nothing less.

6

Valeria stared out the window after Theo moved away. She feared if she looked at him, the desire she felt deep inside for the man would tempt her to go beyond the kisses they'd already shared. She was ashamed of the way she'd propositioned him the day before. Her son was in danger and she dared to think of anything else? She was grateful he was too much of a gentleman to accept her offer. She longed to be with a man such as him. No. That was not true. She only longed for Lord Harrow. Theodore. Theo. His gentle demeanor was a balm to her wounded spirit. Just having him near was a comfort in the midst of her nightmare.

After the suspicious deaths of her parents and the subsequent abuses from her husband and his father, she never would have believed that a man like Theodore existed. It was beyond her experience. But now with this new information, could she dare entrust her heart, her body, and her future to such as him?

He did not have a firm belief in Jesus and that concerned her. He exemplified so many of the qualities she read about the Messiah. Compassionate. Gentle. Righteous. Steadfast. Sacrificial. Protecting. She wondered why, if all his friends were followers of Christ, he had not chosen that path himself. She prayed for faith to trust God. For protection for Dartanian and that they would recover him alive and well. And she prayed for the men who accompanied her on this journey. She prayed for Theo, that his heart would open to understand and love Jesus because she could not imagine spending her life with a man who didn't.

The day dragged on and later in the afternoon it rained. The men decided to stop at an inn for the evening instead of pressing on. Michael, who had been driving, was chilled to the bone. Still, he joined them in the private parlor after he'd donned fresh clothing. They'd only traveled as far as Bedford.

Sitting at the table with the men there was little conversation.

"I was thinking that since we are not that far from St. Neots we could detour there, pick up one of my carriages, and continue on from there." Theo shoved another piece of roast in his mouth and chewed, waiting for his compatriots to chime in.

"Your estate is near here?" Valeria asked.

Theo nodded. His mouth was full.

"I would love to visit it someday."

"As a Marquess it is one of the nicer estates awarded by the King. Theo is the third in his family to hold the title," Phillip offered.

"You are a Marquess? I did not know." Valeria suddenly grew a bit uncertain. "Your parents?"

Theo swallowed hard. "My father died in a hunting accident several years past. My mother was heartbroken. She lost her will to live and was buried within a year of her husband. I was an only child." Theo sipped his port and rose from the table. "I will see you in the morning. Rest well, fair lady." With that he was gone.

"I think we should stop at Hartview tomorrow. Theo has a nice carriage. His groom can take yours in, Phillip, to have it repaired, and we can pick it up on our way back to London." Michael made the suggestion as he sipped his ale.

"He left abruptly," Valeria stated.

The men exchanged glances.

"Theo was very alone growing up. He is two years older than the rest of us and kind of ended up falling in with us at school. He never fit in anywhere else, I guess." Marcus wandered to the fireplace with his ale. "He stayed on as a tutor after he finished school. I don't believe I would have passed without his help."

Phillip leaned back in his chair. "I never realized he helped you, Marcus."

"That would be so like Theo. Helping someone out. Listening to their concerns and never drawing attention to himself," Michael added. He stood and set down his mug. "I'm heading up. We will leave early. We have a lot of ground to cover tomorrow."

"I will come up with you," Valeria said as she rose.

Valeria entered her room and prepared for bed. Once under the covers she could not stop thinking about Theodore. Her body could not help but respond to his gentle embrace and the restrained passion behind his kisses. But he had never gone beyond what she would allow. He never even tried. Today he withdrew from her physically and emotionally. She wondered why. Her heart believed he carried a sorrow deep inside that he hid from the world. She was well acquainted with the emotion. Instead of locking himself away from life he had invested in his friends.

Valeria rose and walked over to the fireplace letting the cold floor seep in through her bare feet. She wanted to go to him. To see him. To know that he was all right. But she didn't dare. She had refused his offer of marriage and had made it clear she would have none of that ever again.

But now she wondered if it would be such a bad thing to be married to a man like him. No. Not a man *like* him. *Him.* Tomorrow she would somehow let him know she might be amenable to that once they were past the current crisis.

Dartanian. She had been so wrapped up in her thoughts about Lord Harrow she'd briefly forgotten about her son. Dreaming about things that couldn't be had been a way to avoid the terror she'd been fighting since her son had been taken. She wrapped her arms around herself. Her prayer lifted to heaven that he would be safe, that they would find him, and be able to rescue him from the evil clutches of the Duke of Diamonte. She crawled back under the covers and longed for strong arms to comfort her and assure her everything would be fine.

The next morning, she arrived in the private parlor early and encountered Marcus, Michael, and Phillip. She sat to pour some coffee and helped herself to some of the food. The sun was beginning to peek past the horizon.

"We will depart as soon as you are ready, Lady St. John," Phillip remarked.

"Where is Lord Harrow?" she asked. She had looked forward to time together with him in the carriage today. Being near him was a comfort she was wondering if she could ever live without again.

"He rode on ahead of us to alert his staff and have the carriage made ready," Marcus stated.

"Oh." She experienced a deep sense of loss and suddenly had no more appetite. She rose. "Let us be off."

Phillip escorted her out the door and assisted her

into the carriage.

The sky appeared ominously dark even as the sun was trying to poke past the trees to the east of them.

The carriage took off at a spanking pace. Realizing they didn't need to make the horses last for long, Marcus ran them so they could reach Hartview in good time.

When they crested the hill before descending into the valley where Hartview was nestled, Valeria gazed out the window in wonder. The woods and the gardens were spectacular. The building was Palladian in style and well-maintained. The stables off to the north were also tidy and well-kept. The sun broke through the clouds casting a golden glow on the mansion and Valeria found herself longing for time to explore the home that Theo had grown up in, as if doing so would give her greater insight into the man she was coming to love.

Love? Did she even understand what that was? It had been so long. But if this was love, she wanted more of it. She wanted Lord Theodore Harrow for her own. The realization shook her to her core.

~*~

Theo greeted the group and moved to let down the carriage stairs to assist Lady St. John. The minute her feet hit the ground he released his grasp of her. He motioned for the group to enter the mansion for a brief rest before they resumed their journey with fresh horses and his own carriage.

Theo was loath to let Valeria go but after the reminder last night of his past, the love that destroyed and took his mother from him, he needed to pull back.

Lady St. John made it clear she did not want to marry. Why would he waste his time pursuing a woman who did not want him? Her kisses drove him wild, but he needed to step away from the temptation she presented. The temptation to love when it wasn't returned came with the vain hope that, someday, she would find him worthy enough. Would any woman? His fingers still tingled for minutes after releasing her and escorting his friends into the house.

The meal was brief, and his chef packed a basket for the carriage.

"Michael, I can drive the carriage now if you would like a breather," Theo offered.

"I'm glad you didn't purchase that matched pair. Given your poor judgement in even considering them, I think Michael should drive." Phillip grinned and nudged Michael who nodded.

"I did not buy that pair. While they were beautiful to look at, they almost killed Lady St. John." All the men glanced at the woman who still wore her arm in a sling. "I have a full stable and a surefooted pair that will likely be able to take us as far as Corby if handled well."

Michael shrugged. "I'm fine riding alongside. It will feel good to not be bouncing my bottom for miles and miles."

"Fine. It is settled. Shall we head out?"

Marcus helped Valeria to rise. She glanced over at Theo with an eyebrow raised but permitted Lord Remington to assist her in entering the carriage.

Theo climbed on top, took the reins in hand and started out. The men joining behind on horseback.

The miles passed with the steady clomping of the horses' hooves and the bouncing of the well sprung carriage over the rutted roads. Theo kept a cautious gaze to the sky as dark clouds drew nearer. He was grateful for his hat and his many caped coat. Even if it were to rain they could make good time if the roads were not too muddy.

The rain did come accompanied by thunder. The horses skittered at the sound and the flashing of lightning.

Michael rode on ahead to arrange for rooms in Corby at the Hen and Rooster.

The rain slowed to a mere sprinkle. Still, Theo looked forward to drying off for a spell before resuming their journey. A tingle went up Theo's spine as they turned a corner in the road and he pulled the horses to a stop at a large tree that had either fallen, or been strategically placed there. He reached for his gun as he tied off the reins and stepped down. He knocked on the door of the carriage. "Stay put and keep your head down."

Phillip and Marcus dismounted and tied their horses to the carriage as they came around, also with hands on their guns.

Theo surveyed the scene. "It was moved. This tree did not fall between Michael's passing here and our arrival."

A scream rent the air.

The three men turned to see a brute removing Valeria forcibly from the carriage.

Theo leveled his gun but the man holding Valeria was hiding behind her with a knife to the side of her throat.

Valeria's eyes were closed but she opened them and spoke calmly. "Theo, promise me you will find Dartanian and care for him."

"There will be no need of that," Theo responded as his gun wavered.

Phillip had managed to move around the far side of the carriage and was working his way up behind the man.

Marcus stood by Theo's side with his gun also drawn but not aimed.

"Go ahead and try to kill me," the thug said. He had an advantage as Lady St. John was taller than him and provided him with complete coverage.

"It would be my pleasure," Theo responded. His eyes bored into Valeria's. He moved his eyes to the side and back.

She got the message. She stomped down hard with her heel on the thug's foot and spun away.

Theo shot.

The man went down.

Theo rushed to Valeria's side as Marcus reconnoitered the area to ensure that there were no other attackers.

Phillip checked the fallen man and looked to Theo.

"He's dead. You haven't lost your touch, Theo. I would hate to ever have to meet you for a duel." Phillip rolled the man off the road and into the ditch and went to find his horse that had whinnied when the gun fired.

Theo helped Valeria to her feet from the muddy road where she'd fallen. She was holding her right arm and biting her lower lip.

"Did you re-injure yourself?"

She nodded and blinked back tears.

Theo brought her back to the carriage and bade her to sit inside without a word spoken. He pulled a flask of brandy out of a pocket in the carriage, unscrewed the top, and handed it to her. "This will take the edge off the pain."

She sipped from the metal bottle. She leaned back against the squabs and her shoulders dropped as she tried to relax.

"This was my fault. I suspected a trap and left you unprotected. Please forgive me, Lady St. John."

"Valeria. I want to hear my name on your tongue." She gazed at his lips, and then back to his eyes. "You have nothing to forgive. I also should have been prepared for this possibility." She reached for her reticule and pulled out a small pistol. She opened the chamber and out dropped the bullet. "I possessed a tool to protect myself and failed to use it. The fault lies with me."

Theo noted the cut on her neck where the knife had been pressing in, pulled out his handkerchief, and applied it to the small wound. Valeria put her fingers over his and he quickly removed his hand, leaving the cloth for her to handle. He swallowed hard. Why was every move this woman made so fascinating to him? He had been terrified when he'd realized the danger she was in. He nodded to Lady St. John and stepped out of the carriage.

Theo never had to kill before, but he had no regrets having done so today. Still, the fear he experienced at seeing Valeria in danger made him want to retch. He stepped off the road for a moment in the woods under the pretense of needing to relieve himself. Instead he vomited the contents of his breakfast. He finally stood up straight and headed back to the carriage.

Marcus and Phillip managed to roll the log off the road.

Theo helped himself to his own flask of brandy as the storm clouds unleashed their fury around him. Despite the rain, they resumed their journey to Corby unimpaired and arrived at the Hen and Rooster later than anticipated.

Michael arranged a private parlour for them as well as lodging for the night.

Theo managed to change into drier clothing and found himself alone in the private parlor. He was into his second tankard when Michael arrived.

"Phillip told me about what happened out there. We may need to come up with a better plan to protect Lady St. John."

"I suppose you have an idea, Michael?" Theo was experiencing numbness with his third tankard of ale. Dinner had not yet arrived.

"I think you need to return to the carriage with her."

"No."

"Why not? You admire her and have not been averse to her company before this. Why not ride in comfort in your own carriage?"

"Back off, Michael."

Michael's eyes narrowed as he came to stand before the much taller Theo. "What is wrong with you?"

Theo slammed his mug down and grabbed Michael by the cravat, almost lifting the smaller man off his feet. "I asked you to leave me alone," he said through gritted teeth.

Michael never flinched as he stared into Theo's eyes, and answered with a low voice. "Or what?"

Theo released Michael with a shove.

Michael wouldn't back down from a fight. He

might be smaller, but he was scrappy and was well-trained in street fighting.

Theo picked up his mug, went to the fireplace, and drank deeply of the bitter brew. What was wrong with him? He had never before been so discouraged.

"Theo?" Michael had righted himself after being pushed back.

"I'm a buffleheaded idiot." Theo turned, threw the mug, and shattered it against the far wall.

Michael ducked even though the mug had not come near him. Theo stormed toward the door and was there when it opened.

Valeria almost ran into him.

Theo stepped back. He looked at the woman he feared he would lose. He swallowed hard. "Lady St. John." He bowed, pushed past her, and rushed up the stairs to his room. Once inside the door he threw some kindling on the banked fire and pulled out a flask from his inner coat pocket that he had filled earlier. He dumped some of the brandy on the fire and jumped back as the flames exploded. Slumping in the chair by the blazing fire, he drank deeply from the flask, relishing the burn as it went down his throat—welcoming the numbness to his senses. He closed his eyes and let his entire body finally relax for the first time since the previous evening.

He never heard the knock on the door but the water splashing on his face got his attention. Sputtering he struggled to open his eyes and found Marcus standing before him.

"Theo. You are three sheets to the wind. I do not know if I have ever seen you like this." Marcus pulled up a straight-backed chair and flipped it around. He sat on it with his legs spread and his arms folded over the back side.

Theo observed as if from some hazy otherworld. "I'll be fine by morning." Theo's tongue had grown two sizes and did not work right. Still, he raised his flask, uncapped it, and drank some more. This time the burn was coming back up on him. He could feel his heartbeat throughout his entire body.

"We've been friends for a long time, Theo. Never once have you threatened anyone, much less tried to intimidate one of us," Marcus stated. "We are worried about you. Ever since last night..." Marcus lifted a hand and rubbed his forehead. "It has to do with your parents, right?"

"I don't want to talk about it."

"How many times over the years have I poured my heart out to you, Theo? Give me an opportunity to reciprocate." Marcus gazed at his friend, warm brown eyes radiating warmth, not a threat.

"I can't be around her, Marcus."

"Who?"

"Valeria. Lady St. John."

"Why? I thought you were halfway to falling in love with her."

"She won't have me. I'm tired of being on the outside."

Marcus's brow furrowed. "I don't understand."

Theo waved a hand lazily at him. "How would you? Everyone always loved you. You never had any doubt growing up that you were wanted and special. Even Josie couldn't deny her love for you for long. But me?" Theo pointed an unsteady finger at his chest and poked himself a few times. Watching his finger was fascinating as it bounced off his chest. He almost forgot the topic of conversation. "No one wants me."

"You have not been our friend over the years out of pity, Theo."

"Perhaps not, but now that you are all happily married and having babies, I'm not content to be the jolly uncle anymore. It hurts," he poked himself some more in his chest, "right here."

"If you want Lady St. John, woo her. Court her. Give her a chance."

Theo waved his hand at his friend. "She's declared she will never remarry. A love affair would be fine but not marriage. But I don't want a mistress. I want a wife. Children. Love." Theo closed his eyes as despair washed over him.

"Come on big guy, let's get you to your bed. We all want those things for you too."

Theo was unsteady on his feet as Marcus looped an arm around his neck and half walked, half dragged him to the bed. Theo fell onto the mattress face first.

"Can't do the carriage tomorrow."

"Why?"

"I might kiss her."

Marcus chuckled. "Theo, only you care enough about her to keep her safe and the rest of us, we're all married. Our wives would not want us in there alone. So, sorry ol' chap, but you're the man for the job."

Theo would have responded but his eyes closed, and his tongue felt like lead. He even heard himself snore as he slipped off into oblivion.

~*~

Valeria did not know what to make of Lord Harrow the following day. He mumbled a greeting as they broke their fast and after helping her into the carriage he climbed in and made a vain attempt to snuggle into the furthest corner. He closed his eyes but she could tell he was not sleeping. He did not look at her or speak.

Michael had spoken briefly with Marcus after Theo left the room abruptly. The broken ceramic mug laying on the floor gave testimony to the tension that had been in the room prior to their arrival. That the argument may have been about her was only confirmed when Michael and Marcus both glanced over at her during their whispering in the corner.

Valeria decided that a day alone in a carriage was painful, but a day in a carriage with a man who refused to talk or look at her was even more so. "Theodore?"

"Hmm?" He opened his bloodshot eyes but did not glance her way.

"Are you unwell?"

"If I am, it is my own fault. Nothing to concern your pretty head over."

Pretty? Well, at least that was something positive. "I am concerned. I hoped we would be friends, but you've hardly said more than a handful of words since the past two nights. I wanted to apologize if I said or did anything to offend you."

At this, Theo looked over at her. His eyes were a pale, bleak gray. His face was haggard in appearance.

"You overindulged last night, didn't you?"

Theo only shrugged and turned his head away.

He never appeared to her to be a man who was given to drink.

"Imbécile parfait," she murmured under her breath.

"I prefer buffleheaded idiot." He gave her a wry grin. "I did not mean to take my foul mood out on you.

You've done nothing to apologize for."

Valeria was confused. She did nothing, yet he seemed to be withholding himself from her. "Why won't you talk to me?"

"I am talking to you. I'm more in the mood for solitude today." He turned and gazed out the window again.

"I'm sure your head is giving you enough noise for now. I will leave you to yourself."

His grimace and wrinkled forehead indicated troubled thoughts. What more could she do for him? He had done so much to protect and care for her and now, now she wished she could return the favor. But how? She asked God about it. Then she turned her mind to her concerns for Dartanian.

Her son was young, and he had been afraid of his father and grandfather as they'd treated him harshly. He had never really opened up and been comfortable around men until Lord Harrow entered their lives. She glanced back at that man who was now snoring softly in the corner. He would make a wonderful father someday. He would be the one she would be willing to make babies with. *Traitorous heart!*

What was it about this man that made her want to give up her vow to avoid men at all costs? She knew with certainty that yesterday when he pointed that gun towards her and indicated that she should act fast, that he would have done anything to save her had it been within his power. She had seen him turn white when the bullet found its home. The sight had shaken her, but he had kept her from looking at the body as Phillip dealt with it. Theo shook as he placed her back in the carriage and without her speaking had understood her pain.

Her collarbone still ached, and she figured it would be a few more weeks before the bone healed. His protectiveness toward her could not be due to that initial accident, could it? She did not want to be loved out of pity, for how long would that last? But she sensed more noble depths in the man across from her. A man who would seek her safety before his own. A man who had killed for her. A man who set aside his comfortable life to help her find her son. A man who commanded the loyalty of friends who were willing to abandon all to assist her. This man was nothing like her deceased husband. Nothing at all.

~*~

The day dragged on and Theo was miserable. The scent of orange blossoms filled the air in the close confines of the carriage. When they would hit a particularly deep rut in the road he could tell it caused her pain even though she made no sound. Never in all his life had he wanted to protect a woman more than this one. It tore him up inside that she wanted nothing to do with him other than to be a friend.

Once Dartanian was rescued and she was safe, he would walk away and never see her again. He could not watch her be wooed and won by a better man, although he hoped she would find someone worthy of her. It humbled him that when facing death, she would have entrusted her son to his care and guardianship. How he would have upheld that against the Duke of Diamonte he couldn't fathom. He still had no idea how they were to rescue Dartanian and keep Valeria safe. What would they do about the Duke? The peerage were above the laws for the common man. As a

Marquess, he didn't face those laws either. A different brand of justice prevailed in these cases. However, when treason was involved? That made things even more dicey.

He wished they could just go in and kill the man and keep him from harming anyone else but unless it was self-defense it would be unconscionable to do that.

He shifted his gaze. His eyes fell on her lips and he instantly grew warm at the thought of how they'd felt when pressed to his. He had the impression she'd never experienced passion before. If anyone was a buffleheaded idiot it was Damon St. John. His gaze came to her neck and the small red mark that remained from that knife point. Anger burned in him at the callousness of her attacker. His eyes traveled lower to the steady rise and fall of her chest and to her hands as they were twisting a handkerchief.

It was his from yesterday. She must have cleaned it last night for there were no stains. That she'd kept it instead of returning it to him gave him hope.

His gaze came up and he found her brown eyes glancing back at him, one eyebrow slightly raised. Her saffron hair was coming loose from its chignon tucked low at the back of her neck.

He groaned and turned his head to view the passing English landscape, the smell of orange blossoms torturing and tempting him to dream of things that were not meant to be.

7

Theo was quiet at the dinner table that evening.

There was no private room, so they had to sit in the common room for their meal. That limited conversation because of the locals around enjoying their ale. The men keep a vigilant watch on any newcomer to the pub.

Theo stayed by Valeria's side.

What the inn lacked in atmosphere it made up for in the quality of the food. Valeria was not sure when she had ever enjoyed such succulent pork, and the potatoes served were far from plain.

The best part of the evening was that Lord Harrow was forced to sit close to her on the bench. Her thigh pressed against his as they ate together. A surprise for her came when it was time to go upstairs to her accommodations.

Lord Harrow assisted her up the stairs.

"Lady St. John."

"My lord?"

"I will be standing guard outside your door through the night. This inn is not as safe as some previous and there were not enough rooms for us all. I just wanted you to know that I would be here watching over you."

"The others?"

"Phillip and Marcus are sharing the only other room available and Michael is bedding down in the stables. Do not worry for him. He has endured far worse accommodations."

"It seems wrong that a Marquess would be sleeping on the floor in a cold hallway."

Theo shrugged. "It is only right that someone stand guard after the attacks that have already been made on your life. Since I may rest in the carriage tomorrow, it falls to me. I promise I will not be drinking tonight." He picked up her hand and placed a kiss on the back.

His lips touching her bare skin sent shivers up her arm and throughout her body. She entered the room and locked the door behind her. She changed for bed. Knowing that the gentleman on the other side would be protecting her was calming. But the air was cold and the hallway unheated. She stoked the fire, grabbed extra blankets, then made a makeshift bed on the rug in front of the fireplace. She wrapped her robe tight, went back to the door, and unlocked it.

Theo turned as she opened the door and peered into the dark hallway. "Lady St. John?"

Valeria put a finger up to her lips, grabbed him by the arm, and hauled him into her room. She quickly shut the door behind him and locked it.

Theo leaned against the wall by the door with his arms folded as he stared at her.

"There is no reason for you to shiver in the hallway. You can just as easily protect me from within." She pointed to the pallet by the fireplace. "I'm sorry it is not more than that. I would not give you the wrong idea. I only could not bear thinking of you alone in that dark hallway without any comfort or rest."

"If this is discovered, you realize you may be forced to marry me." Theo was clenching his jaw. A vein throbbed on the side facing her that was illuminated by the fire.

She sighed. "And would that be so bad?" She turned to move away from him but he grabbed her by her good arm and pulled her back until she was flush against his body. They stood eye to eye, nose to nose. This was not a man who would ever rule over her with an abusive iron fist—but one who would treat her as an equal. Any notions of propriety slipped away as the coolness of his body seeped through her dressing gown. She leaned in closer wanting to warm him.

His eyes turned a dark olive green in the firelight as they searched hers, and then gazed at her lips. His other hand came up to caress her jaw, and she leaned her face into it. His fingers touched her hair, and she could tell it distracted him. She'd brushed it out but hadn't thought to braid it and despised headwear at night. His fingers ran through her locks slowly, and he appeared mesmerized. She loved that small act of gentleness.

His hand came back up and again rested against her face. His thumb moved over her cheekbone and the small scar that remained from the tumble she had taken in the park rescuing Reginald. How long ago had that been now? It seemed like an eternity when it truly was only a little more than a week. She couldn't think. His other arm released her hand and snaked around her waist pulling her closer.

"No. It would not be bad at all. I believe I would find it quite enjoyable."

Theo tipped his head, his lips met hers, and she melted as if she were in the fireplace. She could not help but respond. Her good arm came up and she rested her hand on his chest in between them. His heart beat, strong and steady beneath her palm and all she knew was she wanted him. Reluctantly she pushed back. “I...”

Theo released her. “I apologize. Perhaps it would be better if I return to the hall.”

“No. Please? I would feel safer with you here.”

“Safer from outside intruders, but not necessarily safe from me.” Theo gave a half-grin.

She shook her head. “You, sir, are an irresistible combination of gentleman and rogue.” She stepped away and pointed toward the bed on the floor. “That, my lord, is the best offer you will find tonight.”

“My lady is a heartless temptress, and I am but your servant.” He bowed and moved over to a chair to remove his boots.

She padded over to the bed. Keeping her robe on, she climbed under the covers and watched him, his face in shadows, with the fire brightly burning behind him.

“Sleep well, Theo.”

“Sleep safe, my lady.” With that, fully clothed, he threw the covers up over his body as he settled onto the hard floor with his face towards her and his gun placed under his pillow.

Valeria smiled as she fell asleep.

A few hours later, Valeria heard a noise at the door. The fire was low, and she couldn’t for a moment remember where she was. A rattle at the window sent a shiver of fear down her back.

“Shhh. Where’s your gun?” he whispered. Theo was by the bed to the side of the window and in full view of the door.

Valeria pulled her gun out from under her own pillow.

Theo nodded, a gun in his right hand and a knife in his left. He was in his stocking feet and his coat was off. Even in the scant illumination of the fire and the moonlight the material stretched across his chest and arms.

She took a deep breath and prayed for safety. Peace descended at knowing this man was by her side to protect her.

The door slid open as the person outside managed to pick the lock.

Theo took one look to make sure it was not someone he recognized before he fired. The sound reverberated through the room. He quickly moved to the window, threw up the sash, and kicked his foot out to the body there. A scream rent the air as the would-be intruder fell to the yard below. Theo slammed the window closed and locked it. Turning to the door he went to inspect the injured man.

Valeria's heart pounded but she threw back the blankets, put her feet on the cold floor, and padded to the fire to light a candle. She lit a second one and brought it to Theo, who was now accompanied by Phillip and Marcus, both dressed in robes.

Theo tried to block her view of the intruder. "Go back to bed, Lady St. John. You are safe now."

Marcus and Phillip dragged the body away.

Theo came back into the room and locked the door behind him.

"Is he dead?"

Theo went to sit in a chair by the fire and picked up the poker to prod the flames back to life. He leaned forward with his head in his hands.

Valeria came up behind him and placed her hands on his shoulders. Her right shoulder hurt but she needed to offer comfort. She massaged his shoulders gently.

He slowly relaxed. He sat back and placed one hand over hers. Clasping it, he moved her to his side and wrapped an arm around her waist to bring her to a seated position on his knees.

Valeria cupped her hand on his chin, bent forward and placed her lips there, then over each eye, on the bridge of his nose and his other cheek. She rested her head on his shoulder and allowed him to hold her close.

Neither said a word.

She felt safe—as though she had finally found home.

When she awoke in the morning she was back in her bed, covered up. The fire was blazing and the bed on the floor was gone, all the blankets neatly folded on a trunk in the corner. A cup of something warm was awaiting her as well as some food on a table by the fire. She went to check the door and it was locked. Valeria quickly dressed and put her hair up, sipping the coffee and snatching bites to eat. The sun was well up and the men had obviously chosen to let her sleep after the events of the night.

She was eager to see Theodore again. The man once again saved her life and was winning her heart with his gentle ways.

~*~

Theo assisted Valeria into the carriage. At the sound of a horse riding fast toward them, he pulled out his gun. He would be glad when this was over, and his heart rate could return to normal.

As the horse drew closer Theo squinted. *Jared*? Theo put his gun back in his holster and walked toward the horse as it slowed before him.

"What ho, Theo!" Jared leapt from the horse and as the horse skittered sideways, Captain Jared Allendale brushed off his trousers.

"Why are you here?" Theo asked as he clasped hands with the newcomer.

Marcus had just stepped outside with Phillip and soon all the men were gathered around Marcus Remington's younger brother.

"I made a trip to London. Lord Hughes appraised me of what was afoot and sent me after you." Jared looked at his brother. "Josie, Katrina, and Beth have all removed to Rose Hill with the children and are under guard."

Marcus patted his brother on the back. "I am glad. Thank you for easing my mind."

Michael was leading three horses when he saw Jared. "Whoop!" he yelled as he joined the circle of men.

"I came to lend assistance. Remember that Whitehall would prefer him captured and evidence collected to convict of treason."

"What of Lord Wolton? We believe he may be involved as well," Phillip asked.

"Wolton survived?" Jared's eyes widened.

"From what we understand," Phillip shook his head.

"I wish I had been there for that adventure, Phillip. But I'm glad that you and Beth made a good life for yourselves since that nightmare ended."

"Do you need to rest before we continue on?"

Jared stared at the carriage. "If I can ride in there, I can rest on the way. I wouldn't miss this for the world."

Theo led Jared to the carriage. The door still hung open. Valeria was peeking out. Theo grinned at her curiosity and how she tried to mask it as they approached. "Lady St. John, I would like to introduce you to Captain Jared Allendale, aide-de-camp to Wellesley and younger brother to Lord Remington. He's come to join us on this adventure."

"It is a pleasure to meet you, Captain." Valeria nodded to the newcomer.

"If it would not inconvenience you, I will be joining you in the carriage," Jared said.

"I'm sure that Lord Harrow and I can accommodate you."

"Theo, you are riding inside?" Jared asked.

Theo nodded. "Why would I pass up the opportunity to spend time with a beautiful woman?" He winked at Valeria who slid over on the seat to allow the two men to enter.

"Rear facing?" Jared asked.

"One of us should be in case an attack comes from behind. I want Lady St. John to be in the corner, out of range of any possible gunshot." Theo jumped in and took the center of the rear-facing seat allowing Jared the corner of the opposing one. Theo had not slept much during the night but understood that Jared was exhausted from his travels and needed the rest more.

The carriage took off and Theo tried to relax. His gaze kept going to Valeria.

"Thank you for protecting me last night." She finally spoke when it became apparent that the Captain had fallen asleep.

Theo nodded. What else was there to say after the intimacy of the night before? He'd rested on the floor. The moonlight shone in on her face and made her hair appear as a halo around her head. He longed to lay his head next to hers on that comfortable bed and find comfort in the soft curves of her body. But instead he flipped on to his back and an ache welled up from within as the cold of the floor penetrated the rug beneath him. He watched the firelight reflect and shift in shadows on the ceiling and almost missed the first sound of a scratch at the door.

When he heard it the second time he'd grabbed his gun and knife and crawled along the floor toward the bed. He spied a shadow moving from outside the window, blocking the moon. It gave him good cover, but there were at least two attackers, coming from both directions. He was grateful that she'd encouraged him to be in the room instead of out. He'd have perhaps stopped the outside intruder, but might not have discovered the attacker coming in from the window until it was too late.

He glanced to Valeria. She appeared to have slept well. It had been heaven holding her in his arms after the intruders had been dispatched. To be so close and inhale her scent, was torture and wonderful at the same time. When she finally fell asleep in his arms it was with great reluctance that he'd placed her back in the bed and covered her up without joining her there. He never managed to go back to sleep, reclining on the floor for the longest time listening for any creak or scratch in the old Inn.

He yawned and tried to keep his gaze toward the back window as he leaned his head back to rest.

Soon Valeria sat next to him with her side pressed to his. He dared not move lest he awaken Jared. His eyes opened, and he glanced to the side.

She smiled at him and rested a hand his thigh. The

muscle twitched.

"Rest, Theo. I can keep watch for a while." She leaned forward and kissed his cheek.

He gazed at her and nodded. He had no words to say. He leaned his head back and fell asleep.

At mid-day, they stopped, got out for a stretch and a quick meal while the horses were changed.

In spite of apparent fatigue, Jared flirted with Valeria and she giggled at his comments.

Theo wanted to punch him.

Michael had a grim look on his face.

Theo walked over to his friend. "Michael, about the other night."

"Theo. It's over. We all have our bad moments. We are still friends and I will always have your back. Love can be torture and fighting the Black Diamond raises my hackles as well. We will all be tense as we head into this."

"Do you ever get scared?"

Michael snorted. "All the time when it comes to battles. Part of me gets filled with energy and excitement, but underneath is fear. I want to be able to return home to my wife and watch our children grow. I gave up this line of work because I didn't want to risk leaving her a widow."

"But you willingly joined us on this journey."

"If it were my son, you all would drop anything to be there to help."

"But Dartanian is not your son, nor is he mine."

Michael sighed. "Dartanian is my nephew and he may become your son when this is over. We are friends. We do things like this for each other."

Theo laughed. "We never experienced adventures like this when we were growing up."

Michael patted him on the shoulder. "No, these kinds of things only began when women started taking our hearts hostage. Even Henrietta and Lord Percy had a run in with the Black Diamond."

"Really?"

"Yes, but Marcus doesn't know that was originally behind their marriage."

"But you knew?"

"Yeah, and Jared."

"So, Josie wasn't the first time he's struck?"

"Nope, but then Josie and Marcus, then Beth and Phillip...then Katrina."

"Katrina always held your heart," Theo added.

"True, but I was too dense to realize that treasure for what it was at the time." Michael grinned. "I wouldn't trade any of it for what I have gained." He paused. "Well, I would gladly trade the torture Katrina went through if I could have."

"You've needed to kill people." It was a statement and a question.

Michael frowned. "More than I would care to remember."

"How do you live with that?"

"It was either kill or be killed. Many of those killed would have been responsible for the loss of far more lives on the battlefield. It was never easy to do even though I was good at it. The first few times I became so sick I threw up. Eventually, I was able to shut it out and move on but sometimes, those battles still come back to haunt me."

"I've killed three men on this journey so far. Two with my gun and one with that fall out the window of the Inn. It weighs on me."

"You protected Lady St. John. That's your duty as

a gentleman and even more so if you have lost your heart to her. As much as those deaths leave a wound on your soul, losing her forever would be far more devastating." Michael turned to Theo. "You are a good man, Theodore. Lord Harrow may be your title, but you are a noble man without it. I count it an honor to be your friend." With that Michael strode off to find the men so they could resume their journey.

~*~

Valeria could tell something weighed heavily on Theo's heart. She wished he would share with her, but he had not slept during the night. He took his vigil seriously and he performed so efficiently it had taken her breath away. She was as tall as him but when in his arms, she felt petite and protected. It was something she'd never experienced before. She was beginning to believe she could never be content in life without experiencing that on a daily basis. She bit her lip.

The one thing she'd promised never to do certainly happened. She had fallen in love with a member of the aristocracy. The weight of that set as a lead ball in her stomach. If they did not defeat her father-in-law, any chance of happiness between Theo and her was futile. She would always be hunted. She didn't know what would happen when they arrived at Ashbourne. She only hoped that somehow when Dartanian was safe in her arms again, evil would be vanquished, and she would finally be free to live as she chose. She knew who she would choose to spend her life with.

Theo had stopped mentioning marriage. Not even in a teasing manner. He would gaze at her with longing in his eyes, but a sense of despair enveloped him. Some of that lifted when they'd kissed but he never indicated he desired more. He would not accept her as a mistress. The only thing she could do now was pray.

The rest of the ride was uneventful. Valeria insisted they drive up to Damon's estate outside Ashbourne and walk in. It was now Dartanian's inheritance and as his mother she had a right to be there.

Michael and Jared chose to stay hidden in the woods that surrounded the property, but when they broke through to a view of the building itself, they were shocked by the sight before them.

The estate was no longer there.

The carriage pulled up and before Theo could move to let down the stairs, Valeria was out the door in a state of shock. Her home. Dartanian's home. Gone. All gone. The ashes amongst the shell of stone and brick gave a ghostly appearance. Valeria walked up the front steps and into what used to be the foyer. The marble staircase ascended before her into open sky. She could not step further in to the wreckage due to the layers of brick and stone that had collapsed from the upper floors.

Dartanian was not here. She believed he had not been here when it happened. Weeds were already sprouting up amongst some of the bricks. The Duke must have burned it after she left in revenge for her defection and taking his grandson. She knelt on the ground covered in ashes and cried. She would never miss this as home when the place had been filled with so much evil and hatred. But she grieved for what her son had never really possessed. A home to be loved in.

A place to grow and play. Any chance of that was gone.

Theo assisted her as she struggled to rise. She brushed the dirt off her traveling gown, leaving smudges. Black would have been far more practical for a journey of this nature. When all was said and done she would toss out the lavender shades and adopt happier colors. She'd suffered long enough.

"Michael and Jared will do some investigating and join us later. Let us find lodging and decide our next course of action on full stomachs." Theo helped her down the stairs. When they were in the carriageway he stopped and turned her toward him. He lifted up a thumb to wipe away the remaining tears and pulled out his handkerchief since there was more moisture on her cheeks than a mere thumb could handle. "You will not be homeless. Do not fear that."

"This place was never home, but it was Dartanian's inheritance." She glanced back at the ruins. "In many ways, I'm relieved it is gone. The spectre of the past has been vanquished."

Marcus drove the carriage back to Ashbourne to find a place for the night, as Jared had commandeered his horse to stay behind and investigate further.

Theo held Valeria close as they drove away from the ruins of the St. John property. The scene faded into the distance with every clip clop of the horses' hooves.

Valeria soaked in being so close to Theo. "Will you sleep in my room again tonight?" She moved slightly away so she could watch his face.

Theo glanced at her and away. His face gave no hint of his thoughts or feelings. "Perhaps Captain Allendale will. He's better trained for that sort of thing."

Valeria shook her head. "No. That will never do. It has to be you, Lord Harrow." If only she were free to think of more with this noble man. Her son had to be her primary focus, but she didn't feel safe without Theo close by. When had she ever needed to depend on someone like this? Had she ever met a man so selfless?

His eyes flashed to hers. They were dark steely gray as they met her brown ones. "Why?"

She patted his knee and let her hand rest there. "Because I am only at ease in your presence."

Theo groaned. His much larger hand came and moved hers off his leg.

Valeria smiled to herself. Her presence did affect him. He didn't want to be near her because he was fighting his physical attraction to her. She leaned against the corner of the carriage to think. Did she make it easier for him and withdraw her flirting, or did she use that attraction to make it impossible for him to say no?

~*~

The men were in the private room awaiting Lady St. John before dinner was to be delivered.

"What's our plan? We head to Newcastle-under-Lyme tomorrow morning, but then what? The Black Diamond's been aggressive in trying to get to Lady St. John. How can we rescue a six-year-old boy and keep her safe at the same time?"

"I will be her guard," Theo volunteered.

"You've done a great job so far," Marcus said. "But sleeping in her room? Theo." Censure laced his words.

"You slept in Josie's room when she was injured."

Theo bristled.

"She was injured and bedridden. Once she was up and about I was not there." Marcus's jaw was locked tight as he spoke, daring his friend to question his integrity.

"Valeria is a widow. She has more license than a debutante. No one need know." Theo made eye contact with all four men. "And nothing happened. I slept on the floor."

Michael stepped forward. "Aren't you even the least bit tempted, Theo? You're playing a dangerous game here."

"If I had not been there last night I might have stopped the man at the door, but never the one trying the window."

"What if I took that night shift?" Jared offered.

"No," a female voice interrupted.

All five heads turned to the door where Lady St. John stood. She closed it behind her and walked regally to the circle that opened to include her. "No offense, Captain Allendale, but we are not well acquainted. I want Lord Harrow to stand guard. He has proven himself trustworthy on three occasions thus far."

Jared put his hands up in surrender. "I concede to the lady's wishes. I do not want to be in a woman's bedroom who doesn't want me."

Theo glared.

Jared backed up a step. "Theo, what has gotten into you? If you have staked your claim on the fine lady here, then far be it for me to step in." Jared walked away to the sideboard and poured himself a drink.

The proprietor came in with hot food for the group. The group gathered at the table and Marcus prayed a blessing over the repast.

Theo was seated next to Valeria. He found it hard to focus on his food with the scent of orange blossoms in the air. His mind turned to her in bed, dressed in her nightrail, and her hair spilling in waves across the pillow. Even though he had wrapped his hands in her hair while she slept in his arms the previous night, he found something so beautiful and pure about the golden locks that begged for him to touch them. A few strands were loose from her chignon as she sat next to him and he longed to push them behind her ear. He wanted to touch, hold, smell, and taste her. He finally gave up eating and drank the coffee before him hoping it would help him stay alert.

When Lady St. John was ready, Theo escorted her to her room and unlocked the door. He entered the room first.

Her belongings had been strewn about and the bed covers ripped off.

Pain exploded in his skull and darkness descended.

8

Valeria screamed when the figure emerged from behind the door and knocked Theo senseless. She pulled out her revolver and took aim. The noise was deafening in the hallway. The firearm kicked back causing her pain in the still-healing collarbone.

The man looked shocked and stumbled forward.

She reloaded with shaking fingers and fired again.

The man fell and ceased moving.

She loaded a third time and took a step into the room to make sure there were no more intruders. Valeria knelt next to an unconscious Theo. Her fingers found his pulse. She rose as the other men rushed up the stairs to her door.

"What happened?" Marcus asked.

Valeria pulled out Theo's handkerchief that she had kept and applied it to the dark spot appearing in his light brown hair.

He moaned but didn't awaken.

Phillip knelt down to check the intruder for a pulse. "He's dead." Phillip looked at Valeria. "Good shot, Lady St. John."

Jared, Michael, and Marcus lifted Theo off the floor and on to her bed.

Valeria pulled off his boots and covered him up. He remained pale and unmoving.

"We'll get this guy out of here and contact the magistrate. Jared, can you stay and stand guard in case there are any more attempts on Lady St. John?"

"Be glad to," Captain Allendale checked to be sure

his revolver was loaded. "All set." He pulled up a chair near the fireplace and stirred the embers.

The remaining men dragged the dead body out of the room.

A few minutes later a maid appeared to wash the blood off the floor. The young gal had wide eyes and appeared flighty and nervous but left quickly.

Valeria locked the door and checked the window. She peered down to the yard below. A man couldn't access the room without a ladder. Satisfied that they were safe for the nonce she returned to Theo and sat on the bed by his side. "*Mon cheri,* please wake up."

She picked up his large hand, placed a kiss in the palm, closed his fingers over it, and fought back the tears. She never thought to see this gentle man laid low. It struck her at the risks these men, most especially Theo, were taking to help her rescue Dartanian. She swallowed hard.

A knock at the door had Jared on his feet with his gun drawn. "Who is it?"

"Michael. I brought a doctor for Theodore."

Jared unlocked the door and allowed the two men in.

Valeria rose and moved to the corner. Still shaken, she did the only thing she could think of and bowed her head in prayer. Jumbled pleas to God for Theo, for Dartanian, for all of them tumbled through her mind.

While the doctor assessed Theo's condition. Jared and Michael whispered by the fireplace, but she could not make out their words. She was more concerned about Theo lying so still and didn't think twice about their conversation.

The doctor left, and she returned to Theo's side to keep vigil over him.

Jared came to her as the night grew late. "I can make up a pallet for you by the fireplace, so you can rest." His voice was soft and comforting.

"I prefer to remain here, Captain Allendale."

He sat back by the fireplace and stoked the flames.

Valeria only had eyes for Theo. With startling clarity, her hope of love and joy in the future was wrapped up in this one man. And that love was in jeopardy. She prayed for Dartanian's safety and for God's mercy on them all.

~*~

The pain in his head made him want to retch. He hadn't been drinking, he was sure of it. His chest felt heavy, as if there was a weight on it. He slowly opened his eyes to a dark room, but a light from outside and the breaking dawn illuminated golden hair and a face he had come to hold dear. Valeria's upper body was draped across his chest while she somehow was seated on the edge of the bed with her feet over the edge. She could not be comfortable.

He tried to talk but it took too much effort and the noise in his head was deafening. He wasn't sure he would hear himself, her, or anything else. He gazed at the roughhewn beams above trying to remember how he came to be here. He remembered comforting Valeria when they'd discovered the estate burned to the ground. Dinner. Walking her to her room and opening the door. He reached a hand up to feel the back of his head and discovered the source of his pain when his fingers touched a large bump there. He glanced over to the fireplace and spied Jared. He must have made a noise because the stealthy spy was by his side in only a few steps. "How do you fare, Theo?"

"I've had better days." He gave a grin to his friend.

"You took quite a hit to the head. The man used a broken ax to whack you with. Fortunately, he used the blunt end."

"That would explain the log splitting going on in my brain." Theo winced. "The intruder?"

"Lady St. John dispatched him before we could arrive." Jared raised his eyebrows at the sleeping woman. "She has refused to leave your side, Theo. You are a lucky man." He stepped back as Valeria moved. "Rest now, unless you need some assistance?"

Theo shook his head.

Jared nodded and returned to his post by the fire.

Theo closed his eyes, but his fingers wound through silky strands as if holding onto a safety rope.

~*~

Morning came too early. Lady St. John stirred so Theo released his grip on her hair. He opened his eyes slightly as she raised her head and stretched without realizing he watched her. Even rumpled she was beautiful. Would he ever tire of looking at her? Despite his head pounding he found pleasure in gazing at this woman. He must be insane. Or perhaps buffleheaded.

She moved further up by his side and placed a hand on his chest.

Theo's heart beat grew stronger and he opened his eyes fully to look at her.

Her eyes widened. Her hair was loose around her shoulders, begging to be touched again. He resisted the urge.

"My lord," her eyes searched his.

"I would be yours if you would let me." Theo grinned.

She sat up and her eyes narrowed. "You must be better if you are thinking of such things." She patted his chest playfully.

His hand came up and held hers firm against him. "There is a stampede of horses running through my head and the only way I can stand it is to look at you."

She tried to pull her hand away.

Theo reached up to touch her cheek but the moment was disturbed by a cough. Theo glanced over at Jared. He'd forgotten they were not alone. He dropped his hand.

Valeria grinned at him.

He let his eyes close with her image embedded on his retinas. Such beauty. It brought him peace. The stampede faded into the distance.

~*~

Valeria stood to the side as the men all entered the room and convened by the fireplace. Theo still slept. She grinned as she remembered the way he flirted with her when he'd opened his eyes earlier. But now what were they to do? They needed to rescue Dartanian and they couldn't leave Theo here alone, but he was not up for traveling and the day was quickly slipping by. To make things even more difficult, it rained again reducing the roads to mud, dangerous for the horses and problematic for the carriage.

"I say we leave Theo here and head out," Michael suggested.

"No. That will never do. Theo is Lady St. John's

protector, we cannot take the one without the other," Marcus said.

Protector? That sounded so, *scandaleux.* Valeria turned to glance at Theo only to find he was awake and following the conversation.

He grinned and winked at her. He understood how it had sounded.

Drat the man! He was too injured, or she would punch him in that muscular bicep that was exposed as he tried to raise himself to a sitting position. She tried to keep from blushing as his covers slid down his broad chest.

Jared had removed Theo's clothes after the doctor came and while she believed he still wore his smallclothes, he was naked from the waist up. The sight made her heart beat faster. Damon had been soft in comparison. Even Michael was far more fit than her husband had ever been. Damon had been round all over. She glanced at Theo and his eyebrows rose. She waved her hand and listened to the conversation.

"I would say that Theo is the one in need of protection," Phillip stated, but realizing how horrible it sounded, he backtracked. "Pardon me, Lady St. John. I had no desire to cast aspersions on your character."

Heat rose in Valeria's cheeks again. He was not far from the truth if she were honest. The more time she spent in Lord Harrow's company the harder it was to restrain herself from touching him or doing even more. That did not honor God, and yet she was even loathe to pray for protection from the temptation that the man beside her presented.

"Lord Harrow cannot be left behind and neither can I. I suggest we wait for the storm to end and set out in the morning." Valeria sat down in a chair next to the bed and folded her arms across her chest. She had handed Dartanian's safety to God despite her fears, and as far as she was concerned, the matter was settled.

Jared walked to the window. "The lady has a point. I would be loath to slough through the mud with any horse and Theo's carriage would likely get stuck. Better to wait until tomorrow."

"But what about Dartanian?" Michael asked.

"We will pray for his safety. The delay cannot be helped," Marcus conceded, and then glanced over to Theo. "Put a shirt on, there is a lady present."

Theo's cheeks turned pink.

Valeria quickly turned away.

Jared handed Theo a shirt.

When Theo finished dressing he quietly said, "I'm decent now."

Valeria laughed, grateful that Lord Harrow was recovering from his blow to the head and also that the darkness that had been radiating from him had seemed to disappear. At least for the moment.

"Now we only have the challenge of who will keep guard over Lady St. John."

Valeria looked at the men. "I think it is time we use our names. I'm beginning to think I have several big brothers watching over me. I am Valeria. You may call me that. And I will take the liberty to call you all by your names. Jared, Marcus, Michael, Phillip, and Theodore."

The men nodded.

"Now as for sleeping arrangements. I believe we will do what we did last night. Allow Jared a place to sleep for now so he can rest, and he can keep guard again during the night and I will stay here by Theo's side lest he need anything."

The men looked past her.

Valeria followed their gaze.

Theo smiled and shrugged. "Sounds like a good plan to me."

"You would deny a lady her bed so you can be pampered?" Marcus shook his head in disbelief.

Valeria bit back a grin.

Theo looked down at his hands. "I can move to the floor."

"You will do no such thing. You need to rest and this is the ideal place for that. I will be fine in the chair or on the floor myself. I have slept in worse surroundings in the past. I will survive."

Phillip shook his head. "I do not like what this could do to your reputation, Lady—Valeria," he corrected himself.

"All I want is my son back and to take the next packet to the Colonies, so I can be far away from this bedeviled island."

"America?" Theo squeaked.

Valeria folded her arms and refused to look his way. "Yes. I doubt my father-in-law would find Dartanian r me there."

Silence hung heavy.

Theo slid back down onto his pillow and rolled to his side, away from the rest of the room. His back was all that presented itself.

Oh, my, what had she gone and done now?

The other men left the room, including Jared, with assurances he'd be back.

Valeria and Theo were alone. Her gun was nearby in the event of any unwanted visitor. "Theo?" No response. She was not sure if he was sleeping, but she sat on the bed and placed a hand on his arm. "What have I done to offend you? Please forgive me so we can be friends again."

She thought he understood that in spite of the growing attraction between them, that she would need to leave once Dartanian was found. She could not risk Theo being taken or possibly killed. Staying would only endanger the man. "If anything should happen to me, I meant what I said the other day. I want you to take Dartanian and raise him."

Again, no response. Valeria left the bed and sat in the rocker, wrapping a blanket around herself. Soon she was asleep.

~*~

Theo did not rest well that night. He could smell her near. Everything in him longed to take her in his arms and kiss her into agreeing to stay in England and be his wife. She had said she felt as if she was being taken care of by big brothers. Did she consider him more as a big brother than a potential husband? He didn't desire a sister. No. What he desired was the woman so close and yet unattainable.

The next morning, he rose and quickly dressed behind a screen that had been brought in for privacy. He experienced dizziness but could not rest helpless in bed any longer.

Dartanian was in danger and they needed to rescue him so they could seek safety. If she wanted to be gone then it should happen quickly before he fell more in love with her and had his heart broken.

He suspected it was already too late.

The carriage ride to Newcastle-under-Lyme was

uneventful but slow due to the mud.

Jared chose to sleep in the corner of the carriage. Jared and Michael planned to survey the property before the rest of them sought to perform a rescue. Valeria was both a blessing and a curse in the process. She was well acquainted with the property and places where Dartanian might be held prisoner, but she also insisted that she go in with them for the rescue.

Dartanian would want his mother, but it also meant greater danger in trying to keep her and the boy safe.

Anxiety ate Theo up inside. If they rescued Dartanian, she would leave, but the rescue itself endangered them all. The teasing mood from the previous morning had dissipated in the light of the dangers that were ahead. For the first time, he was almost ready to pray for God to let him die so he would not need to face a future without her.

~*~

The carriage pulled up to a pub across from the village green at Newcastle-under-Lyme. It was late afternoon.

Michael and Jared got a change of horses and took off for the estate to check if Dartanian could be found.

Valeria paced in front of the fireplace in the public room. Some townsfolk were present and recognized her and while they gave her warm greetings, they also kept a distance.

Valeria had been burdened by Theo's dark mood the entire day. He resisted any attempt at conversation. She consoled herself that she would be on a ship bound to the Colonies, perhaps within the week if it could be arranged. Michael told her he would fund the trip as a gift to his sister-in-law and nephew and asked that she keep him appraised of their progress when they had settled there.

She suspected Theo's withdrawal was because of her stating her need to leave the country. The likelihood of the Duke, whom they referred to as the Black Diamond, possibly being killed was small. He was a powerful man and above the laws. Even if they rescued Dartanian, they would never be safe as long as the Duke was alive.

She only hoped his power could not extend to America. She suspected that since his energies were focused on France and his dream of ruling there with Bonaparte, she would be safe. She'd change her name. Perhaps dye her hair. Whatever it took for her son to grow up happy and strong.

But now leaving left a bad taste in her mouth knowing that Lord Harrow existed and stirred feelings in her she'd never dared hope for. He tantalized her with dreams of a future that could never be theirs.

Several hours later Valeria and Theo went up to the room they were to share. It felt odd to be entering a room again with him after the last attack, but Theo once again entered before her. The room was untouched, and he locked the door behind them.

Valeria grabbed blankets and a pillow to make a bed for Theo by the fireplace. "I hope this will be the last night we need to do this."

"Why. Do I snore?" Theo asked with eyebrows raised.

"Well, as a matter of fact, you do. But it's not bothersome." Valeria reached out to touch his arm and experienced a jolt of energy that seared her to her toes.

Theo took a step closer and placed her hand on his chest.

Valeria swallowed and broke eye contact to gaze at his lips. She leaned in.

They kissed. Slow. Sweet. Bliss.

Valeria pulled back and gazed into his eyes now turned a deep green.

His arm snaked up behind her head and pulled out her pins. He ran his fingers through her hair and groaned. His hand came up behind her neck. He brought their heads together again and their lips met in a seductive dance.

Valeria broke it off and stepped out of his arms. Her breath was ragged. "We cannot go on like this," she whispered.

Theo frowned. "I could have gone for far longer."

Valeria couldn't help but be pleased at the admiration in his eyes and the longing in his voice. She didn't want to start something she was not prepared to finish and if she went further with Theo it would be impossible to say goodbye without leaving her heart in England. She could not afford to do that. She took off her slippers, and fully clothed, she slipped under the covers with her face turned away from him. Her attempt at sleep was for naught. She tossed and turned all night.

Theo was not sleeping well either.

Anxiety over what might transpire on the morrow warred with the desires that longed to be filled tonight. She could not give in. She could not do that to Theo. She did not want to leave his heart crushed when they finally parted. He had so much to give a woman. She tried to pray that God would bring him a bride who would be perfect for him, but inwardly she rebelled at the thought of another woman pressing her lips to his.

~*~

Dark clouds once again spanned the sky above them as they drove to the Diamonte estate.

Theo grew uneasy about the plan. For Valeria to walk in and ask for her son seemed like foolishness. Yet, the men would be nearby, armed and ready to assist.

Valeria hoped that they could achieve their goal without a fight. Her back was straight and her hair braided, wound into a severe bun. She wore the plainest of dresses and had a look of steely determination on her face. She made it clear this morning in front of everyone that if anything happened to her today, she wanted Theo to raise her son.

Michael, claiming kinship as the boy's uncle, stated he would see that Theo did his duty and if for some reason he could not, then Dartanian would be welcomed into his own household.

Valeria listened to Michael and nodded her head. After her initial fear of him she'd grown more comfortable in his presence and even chuckled at some of his jesting, especially when Theo was the brunt of the humor.

~*~

Theo grumbled to himself. He suspected she was up to something and that he would not like it. They'd not talked much since she'd announced she would leave when this was over. Was she really a tease or as uncertain about her feelings for him as he was about her? Theo had not slept well. He could not shut off the memory of her body pressed against his and the taste of her lips that left him wanting so much more.

The carriage pulled into the long drive to the Diamonte estate and Valeria sucked in a breath.

He glanced over at her.

She stared at him with hunger in her eyes. "You will care for Dartanian, *Oui*?"

Theo nodded. He knew nothing about being a father and he hoped it would not be necessary, but his friends would help.

"You are not planning anything foolish are you, *Madame?"*

She bit her lip but gave no response as she turned to the window.

Fear gripped Theo in that moment. She was gone from him. It cut like a knife twisted deep inside his torso. He wanted to cry out from the pain of it. He wanted to drop to his knees and beg her to marry him, to be with him forever and yet he knew what her answer would be.

If they survived today's rescue attempt, she would be gone on the first boat west.

Theo closed his eyes fighting the fatigue and fear. He vowed to himself he would do anything to keep her safe. Anything. Even if he died doing it. For the first time in forever, Theo prayed.

9

Valeria struggled not to throw herself into Theo's arms in the carriage as they rode. To tell him how much she loved him. To beg him to understand. To experience one last taste of heaven from his lips. She cried out to God during the night, asking why she would finally, after all her years of loss, pain, and heartache, find the one man she could love and live with. Yet she needed to walk away from the country once her son was safe in her arms. It was too cruel for God to lead her on this path.

She prayed for Dartanian, guilty that her heart kept pulling her towards Lord Harrow when her son could be injured, dying, or worse. She could not bear to think of the fear and anxiety her son had suffered at the hands of his cruel grandfather.

Legally the Duke of Diamonte had full authority to do what he had done. But she could not allow it and swore she would do whatever it took to see the Duke dead today. Vengeance for the pain she had suffered. Vengeance for Dartanian and perhaps for the women who had also been affected: Josie, Elizabeth, and Katrina. She prayed that their husbands would prevail and return home to the loving arms of their wives. She loved them all as a family in a way she had never before experienced.

She glanced over at Theodore. Her heart ached for him. He deserved a woman who would love him. She recognized how lonely he was and how his single state was now a curse compared to the blessings his friends had found with their wives. "Theo."

He turned towards her, startled. "Hmmm?" There was despair in the cool grey of his eyes.

"May God protect you."

He nodded. "And you as well, Lady St. John."

The carriage rolled to a stop. Valeria straightened her back and patted her pocket where her gun was kept. A knife was sheathed to her outer thigh under her gown. She was as ready as she would ever be.

Theo assisted her out of the carriage and walked up the front steps with her arm on his. She left her sling behind. She risked further injury but could not show any sign of weakness before the Duke lest he exploit it. He was a crafty man. As wily as Satan in the Garden of Eden. The Duke would do whatever it took to get what he wanted. He wanted Dartanian and she was the obstacle. She figured he had to be frustrated at the failed attempts thus far to eliminate her. That made him all the more dangerous.

"Ready?" Theo asked.

She nodded. "Ready."

Theo lifted the knocker and banged it three times on the heavy, ornate, oak door.

The door opened, and Valeria tipped her head. "Watkins. How very good to see you again. I believe the Duke is expecting us?"

The elderly servant's face gave a flash of fear, but it was gone and replaced by a cool reserve. He was a wiry old man with a bald head and several inches shorter than her. He had always treated her with deference, but he would never cross his employer. Watkins escorted them into the main drawing room and closed the door firmly.

A click sounded as it locked.

Theo glanced at her with concern.

"*Maman*?" a soft little voice whispered.

"Dartanian? *Mon enfant*?" Valeria's heart leapt at her son's voice. She came around the furniture to find him lying on the settee with his head on a pillow and Mittens curled upon his chest. She knelt beside him. *"Vas-tu bien?"*

"Je suis malade," he groaned, clutching his middle.

She became aware of the smell of vomit and a pot on the floor. He obviously had need of it. She placed a hand to his forehead.

Theo quickly made the rounds of the room but kept an eye on the door. Light poured into the gloomy space.

"He has a fever."

Theo's eyes narrowed.

It warmed her heart that he cared.

"I unlocked the windows and pulled back the drapes." He came back to stand by the fireplace. He urged the embers into a flame and stood with his back to the wall next to it to keep an eye on the entire room.

Valeria turned her attention back to her son. "How long have you been sick, Dartanian?"

"Shortly after *grand-père* took me from the park. I told him I did not want to go with him. I wanted you, *Maman*. He said you would come for me. I am glad you are here. *Tu me manquess*."

"I missed you, too, *mon petite*." She gave her son a hug and the cat purred against her ear. "Mittens has kept you company?"

Dartanian nodded. "*Grand-père* does not like cats. Says they make his eyes itch."

"Have you been treated well?"

Dartanian frowned. "They feed me, and I like the

candy he gives me, but I am bored and lonely."

"How long have you been in this room?" Theo asked softly.

"Since we arrived. *Grand-père* will not let the cat in a bedroom and I will not be without Mittens." He stroked the white fur on the kitten as it nestled back into a ball on his chest. "I am scared, *Maman*. *Grand-père* said you will get what you deserve. I think you deserve a husband. He does not agree with me."

"A husband? You want me to remarry?"

Dartanian nodded.

"Have you picked a man out for me?" Valeria asked, astonished.

Dartanian nodded again.

"And who do you suggest I wed?" Valeria gave her son a small smile.

"*Grand-père* said you belong to him but Lord Wolton has been begging to be your husband. He hates me. I want Lord Harrow as my new daddy."

Theo's gaze met Valeria's. He was as startled as she at her son's declaration.

"Never fear, I will not be wed to *Grand-père* or Lord Wolton." Valeria patted Dartanian's shoulder and pulled a blanket up over him to just below where the kitten sat.

A door opened and closed.

Theo tensed.

"Ah, what a touching scene. The mother returns for her son. You are predictable, Lady St. John." The heavy-set man wandered toward the center of the room. "You brought a visitor. Pray, introduce us."

Valeria rose. This man frightened her and made her want to retch into the pot her son had been using. "Lord Wolton, meet Lord Harrow."

"Ah, so this is the man you took as your lover?" Lord Wolton came forward until he was close to Valeria. He clasped her hand and raised it to kiss as he watched her eyes. She tried to hide the shiver of revulsion that rippled through her. "So, you are not indifferent to me, my dear." He gave an oily grin and his eyes narrowed. "It is always good to have witnesses to a marriage."

Theo was behind her.

She slipped a hand behind her back and he placed something in her palm. *A knife!* She pasted a smile on her face. "You must misunderstand. Lord Harrow is but a friend. We are not engaged to be married."

Lord Wolton walked a few steps away and laughed. He went to pour himself a drink and nodded to Theo. "No? Lord Harrow, it has been a perilous journey north and you have had little sleep. With a temptress such as Lady St. John it is no wonder." Lord Wolton turned his attention back to Valeria. She moved her hand down to hide the knife in the folds of her skirt. "You cannot marry Lord Harrow, my dear. You are pledged to be married to me."

Valeria placed her free hand over her chest. "To you? *Pardon,* my lord, but you failed to propose."

Lord Wolton waved a hand at her in dismissal. "Tis all arranged by your father-in-law." He moved over to Dartanian. "But the boy will stay with him. I do not need a brat around the house."

Theo pulled on the back of Valeria's skirt to keep her from lunging forward.

"I will not be parted from my son."

"You will do whatever your husband bids you to do." Lord Wolton's visage was hard and his eyes cold and lifeless. He scanned her figure. "I only hope you are not pregnant with his by-blow. Not that it matters, the child could be put to good use and Lord Harrow will not live to care anyway." He took a few steps across the room and sipped his brandy. "I just recalled, you have no direct heir do you, Lord Harrow?" He laughed. "I delight in rubbing out more of this foolish British aristocracy."

Theo's silent strength remained behind her. He released her dress. She wondered if there was pain in his eyes at the disparaging remarks this man made.

Dartanian had curled up with the kitten and had fallen asleep or was pretending to be. *Good boy.*

Valeria struggled to think of how to buy time to do what she needed to do—kill the Duke and get Dartanian to safety.

The killing part was not something the men agreed to. They first wanted to get Dartanian safe, and then seek, through political and peer pressure, to get the Duke to leave the country.

She hoped they could get Dartanian to safety. But she would take care of the Duke. She believed murder was wrong…but she also understood how evil this man was. Sometimes she even doubted he was a man. He had taken more and more of the form of a demon sent to torture her.

A sound came from the window and the wind moved the drapery.

Lord Wolton's eyes narrowed as he wandered over. "I wonder how that window got open. The cool air is not good for a sick child." Wolton leaned to shut it.

He let out a startled yelp when Phillip grabbed him and put a knife to the man's throat. "So, we meet again, Lord Wolton," Phillip spoke in a low, menacing tone of voice. "My wife sends her regards."

Lord Wolton's face lost all color as the metal blade pressed against his throat. "Let me go. I let you have her. And your spawn."

"Do you miss your cohort, Lord Follett? Did you realize he put in writing all he knew about your treasonous deeds? Those papers are at Whitehall, by the way. They have reserved a lovely cell in the Tower for you."

Valeria walked over to Wolton and Phillip. "May I do the honors, Phillip? It would be a shame to put a man such as Lord Wolton through the embarrassment of a trial and suffering the same fate as his friend Sir Bastion."

Lord Wolton made the mistake of nodding and a trickle of blood emerged along the edge of Phillip's knife.

"What did you have in mind, my lady?" Phillip asked as he grinned at her.

"Murder."

Phillip's eyes grew wide and he shook his head. "Maim him, certainly, but no, we never agreed to murder."

"I never asked your permission, Phillip." Before she could raise the knife that Theodore handed her, she found her hand grasped from behind.

"I think we need to find a better solution." Theo sheathed the knife and hauled Valeria away.

Valeria seethed with anger and pulled away from Theo. Pain and humiliation crashed through her. They had no idea how that man had abused her, had treated her like less than an animal. How her husband and father-in-law forced her to be with him. The man was pure evil and while she should be concerned for his eternal salvation and forgive him, she struggled to do so.

Theo tried again to wrap his arm around her shaking form.

She shrugged him off and went to sit next to Dartanian, determined to shed the tingling senses that screamed danger.

Phillip and Theo tied up Lord Wolton, gagged him, took him to the window, and rolled him over the edge of the balcony to the yard below.

Valeria winced as she heard the large body hit the ground.

Marcus, Michael, or Jared would attend to him.

"*Maman*?" her son called weakly.

He was sweating and shivering under the blankets and looked so pale it frightened her. Were they too late?

"Dartanian?" Valeria pulled back the eyelid when he did not respond to her anymore.

His eyes rolled back in his head. He stopped shivering and stilled.

"Dartanian?" She couldn't feel a pulse and it terrified her. "*Mon enfant*. Dartanian."

Theo reached down to find a pulse. "He still lives, my lady, but we need to get him to a doctor quickly." Theo assisted Valeria to her feet and bent to scoop the little boy in his arms. The kitten jumped off to the floor and mewed at Valeria's feet.

Phillip motioned for Theo to come to the window. He gave a low whistle and Marcus appeared below them. "We have Dartanian, he is ill. We need to get him to a doctor quickly."

Marcus nodded. "Can you lower him down to me?"

Theo leaned over the railing. "If I drop him low can you catch him?"

Marcus nodded.

Theo lowered the boy as far as he could lean before dropping him into Marcus's arms.

Marcus looked at Valeria. "I will care for him as if he were my own." He took off into the woods.

Theo and Phillip escorted Valeria back into the room and closed the windows behind them. They were not latched so that an escape route would still be available should they have need of it.

Valeria slumped into a chair petting the kitten.

The door opened.

Two large men entered the room, dragging the limp body of Sir Tidley between them. They dropped him onto the carpet before her and stepped away. Michael lay with his face to the side against the carpet, but a pool of blood could be seen spreading from beneath him.

Firm footsteps echoed in the hall before the Duke entered.

"Ah, my dear, Lady St. John. What a pleasure to have you back home again. You brought some unexpected guests. You should have known that I dislike visitors I have not previously been introduced to." The Duke's hair was a salt and pepper gray and he stood as tall. He held many similarities to the man at her feet, and her deceased husband.

Valeria could not hide her contempt. It took all within her to not retch into the pot that Dartanian used. "I have not come to stay, my lord." She rose from her chair, leaving the kitten. She dropped to the floor by Michael and pressed a finger to his neck. Thank God he still breathed. She would hate to face any of the wives of these brave men should anything happen to them. She lifted part of her dress to reveal her linen underskirt and ripped a strip of material off.

"How quaint, my dear. You tending to your half-brother-in-law. It is pointless. I have wanted him dead for quite some time. As long as he stayed out of my business I was more than happy to let him continue to live, but he is now obviously very much in my business if he is in my home." The Duke threw his head back and laughed. "Lord Westcombe and Lord Harrow. I wish I could say I am pleased to finally meet men who have sought to undermine my plans in recent years, but," he glanced at his fingernails on his right hand, "I am sorry to say your visit here has not come at a good time."

"There was never any pleasure intended in our visit," Phillip spoke in an even tone of voice.

The Duke grinned broadly. "How do you like your lovely wife, Lord Phillip? Did she tell you that she had an acquaintance with me a few years back?"

Phillip kept his face blank.

"No? Well, she was a tasty little morsel, but I'm sure you are aware of that. She wasted no time wrapping you around her little finger…or other body parts." His laugh was dark.

"And Lord Harrow. I am confused as to where you figure into this. Just a well-intentioned oaf who trails after his friends for adventure? Has my lovely Valeria let you taste of her charms yet?"

Lord Diamonte stepped toward Valeria and leaned down to clasp her face in his left hand. "I do not like to share, *Madame*. For that you will, of course, be punished." He glanced to the settee that was now within his view. "Where is my grandson?"

Valeria shook his hand from her face and bent to continue wrapping the strip of linen around Michael's head. He moaned, and she rolled him over.

"I asked where is Dartanian?"

She refused to answer. She only prayed that Lord Remington made good his getaway and that her son was in the capable care of a physician.

"It does not matter, he will soon be dead. But I have plans for replacing him."

What had he done? She wondered why her son was so sick. Had he been poisoned? *Lord, please keep mon enfant safe!*

The Duke kicked the unconscious man in the ribs and another moan was heard.

"Too bad Michel was on the wrong side of this war. He would have been a wonderful substitute for my son to help you bear me more heirs for when we triumph in France." The Duke's face was hard and his eyes like flint as he hovered over her.

Why were Phillip and Theo not doing anything? Fear welled up in her at facing down her darkest fears in the form of her father-in-law. She rose to her feet and reached for the kitten sitting on a nearby chair. Not that an allergy to the cat would stop the Black Diamond from accomplishing his plans, but as small as that kitten was, it gave her comfort in the midst of this situation.

"Well, now, what shall we do about our little welcoming party? Sam and Neil here will escort you gentlemen to other accommodations. Lady St. John and I have unfinished business to attend to."

One of the thugs spoke up. "What about da bloke on da flur?" The men were punching fists in to their opposite hands.

"Leave him. He can do no harm there." He turned back toward Valeria. "I have waited a long time for this night. You will not disappoint me or you will regret it."

~*~

A jealous rage boiled up inside Theo like he never experienced before. He had heard bits and pieces of the terrors that some of his friends' wives had endured at the hands of this evil man and his minions. To witness him so blatantly abusing Valeria and trying to strip her of her dignity exposed something new and primal within him. His hands clenched.

Phillip's gaze cautioned him, although Theo's friend was prepared to fight if his clenched jaw was any indication.

Theo banked his anger. He slowly reached back to unsheathe the knife he had taken from Katrina. Where was Jared? He was the only one unaccounted for and able to help them out of this bind.

He admired Valeria's composure and wished he could wipe the leer off the older aristocrat's face. Why were they unable to kill him? Had he not done enough to ensure the deaths of so many British soldiers through his treasonous acts?

Valeria refused to turn toward Theo. She was probably trying to keep the Duke's attention on her. Foolish woman. She held that silly kitten as if it was the most important thing in the world.

They could never leave her with the Duke. It was obvious what his plans for her were. Theo struggled with the urges this peer of the realm was fully bent on unleashing on Valeria. They were not far from the desire for her that he struggled with when he was alone with her. The difference was that he would never hurt her and this man was notorious for hurting women. It galled him to think of the Duke putting one finger on her in a dishonorable way.

He glanced at Michael, filled with concern. Michael was one of their scrappiest fighters and it surprised him that his friend had been captured and beaten to the point where he lay so still on the floor. Katrina would kill him for embroiling him in this fiasco if any harm befell her husband. The fact that he almost pummeled his friend himself a few nights past was not lost on him. Was he really any better than the brutes who stood by the wall eying them?

The two thugs advanced on Phillip and Theo.

Phillip stood, appearing calm, as if waiting to be politely excused from the room.

Theo fingered the blade hidden in his hand. He would reach for his gun, but he didn't want to draw attention to any weapon and his was hidden in the small of his back. He was suddenly unsure if they would prevail against these much larger street fighters.

The Duke was lifting a finger to touch Valeria's hair.

The rage that flamed up within him gave Theo the confidence that he needed. There was too much to lose if he didn't. He didn't reflect on the fact that he had already lost Valeria with her plans to set sail once this was over. He could not let anything bad happen to her now. Not after they had already survived so much.

"Now come along nice like 'n we'll make yooz right comf'terble," one of the men said as he neared them. He had a gaping hole in his smile where teeth had been at one time. He was unshaven and something foul emanated from him.

The man reached out to grab Theo as if he really expected them to go quietly.

Theo ripped the man's arm around and stuck the knife into his back as he now faced away from him. He could not see how Phillip was engaging with his counterpart, but a scuffling arose from that quarter as well.

The man Theo held rammed his head back making contact with Theo's nose. Theo jammed the knife in harder through the roughhewn clothes and shoved the man away from him. The man fell forward, but quickly turned to rush at Theo. Theo side-stepped him and tripped him into a desk, kicking him as he fell to the ground. The brute stood again and wobbled a bit before pulling a gun on Theo.

Theo managed to shoot first, not even aware of when he'd grabbed the pistol now in his hand.

The man fell to the ground, his eyes rolling back in his head. Theo lunged to assist Phillip who was underneath a brute on the ground. Theo pulled the man up and punched him, kicked him to the side, and hauled Phillip up to his feet.

The two of them rushed the man as he wobbled to his feet and with the force of their running and his falling, pushed him out the window and over the balcony. He fell to the ground with a *thump*.

Clothes torn, noses bloodied, and black eyes forming, the two men turned.

Valeria was being held in front of the Duke with his gun pointed at her head.

The kitten was on her other shoulder climbing from Valeria to the Duke.

"You surprise me, gentlemen. You are not as soft

as you appear. I'm terribly sorry that you will find your battle for naught." The Duke sneezed. "Lady St. John is my kin and I need to take her with me. However, should you choose to follow, I am more than willing to dispatch her. I can always find other breeding stock." The Duke blinked and looked at the kitten sitting on his shoulder. He could not dislodge the cat without letting go of Valeria. He held firm to his victim while growling at the kitten. "I already broke this one in and she is 'family'. It is more convenient to keep what is already mine than to find someone new." He sneezed again, and his eyes were rapidly swelling and watering.

"It must be hard to find someone new when you spend your life in hiding," Theo said with a bored voice that did not reveal the terror that welled up within him at the danger Valeria now faced.

~*~

Valeria tried to remain calm. Theo had put up a valiant fight, but it hurt her to see him being pummeled. His hair was wildly out of place, his nose bled, and he appeared more handsome to her than ever.

The Duke spun her around to watch as he held a gun to her temple while his other arm held her iron tight against his chest.

The kitten was moving to his shoulder and the Duke's allergies were affecting him. Perhaps she could use that to her advantage.

The fight was over in a matter of seconds, although it seemed longer.

Theo stopped in his tracks when he recognized the

danger she was in.

She wanted to convey the depth of her love for him, but she was not sure he was getting the message. Unless a miracle occurred she would not be alive for much longer. If the Duke did leave her alive, she would most likely wish she had died.

Michael stirred.

The Duke kicked him in the head.

The body on the floor stilled.

It broke her heart. Michael appeared identical to Damon, but he was a different person, someone whom she'd come to like. It saddened her to see him bested by his father. But Damon had never been very good at standing up to his father's bullying either.

She thought of Damon and for the first time experienced pity for him instead of resentment. He was weak. He would never stand up against his father but only did his bidding and often suffered for it. Not as much as she did, but he had suffered none-the-less. The fact was, she was not sure if Dartanian was really Damon's—or her father-in-law's. She shivered at the memories of liberties stolen and grew suddenly stronger. What did it matter if there was a gun to her head?

The Duke was sniffling and sneezing and the gun wavered each time. He could accidentally shoot her.

She gave Theodore a smile.

The men stood still, lest any move on their part cause the Duke to pull the trigger.

Valeria glanced to Michael, and then over to Theo and Phillip. Dartanian was safe with Marcus, but even his survival could not be guaranteed. She recalled all the times in the past when she had been a victim of this evil man and how the wives of the men who had given everything to come and assist her, had been traumatized. Men were dying because of the evil this traitor had perpetrated. Enough was enough.

~*~

Theo held his breath.

All were focused on the gun aimed at Valeria's temple.

Her eyes were trying to tell him something, but he wasn't sure he was getting the message. When she smiled, his heart dropped. She had a plan. She was going to risk it all. Theo glanced at Phillip.

He was aware. His friend was wound tight, ready to spring into action at a second's notice.

Where was Jared? What had happened to him? He hoped that Marcus would return, but anticipated that would not happen or if it did, it would not be soon enough.

So, he prayed. *God, I do not deserve You. I failed at living my life on my own. Please help us here. Save Valeria. Even if I need to let her go, please let her survive this to raise her son. I want to believe in You as my friends do. Please show me Yourself.* Did one need to say Amen?

~*~

Valeria prayed she would prevail. The God of the universe was more powerful than the lord of this world. She understood first-hand that Lord Diamonte came by his power, not through persuasion, but through his worship and dedication to Satan. Had she realized this truth about this charming and powerful man when she was a young woman, recently orphaned—she would have run away. Anything would have been preferable to what she ended up with.

But could she really regret it completely? She had Dartanian and now her heart yearned for Theo. If they could eliminate this evil she wouldn't need to leave the country. Maybe she could find a happier future as Lord Harrow's wife.

Theo now understood the depravity to which she had been subjected in her marriage. Would he still want her?

There was nothing left to lose. She prayed for God's aid and protection.

The cat meowed, and a tiny paw come up with claws out.

With everything she had Valeria stomped her heel into Lord Diamonte's foot.

The Duke yowled, startling Mittens, who reacted in fear. Claws scratched at The Black Diamond's face, one hooking into his eye.

Valeria tried to shake off the arm that held her tight. The gun was not near her head anymore, yet a shot rang out in the room. The arm around her went slack as the Duke fell down behind her.

The kitten jumped free with a loud *meow*, tearing across the room to cower in a corner.

Valeria dodged away, too.

A circle of blood stained the Duke's light blue coat and waistcoat. His eyes were closed. The Black Diamond did not move.

Jared stood in the doorway checking his gun. "I'm surprised he didn't have more thugs around this property." He stopped and knelt by Michael. "Come on, wake up sleepy head." He slapped Michael's face and grinned. He went over to the sideboard and poured a glass of Irish Whiskey. Raising Michael's head, he poured the alcohol past Michael's lips.

Michael sputtered and gagged, then reached up and punched him.

Jared reared back, laughing.

Phillip checked Lord Diamonte. "He is still alive."

"Good. Let's bind his wound and put him on a ship to France. If he survives the trip over the channel he can live out his days there. He will no longer find a welcome in England. The new Duke will be Dartanian." Jared had taken charge.

"Dartanian cannot be Duke while Lord Diamonte is alive." Valeria pointed out the obvious.

Jared raised eyebrows. "Is he alive?" He glanced to Phillip. "Is he alive? I don't see a living Duke in this room, do any of you?"

Phillip grinned and came to Valeria. He lifted her hand and placed a kiss on it. "You were spectacular, my dear." He bent down to help Michael up with Jared's help. They left the room, and then returned for Lord Diamonte.

"The carriage is full, Theo. Do you think you can manage to get Lady St. John back to the Inn with my horse? The animal is tied up outside the door." Jared scooped up the kitten.

Theo nodded.

The door closed behind Jared and they were finally alone.

Theo placed his hands on her shoulders and gazed into her eyes. "Valeria?" She reached up to touch by his eye that was almost swollen shut and traced a light finger down his nose that must surely be broken. Her heart swelled with gratitude for the faithfulness of this man. "*Veuillez me tenir,* Theo. Please, just hold me." She was safe in his arms as she wept.

10

Theo was drained and inept after all that happened. Jared saved Lady St. John but he wished it had been him. He held her close in his arms and she shook as she released all her pent-up fear. He treasured holding her close as they rode Jared's horse back to town. At least Jared allowed him that.

They entered the inn and Marcus informed them that Phillip and Jared departed with a hired carriage to transport Lord Diamonte to the coast. He was still alive.

Jared insisted they leave immediately as he needed to report to Whitehall and make sure that Lady St. John and Dartanian were guaranteed full access to the estate and funds. Dartanian would now be the Duke of Diamonte.

Lord Wolton had escaped. Again.

Dartanian was not well. The doctor tending him expressed grave doubts about him surviving the night. He had been poisoned. He suffered the side effects of the drugs as well as influenza.

Theo grieved with Valeria for the safety of her son.

Michael also rested in a room with broken ribs and a concussion. Theo suspected that Jared fled for the coast to avoid the wrath of Michael which was due to come eventually for the cruel way he awakened him.

"Whiskey? I hate the stuff. Why couldn't he have splashed my face with water?" Michael grumbled to Theo before lapsing into unconsciousness once again.

Theo chuckled even as he put a raw steak over his

own eye and tried to rest on a pallet on the floor of Michael's room. He hoped that it would not be too many more days before he would be allowed to sleep in a real bed. If that bed also contained a certain tall, blonde woman with deep brown eyes, he would be even more content. At the moment, there was nothing more he could do to further his goals in that regard while Dartanian lay so sick. It would be tragic if after all they had gone through they lost the young boy now.

~*~

Valeria was exhausted. She nursed her son through the night and was unable to sleep. Every cough or sniffle jarred her into full wakefulness.

Marcus came that morning to beg her to at least go eat and he would sit with Dartanian while she broke her fast. "You will do him no good if you get sick as well, Lady St. John."

She agreed with his wisdom. Dartanian was delirious and hardly cared who was with him. She trusted Lord Remington and recognized that he would do all he could to keep her son comfortable.

The private parlor's lone occupant was Lord Harrow. His face was a myriad of colors and his hair had not been restored to its normal tidy appearance. His apparent fatigue did not hinder his appetite because his plate was full of of eggs, toast, and fruit.

She came into the room, shutting the door behind her. "How do you fare, Lord Harrow? I have not seen you to thank you for your care last night."

Theo stood as his face turned pink. "I fare well enough, my lady. How is Dartanian?"

"Not well, but he survived the night."

Theo pulled a chair out for her. He poured her a cup of tea, filled a plate of food and set it before her—all before he sat down to resume his own meal.

"Thank you, Theodore."

"My pleasure, my lady." He focused only on his meal.

She applied herself to the food in front of her but found she had little appetite. She leaned back in her chair, sighed, and sipped her tea.

"You need to eat to keep your strength up."

"So Lord Remington reminded me. I hoped that I would feel different once we had rescued Dartanian and were safe."

"How so?"

"I thought I would be elated. I anticipated fleeing the country and now I do not need to. I will not need to work. I will be myself again, if I ever figure out who that is. I will have to find a place to live and try to figure out what to do with my life. It is overwhelming."

"But none of that will mean anything until Dartanian has recovered."

"Dartanian. *Mon petit*. It is terrible what he suffered due to his *grand-pere*. How do I explain all that has happened to him when he grows older?"

"When he is older, tell him the truth." Theo patted his mouth tenderly with a table linen. With a split lip the motion had to be painful.

She sighed. "The truth is ugly."

Theo sipped his coffee. "The truth is you are now free from the horrors of the past. You do not need to live there anymore or walk in fear. Dartanian does not need to carry that with him either."

"When did you get so wise, Lord Harrow?"

Theo shrugged and grew quiet.

Did he still desire her after all they'd been through yesterday? Heaviness weighed on her soul. What man would want her after all that had transpired? She was not only a widow, she was damaged goods. She really was not worth more than being a lover to a man like Lord Harrow. Even as the mother of a Duke, she had too shameful of a past to be worthy to step out amongst the *beau monde*. She did not belong in such exalted circles even though she was the daughter of a French *Comte*. All that had burned in the revolution. She was not a citizen of Britain and did not really belong anywhere. Once Dartanian was old enough to assume control of his vast inheritance she would be without value or purpose. She cleared her throat. "Theo."

"Yes?" He looked up at her with a fatigued expression.

She went over, stood behind him, and placed her hands on his shoulders. "Relax." She massaged his shoulders under the fine fabric of his coat.

He leaned his head back and closed his eyes.

She bent down and kissed the top of his head and her fingers followed, massaging his scalp and loving the feel of his soft sandy-colored hair in her fingers.

He let out a sigh of contentment and reached up to pull her around. He pushed his chair back from the table and sat her across his lap.

She gazed into his eyes. For once she was actually taller than him. His large hands, with their bruised and cut knuckles came up to gently touch both sides of her face and pull her head down toward his. He did not encounter much resistance as she wrapped her arms around his neck and met his lips in a soft kiss. When the kiss broke, she pulled her head back and smiled at him.

"I'm beginning to want to thank God for having your horses run me over and bringing you into my life."

Theo groaned and closed his eyes.

Valeria leaned down and kissed each eyelid. "You have been a hero ever since that day in every way possible."

Theo opened his eyes, they were deep mossy pools of green. He pulled her back to him and deepened the kiss.

Valeria sighed as she leaned in further to taste more of him. Had she ever wanted a man like this before? No. Never. The desire swirling within her fueled by the aftermath of yesterday, her anxiety over Dartanian, and her fatigue all combined to weaken her defenses and make her want everything this man had to offer.

Before she realized it, she was on her feet and Theo was across the room messing his hair with one hand.

"I would never so dishonor you, my lady. I apologize for my inappropriate actions." He pulled a hand down over his face and groaned.

Valeria grew bereft of his presence. It felt so much like rejection. Anger built inside her at her own stupidity at being so forward and giving into her baser emotions. "You did nothing that I did not allow you to do. I'm sorry you found me so distasteful." Valeria strode to the door and delivered her parting shot. "I will not so importune you again, my lord." She slammed the solid oak door and trudged up the stairs realizing she never ate a bite of her breakfast.

When she came to her room she asked Marcus to have a maid bring her some tea and toast. She crawled into bed to lay next to her son and holding his little body close, she cried herself to sleep.

~*~

Marcus strode into the parlor to find Theo standing by the window. "What did you do to upset Lady St. John?" Marcus filled a plate and began to eat.

Theo ignored him. What did he have to say for himself? The minute that woman touched him all he wanted to do was bury himself in her golden hair and comfort himself with her touch. Her scent. The way she tasted. Everything within him had longed for this woman from the day he had run her down by accident. He wanted to be honorable in the way he treated her, but when she came near him his brain shut down and he was lost in these new and uncomfortable emotions. There had been nothing honorable in the thoughts that accompanied their kisses. He was sorry if he hurt her by rebuffing her advances, but he did not know what else to do. He shook his head as he glanced over at his friend.

Marcus raised an eyebrow.

The uncomfortable truth was he had never been with a woman. His friends thought he had experience, but he was as much a virgin as Marcus had been on his wedding day. He'd never met a woman who tempted him to want to bare his body and soul in such a way as to act on the urges that he now struggled with. Valeria had experience. If he married her would she find him satisfactory?

Memories from the past rose up to taunt him. Friends early on in school questioning his masculinity. His first time to a brothel, forced there by his father. He was so intimidated by the woman hired to initiate him that he could not perform and ended up leaving in shame. His father taunted him with his failure up until his death. Through all these years he'd wondered if he was even normal. He would dance and flirt with the women, but had no desire for them.

Never once was he tempted to steal a kiss and never before had any woman tempted him to think about marriage. Classmates shamed him incessantly for his lack of desire to pursue women. He loved women. He adored his mother, but he had also seen her pain at her husband's infidelities. He never wanted to treat a woman that way. He despaired he would never find one who would make him want to take the risk of humiliation smilar to the past.

It took three women to show him how wonderful marriage could be. Josie, Elizabeth, and Katrina all doted on their husbands and Marcus, Phillip, and Michael were equally besotted. He felt left out and jealous. It was not until he had met Valeria that his heart found peace. He wanted her at his dinner table. He wanted her holding their children. He wanted her beside him when they went to bed at night and he wanted her to be there when he awoke in the morning.

His friends never knew about the brothel debacle. They'd never met his father and he preferred it that way. He admired Marcus for his choice to stay pure until marriage. But for Theo it had not seemed like a choice. More like a failure and it had gone on for so long now he wondered if he would ever be physically attracted to a woman. Until Valeria.

Theo came back to the table and sat across from Marcus. His food was cold, and he pushed the plate away. His coffee was tepid, but he drank it anyway.

"Care to talk about it?" Marcus asked.

Theo started to open his mouth but closed it again. Why the hesitancy? Marcus was a good friend. He kept confidences and he led a virtuous life. There was no one he could trust more than the man sitting across from him. Marcus may have been two years his junior but in so many ways he was older in spirit than the rest of them.

"Let me guess from what I've seen. You care for Lady St. John, desire her, and that scares you." Marcus's brown eyes held compassion.

"That would sum it up well."

"There is no rush to marry, is there?" Marcus was asking the trick question.

Theo sighed. "That depends on what it means to compromise a widow."

Marcus raised an eyebrow and frowned.

"I have not bedded her." Theo's face grew warm. "But I wanted to."

"You are a man. Temptation comes to all of us."

"Did it come to you before you met Josie?"

Marcus shook his head and grinned as if he remembered their rocky courtship. Or perhaps it was their wedding night. "Never did I physically desire a woman before her. I am glad that I did not taint our wedding night with memories of other women."

"I would bring that purity to my marriage bed as well and that terrifies me." Theo sighed.

Marcus dropped his fork. "Really? Theo. You never indicated that you were not, well, active in that."

"I never desired to before now."

Marcus nodded. "It will be worth the wait. Trust me."

"But she has been married before. I fear I would not measure up to her expectations."

"Given the heat I sense between the two of you I do not think that would be a problem. I would suggest a short engagement or a special license."

Theo laughed. "Has any one of us had a traditional wedding yet? It seems that getting a special license is a rite of passage for us men."

"Michael had not needed a special license. He had the banns called and yet he was the only one whose wedding we were unable to attend."

Theo laughed. "Poor Katrina. He put her through a lot when he got his memory back but didn't remember the wedding."

Marcus sobered. "It was heartbreaking for her when she discovered she was with child and lost her husband."

"In the end, it worked out though. I can hardly believe they are on their way to a second child already."

Marcus smiled. "We are, too."

"Really? Congratulations!"

"Thank you, Theo." Marcus sipped his coffee. "There is something wonderful about marriage and children. But I'm glad I waited for the right woman to share my life with."

"After Michael and Katrina, I decided I needed to get serious about searching for a wife. I hoped to avoid the drama you all endured."

Marcus laughed and couldn't stop.

Theo joined in. "I guess I had that one wrong, didn't I?" Theo chuckled.

"Women and drama kind of go together, Theo, but in the end they are worth it."

"I wish I knew if in the end, I was getting what I want."

"Has she seemed unwilling? I thought she had taken a shine to you?"

"I thought so, but she runs hot and cold. I lose confidence. She was going to leave the country and I lost hope of ever having her for my wife. Now that the Black Diamond is on his way out, she would be free…"

"But so much has happened that she will need some time to adjust."

Theo nodded. "I don't want to rush her, and I do not want to take advantage of her emotional vulnerability right now."

"Plus, her son is unwell. A woman often has no thought for anything else when her child is sick."

Theo nodded but grinned. "I'm not so sure about that."

"Oh?"

Theo shook his head.

Marcus stood. "Shall we go up and spend some time with Michael or do you need a bed to really sleep in for a few hours?"

Theo yawned. "I'll borrow your bed if you are willing to babysit the invalid."

Marcus smiled. "I'll be praying for you and Valeria, too."

"Thank you."

~*~

Valeria woke a few hours later, weary.

Dartanian was awake. "*Maman*? I am thirsty."

She rose to get some water and helped her son drink. His forehead was cool. "*Mon enfant*, your fever broke. We will get you a bath."

Valeria left to find a maid and request a bath be set up in her room, so she could bathe her son. She returned and helped him sit up. "I am so glad you are better, *mon petit*."

After bathing her son, changing his clothes, and supervising him drinking some broth, she tucked him into a bed of fresh sheets and left the room to let the men know. She searched in the private parlor, but no one was there. She asked the innkeeper to give a message to the men.

Marcus arrived a little while later. "Lady St. John, I hear that Lord Diamonte is recovering?"

Dartanian looked around. "*Grand-père* is here?"

Valeria grinned and tousled his dark locks. "No, *Grand-père* is gone and now you are the Duke."

The little boy sat up and puffed out his chest. "Really? I am the duke?"

Marcus laughed. "You are, my lord." He bowed before Dartanian.

The little boy laughed. "I am a higher rank than a Viscount."

"That would be true, Lord Dartanian."

Valeria turned to Marcus. "I am eager to leave. How soon will Michael be able to travel?"

"He is awake. We could leave tomorrow if we take the journey in slow stages."

"I believe that would be good."

Marcus nodded. "Rest up, we will leave early in the morning. We will make Rose Hill our destination. After Phillip helps Jared get Diamonte en route to France, he will reunite with us there."

"Rose Hill?"

"My principal seat outside of Didcot. Michael's home is nearby."

"That will be fine. From there I can decide where we will go next."

Marcus nodded. "You are welcome as a guest in my home for as long as you need."

"Thank you."

~*~

It was late in the evening and Theo rested in bed. He was not sleeping after his nap during the day. His sore ribs would not tolerate the hard floor. Tomorrow he would be driving his own carriage with Michael, Dartanian, and Valeria riding inside, and Marcus riding alongside. The journey south would probably be far more peaceful without Diamonte's thugs pursuing them.

He wandered to the window and opened it to lean outside. He inhaled...smoke. The distinct odor was more than what would have been coming from the kitchen. He peered out the window.

Smoke came from the room next door.

Fire!

"Michael, wake up, grab your stuff, and get out immediately. The inn is on fire."

Theo ran out of the room into a smoke-filled hallway and knocked on Marcus's door. "Fire, Marcus, get out!"

He ran down to Valeria's door and found it locked. He knocked, but there was no answer. He tried to ram the door with his shoulder but was unable to break through.

Marcus appeared and together they broke through the door into a room filled with smoke and flames licking up the drapes.

"You take your lady, I'll take the boy." Marcus picked up Dartanian and ran out to the hallway.

Theo tried to rouse Valeria, but she wouldn't stir. He grabbed her roughly, threw her over his shoulder and headed for the door, into the flames and smoke that threatened to overwhelm him. His ribs screamed in pain. Escaping outside he found the innkeeper and his wife in the courtyard of the inn.

Marcus had Dartanian on the grass in the village green and was trying to rouse him.

Michael knelt nearby coughing.

Theo gently reclined Valeria on the grass before bending over to cough. She lay so still. He checked her pulse. She was still breathing. He shook her with no response. Marcus was having the same results with Dartanian. The men looked at each other and mouthed the word at the same time.

Poison.

Another attack came without them expecting it and if he had not been awake they would have all been burned to death. Theo knelt with his hands on his knees gasping for breath.

The fire burned even as the servants and neighbors nobly tried to save the structure. The stables had been spared.

The moon was bright. Theo collapsed onto his back into the damp cool grass as he tried to fill his lungs with fresh air. His chest spasmed with pain. His clothes had been singed but thankfully he had his boots on. Michael had grabbed his and Marcus had gotten his on quickly, but other than that they had no other belongings.

"Mittens!" Theo jumped up and went around the perimeter looking for the cat. He tried calling but doubted the animal would hear him above the crackling flames and the building falling apart from within.

A little figure emerged from the grass. now slightly gray and uttering a wheezy meow.

"I'm glad you are safe, little one." Hugging the kitten he walked back to his friends.

"I suggest we hitch up the carriage and head south. We'll keep trying to wake Valeria and Dartanian and seek a doctor in the next town." Theo set the kitten down next to Dartanian and it curled up around him. "We have nothing to stay for. It will be cold. Did any of you leave any of your clothing on the coach?"

Michael shook his head. Marcus shook his as well.

Theo stood. "I have blankets inside to keep our passengers warm. We can buy clothes after the sun rises." He glanced at Marcus. "You could ride inside for now and we can pick up a horse after we get warmer clothes." Theo was in his shirtsleeves, a waistcoat, trousers, and boots.

"What about you? How will you manage to drive?" Marcus asked.

"I will manage because I am alive. I can drape a rug across my legs to help. What other choice do we have?"

"We could take turns, so you could warm up inside."

"We'll see." The two men exchanged glances and Marcus nodded. Theo needed to do this.

Soon the carriage was hooked up and the still unconscious Lady St. John and her son, the new Lord

Diamonte, were loaded in along with a slow-moving Michael and Marcus.

Theo put on driving gloves that he had stored in the carriage and threw a rug over his legs before he picked up the reins and took off from Newcastle-under-Lyme with his passengers. The horses were fresh but sluggish at three of the clock in the morning and there were a few more hours before sun would break through the horizon. Theo headed south toward the village of Stone, hoping that by the time they arrived they would be able to get a meal and some clothing. He prayed that somehow his two sleeping passengers would awaken by then.

He was cold. He still coughed from the smoke he inhaled. He shivered and perspired at the same time. After a few hours of driving the sun illuminated the road and Theo grew weaker. When he finally rolled into Stone and pulled up to The Boar's Nest, he was ready to collapse. He threw the reins to the ostler, pulled off his gloves, and shoved them into the storage space under the seat. He got down and stumbled into the inn to request rooms.

He returned to open the carriage door. Michael needed a hand.

Marcus followed and assisted Lady St. John, who had awakened during the journey. A groggy Dartanian got out on his own, but staggered until Marcus picked him up. The ragtag group marched into the Inn and were given a private parlour.

Theo went straight up to the room assigned to him. Once there he collapsed on the bed, fully clothed, and pulled every blanket available over him. Shivering and achy, he fell asleep.

~*~

Valeria was surprised to awaken in a carriage with Dartanian resting against her and Michael and Marcus on the opposite seat. Marcus explained about the fire. That explained why she was in her nightgown. She wrapped her blanket closer around her.

Dartanian took longer to wake up and when he did he needed to use a container to throw up.

Marcus explained the two of them had been drugged.

She didn't get to speak to Theo when they arrived at The Boar's Nest. Soon the innkeeper's wife provided her with a dress that was too large and too short—but at least something decent to get her to the marketplace to find some new clothes for her and Dartanian.

When she returned, she bathed and dressed, while Marcus spent time with Dartanian. She then bathed her son and put him in fresh clothes. Still weak from his illness he went down for a nap. "Where is Lord Harrow?" Valeria asked.

Marcus was shuffling cards for a game with Michael in the private parlour. "I believe he went to his room when we arrived. I've not seen him since." Marcus had fresh clothes and no longer smelled of smoke.

"The day is getting long and if he is to get fresh clothing he should do that before the shops close."

Michael spoke up. "He didn't look too good. Why don't you go up and check on him, Marcus? It would have been a pretty rough ride this morning in the chilly damp air."

"Theo's a hardy sort. I'm sure he was just tired. But I'll go rouse him, so he can get some clothing and we can head further south tomorrow to Rugeley or Lichfield." Marcus tossed his cards down and left to find Theo.

11

When the door closed behind him Valeria walked to the window. "The fire was an attempt to kill both Dartanian and me." She shivered at the thought.

"It would appear so, my lady," Michael affirmed.

"So how do we stay safe now?"

"Perhaps Theo can sleep on your floor again and keep watch over you and Dartanian tonight?"

"I would feel safer knowing he was there," Valeria added. She experienced a little spurt of delight at some time alone with him. Even if Dartanian was there, he would sleep easily enough, and they could at least talk.

Marcus re-entered the room with a frown on his face.

"How is Theo?" Michael asked.

"Burning up and delirious. I've sent for a physician and I'm heading out to get him some fresh clothing. I will return shortly." Lord Remington left the room and shut the door.

Valeria sat down by the fireplace. Theo was ill? He hadn't really spent any time with Dartanian since he had become sick. Had he? She only remembered him once sitting with Dartanian and telling him silly stories. It had warmed her heart. Lord Harrow would be the kind of father her son needed. And the thought of making more children with him made her heart flutter. The man who had rescued her from the fire, who had been pummeled, shot, and had slept on hard floors all to protect her, was ill.

"He's a strong man."

"He's human, Michael."

Michael rose to bring her a glass of brandy. "Here."

"Thank you." She sipped and relished the warmth that spread through her body.

"We will have to come up with another plan to keep you and Dartanian safe tonight since Theo is ill and unable to stand guard."

"Perhaps I can nurse Lord Harrow and Marcus can guard Dartanian?"

"Why do that?"

"Because Marcus is married and would not be comfortable guarding me. And you are too injured to do the job. If I stay awake to watch Lord Harrow tonight, I can always rest tomorrow during the day."

"You are assuming that you are safe during the daytime hours."

"I hoped that I was safe now that Lord Diamonte is gone."

"Perhaps his cohorts did not realize he was no longer ruling his treasonous empire."

"Will he be able to do damage from France?"

Michael winced. "Possibly, but much less. And that is only if he somehow survives his gunshot wound and the crossing."

"It seemed inhumane to deny him medical care."

"He is responsible for the deaths of many British troups, he poisoned your son, made several attempts to kill you and Theo, and practically had me beaten to death. And you wanted him treated humanely?"

Valeria frowned. "I see your point."

"We did not kill him, and we offered him safe passage to France. That was more than he deserved."

"What do you think God thinks of all this,

Michael?"

"I believe He hates evil."

"But He still knew all of this would happen and allowed it, didn't He?" Valeria took a sip of her brandy. "I don't mean to cast aspersions on God, but I'm new to this Christianity and there is still so much I do not understand."

"I did not realize you were a believer."

Valeria's heart sank. "I am not a good follower of Jesus, but I am trying."

"No, it is not that, Lady St. John. You have come from such dark evil in your past that I find it surprising that you know about Christ."

"I only learned about Him after I buried my husband and escaped. I speculated that there had to be a God. For how could the world be so beautiful at times when there is such darkness?"

Michael nodded but said nothing.

"After we left we found sanctuary with a pastor and his wife until I was able to find a job. They asked no questions and loved Dartanian and me as if we were family. They talked to God as if He was right there with them in the room. I asked questions and they shared about sin and the consequence of eternal death and Jesus dying in my place so that I could have a relationship with God. I read the Bible they gave me, and I prayed and experienced such peace as I ventured out on my own." She stared into the fire. "I naïvely thought that perhaps God would rescue me from Lord Diamonte. That I would be free from him." Tears welled up in her eyes.

"But don't you see, Lady St. John?"

"See what?"

"He did rescue you. What seemed like a terrible

accident with Lord Harrow running you over with those silly horses, ended up connecting you with us. People who know first-hand the evil of the former Duke of Diamonte. People who were willing to risk anything to protect you and Dartanian. How many people do you think you could have found in all of London who would have been safe for you to share your secret with? Every step of the way God has led you and brought people around you to care for you and protect you. We've not been perfect by any means, but we are all still here. We all survived. But even if we hadn't, we would have given all so that you and others would no longer be in harm's way. I long to see my wife and watch my children grow, but I was not afraid to die should that have been required. I know where I'm going." Michael frowned and bit his lip.

"What is it?" Valeria asked.

"Theo."

"Theo?"

"He is the only one of us who has not taken that step of faith. Marcus has been sharing with us for years, but it was not until each of us got attacked by the Black Diamond that we really took our eternal destiny seriously and accepted Christ. I've tried talking to Theo about it and so has Phillip and Marcus."

"But he does not know Jesus?"

"Oh, he knows of Jesus Christ and he understands a lot about God and I would guarantee he could tell you much about Jesus's life here on earth. But has he accepted him as Lord? Bent his knee to submit to His authority?" Michael shook his head. "That I have no assurance of."

"I did not realize. I had hoped..."

"Why did you think he had?"

"He has risked everything and been so honorable towards me even when in my weakness, I tried to tempt him." She sighed. "I thought that came out of a heart like Christ's."

"Love can do that to a man, make him rise to new heights. I pray that somewhere along this journey he has taken that step of faith. Theodore is private. He doesn't always say a whole lot about himself. I never saw him grieve his father's death. I did witness it when his mother died shortly after. That devastated him. But beyond that he has always been that gentle, even-tempered man you met." Michael laughed. "This journey has definitely brought out new sides to the man I had not seen previously. I've never seen him lose his temper before. Did you now he almost beat me up?"

"Theo?"

Michael nodded and grinned. "Seems like a certain woman has gotten under his skin and he's not quite sure what to do about that."

Valeria grinned. "Maybe I need to make it a little easier on him?"

Michael raised his hands. "You didn't hear it from me. I'm staying out of this." He set his hands down on the arms of the chair and grinned. "But I'll be praying for your success, my lady."

Valeria grinned in response. She liked Theo's friends.

~*~

Theo felt like he had been run over by a carriage pulled by at least four horses. He coughed, and his lungs ached. His lips grew parched but soft hands lifted his head and cool, soothing water passed through his lips. He could not make out the voices but he recognized someone was there on the fringes of his consciousness. Valeria. Where was Valeria? Was she all right? He remembered a gun to her head. What happened after that? He remembered her close to him wrapped in only a cotton nightrail, her form thrown over his shoulders. Flames. Smoke. Terror that he had not been in time. Was she all right? Had she awakened? He tossed his head trying to remember but soft hands and a cool cloth were placed across his forehead.

A little while later his body was stripped of his clothes and he was half-dragged, half-carried to a bathtub. He shivered even though the water was warm. Whoever was torturing him poured water over his head. He was dried off and dressed and soon he found himself wrapped up in a cocoon of blankets. He smiled. Finally, he could rest. But Valeria. Where was she? Why couldn't he know if she was all right? A soothing voice and a gentle hand eased him as he drifted into a fitful sleep.

~*~

Valeria stayed with Theo most of the time. At night Marcus slept on the floor with Dartanian near the fireplace as she rested in a chair by Theo's bed, watching over him.

Michael helped keep guard during the day.

Theo kept calling her name and she tried to soothe him, but he seemed fearful. It warmed her heart that his concern was for her safety and well-being. It made her sad that he was being tortured by dreams of recent events with no consolation that they resolved well.

Dartanian was enjoying his time with Marcus and Michael as they worked at teaching him how to read and play simple card games. Marcus would also take him out for long walks to help tire him out.

Theo remained sick for three days. Marcus sent a note to Rose Hill to inform them of their delay and that they hoped to be en route soon.

Valeria spent much time praying for Theo and reading out loud to him from a Holy Bible the innkeeper lent her.

On the third day, he opened his eyes and they no longer held that glassy look. He took in the ceiling with its wooden beams, the far wall, and finally his gaze rested on her. "Valeria? What are you doing here?"

"You have been very ill, I have been nursing you back to the land of the living."

"I'm warm under all these blankets." He moved to take them off but realized quickly how little he was wearing underneath them. "Perhaps someone else can come to help me?" The color rose in his cheeks.

She bit back a smile. "If you insist. I will see if Lord Remington is available." She rose and left the room.

~*~

Theo needed to use the chamber pot, but a lady was in the room. As soon as she left he threw back the covers and welcomed the cooler air. His hair felt damp. He must have had a fever because he was weak. He managed to take care of his needs before he collapsed back into the bed. He threw one sheet over himself in case Lady St. John returned.

Someone knocked at the door.

"Who is it?"

"Marcus."

"Enter."

Marcus came into the room appearing hearty and whole. If he remembered correctly Marcus and Jared were the only two to come through their adventures unscathed. "What happened? How did I get here?"

Marcus sat down. "I have a maid coming soon with a bath for you and some food."

"My question?"

Marcus laughed. "You never used to be this impatient, Theo. You had influenza. Between rescuing Lady St. John from the fire and driving that carriage with insufficient clothing through the damp and cold early morning hours, by the time we reached Stone you were barely functioning. You got us our rooms and went straight to bed. It wasn't until later when I came to check on you, that we realized how ill you were."

"How long?"

"Three days."

Theo groaned. "Is Dartanian safe?"

"We've managed to keep everyone alive for the nonce. I even purchased some clothing to replace your singed articles. We will see how you fare today and perhaps we can depart tomorrow and make Rugley or Lichfield. I will drive the carriage since neither you nor Michael will be physically ready for that."

"True, but am I ready to spend days in a carriage with Lady St. John?" Theo asked.

Marcus grinned. "Whether you are ready or not, you will need to. Perhaps in a few days we will reach Rose Hill and you will be free to leave if you desire and return your carriage to Hartview."

"If I desire." Theo grimaced. "That seems to be the crux of my problem, Marcus—desire."

~*~

Valeria didn't know what to do or say as they entered the carriage the next day. She hoped to talk with Theo privately but after he awakened from his fever she was denied access to his room.

Dartanian recovered from his illness and the fire in fine form and was as chatty as he ever could be.

"Dartanian, how does it feel to be a peer of the realm now?" Michael's cheeky grin was back.

"I'm more important than Lord Harrow!" the boy crowed. His eyes were bright, and he bounced in the seat.

Theo smiled kindly at the boy's antics.

"Dartanian, no one is more important than anyone else. We all have equal value in the eyes of God," Valeria said.

"But, *Maman,* I'm a lord now. Isn't that like being God?"

Theo laughed. "Oh, if only that were true, Dartanian. Then you and I could have anything we would want and would not need to work for it."

"I want a pony. Can I have a pony, *Maman*?" The boy put pressure on Valeria's right arm and she winced.

"Young man, be gentle with your mother. A gentleman always treats a woman with respect." Theo's tone was serious.

The boy's eyes filled with tears. *"Maman je suis désdé."*

Valeria wiped her son's tears. "I forgive you, *mon enfant.*"

"I'm not a baby anymore, *Maman*. I am a lord and I want a pony." The young boy set his jaw and narrowed his eyes.

"We will need to see what the trustees of your estate will say about that. Lords do not have as many choices until they are grown."

"Like Lord Harrow?"

Valeria smiled. "Yes, like Lord Harrow."

Theo mustered a weak grin.

"Do you get whatever you want, Lord Harrow?"

Valeria found Theo's gaze boring into hers, his eyes a deep green. "No, son, I do not." He broke the gaze and turned to her son. "I have many material blessings due to my wealth and title, but love cannot be bought."

"We will love you, won't we, *Maman*?"

Theo wordlessly gazed out the window.

Valeria's heart ached for him because she understood exactly how he felt.

~*~

Theo was thankful that Valeria was alive and well sitting across from him. Dartanian had survived. God had answered his prayers and even helped him rescue her from the fire.

He promised God that he would give up Valeria if God would spare her life. Theo was, above all, a man of his word. If she was leaving the country it would be easier to bear, but now? Now she would be able to mix amongst the *beau monde*. He would see her on a regular basis. He would stand by and watch her flirt and dance with everyone but him. She was off limits.

He'd prayed a lot in his room yesterday as he rested. A Bible had been left. He had spent time reading it and he asked Marcus pointed questions about faith and if he really was now a follower of Jesus.

God had rescued them. He could no longer deny that God was what he needed to fill the empty void in his soul. He was at peace for the first time in forever. His father may have shamed him and his mother died leaving him lost and alone. He had never experienced the love of a woman and now his heart broke because the one woman he hoped for and desired sat across a carriage from him, tantalizing him with her honey-colored hair. Even her premade, homespun dress did nothing to hide her elegance and beauty.

But lords did not get everything they wanted in life. He'd learned that long ago. God showed him that Jesus provided everything he needed. He had friends who were willing to sacrifice to help him. Friends who never left him out in the cold, who never failed to show him and tell him about God's love for him. He was such an idiot to have taken this long to finally surrender to Christ.

But now that he had, he could not forsake his vow. God answered, and Theo would step aside and trust that somehow God had someone better for him to take to wife. He could not imagine anyone more perfect for that role than the woman across the seat from him. One look at her delectable lips and he was transported back to what it was like to kiss her. To taste her. To hold her in his arms.

Lord, please take these memories away! But did he really want them gone when he was alone at Hartview or in his townhouse? Would those memories comfort or torture him in the years to come? And would any woman be able to surpass the emotions this woman evoked in him?

He didn't have any answers. Only questions. He was anxious to get to Rose Hill so he could depart as quickly as possible and avoid seeing the woman of his dreams again. A black cloud settled on his shoulder with these thoughts. He would study God's word, try to grow in his faith, and trust that God, as the true Lord, would provide.

~*~

Valeria and Dartanian slept during parts of the carriage rides.

When awake, Michael would try to entertain them, but he was still in considerable pain from his beating, and the jostling of even this well sprung carriage was taking a toll on his energy.

Dartanian was undaunted by the adventure. He asked Theo questions about what his future responsibilities would be, and Theo and Michael told him what to expect when it came time to go away to school. Dartanian was not too sure he wanted that.

Valeria giggled at some of the tales Michael told his nephew and she was grateful that Dartanian still had one family member in his life who was worth looking up to and modeling after.

Theo was polite and respectful. He told stories with Dartanian sitting in his lap as if'd he always belonged there.

Valeria's heart ached for Dartanian to know someone like Theo as a father. Gentle. Patient. Sweet.

Another night and another inn and Valeria still felt

shut out from the man who had stolen her heart and made her want to believe in love.

"Lady St. John. Come take a walk with me in the garden." Marcus extended an arm to her and escorted her out of the inn. "If the weather holds and we escape any trouble, we may reach Rose Hill tomorrow night."

Valeria smiled.

As they entered the garden she dropped her arm and walked side by side with him. "I look forward to getting better acquainted with Josie, Beth, and Katrina."

"You are welcome to stay with us as long as you need to. You belong to a unique group of women who have all been impacted by the Black Diamond in some way or another. I am fortunate that Josie was spared worse than what she endured with Lord Bastion."

"Archibald was a dirty dish," she said flatly and gave an involuntary shiver.

"Did he…? Wait. I do not really wish to know." The handsome Viscount frowned.

Valeria bit her lip. There were so many things she wished she did not know.

"I wanted to share that after you were booted from Theo's room, he and I had several hours to talk."

She raised an eyebrow but said nothing.

"Theo has accepted Christ. He did so while at the Diamonte estate."

Valeria smiled. "That is wonderful news. Why has he spent the last few days looking as though someone has died?"

Marcus shrugged. "That I wish I understood. He admires you greatly. But why he is so distant, I cannot tell you for he has not confided in me."

"Thank you for enlightening me as to his spiritual

state. That eases my mind."

"I think you need to know that he plans to leave Rose Hill the day after we arrive."

"By himself?"

Marcus nodded. "He plans to return his carriage to Hartview."

"There is a rush to return?" This made no sense. He pursued her, now he shut her out and was running away.

"No one awaits him at home. He truly has no one but us to call his family."

"This makes no sense."

"I agree. Have you had some sort of disagreement?" Marcus frowned.

Valeria shook her head.

"I am sorry. I had hoped..."

"So had I."

~*~

Valeria tucked her son into bed that night and experienced a deep sense of loss.

Marcus knocked. "I can sit with the lad for a while."

She went to seek out Theo.

Michael was leaving the parlor when she came to the bottom of the stairs.

"Lord Harrow?" she asked.

"He is within," Michael said. He gave her a wink before ascending the stairs.

She entered the parlour.

Theo sat by the fireplace with his head back and his eyes closed.

She walked as softly as she could, thankful for

slippers instead of the harder soles of her boots. She came up behind him, placed her hands on his shoulders, and began to work out the knots.

Theo jumped at her touch but let out a deep breath and relaxed into it. Neither said a word.

Valeria started to massage his head and reveled in the feeling of his soft hair. She massaged his scalp and worked her way to the furrows on his forehead and between his eyes. She even massaged his jaw which was clenched together tightly. She came around to the front of his chair and leaned in to give him a kiss.

Theo's eyes popped open, He gently pushed her away and strode to the other side of the room where he commenced pacing.

"What is it, Theo? What have I done to offend you?"

"Offend me?" Theo turned to her with wide eyes. "What makes you think you offended me?"

"You avoid me. You do not talk with me. You won't even let me kiss you." Valeria walked towards him.

Theo put a hand up. "Do not come closer. Please."

"But why? You used to have no trouble being close to me." Valeria hugged herself and bit her lip to hold back the burning of tears.

Theo swallowed and continued pacing. "I cannot do this. I want to behave honorably to you. I vowed I would. You tempt me too much. I am sorry." With that, Lord Harrow left the room. He took the stairs two at a time, if the speed he went up was any indication.

Valeria went to her room, locked the door, and prayed for a way to regain what she had somehow lost with the gentle Marquess.

12

Theo was shaking when he left Valeria in the private parlour. Everything in him wanted to kiss her senseless but he had no right to do that. He was not her husband and never would be. Marcus told him that God gave a way out of temptation and that sometimes fleeing it was best. Flee was exactly what he planned to do. He knocked on Michael's door.

"Theo?" Michael had not undressed yet but had removed his cravat and boots. "Come in."

Theo shook his head. "No time. I wanted to tell you I'm leaving. I will hire a horse and head to Rose Hill."

"Why?" Michael tipped his head, compassion written in his brown eyes.

"I want to do what's right before God. I cannot stay any longer." Theo hoped Michael understood what his words would not say. "I believe you and Marcus are capable of looking after Lady St. John and the boy."

Michael frowned. "We will see you at Rose Hill?"

Theo nodded.

"Travel safely, my friend." He put a hand on Theo's shoulder and squeezed. Theo returned the gesture. They both stepped back in silence as their arms fell.

Theo nodded. "Safe travels to you as well." He fled down the back stairs to avoid seeing Lady St. John.

Theo hired a horse and rode through the night. It was almost too dark for safe travel on the roads. He took care when he could not see far in front of him. He patted his revolver to ensure that he was ready should there be any ne'er-do-wells about. He possessed nothing of value to steal anyway.

Theo arrived at Rose Hill before sunrise. He rubbed down his horse and fell into a bed of hay so he would not disrupt the household. He was awakened to someone kicking him gently.

"Theodore! We have plenty of rooms in the house. If you wanted to sleep, we were more than ready to accommodate you regardless of the time of your arrival."

Theo slowly opened his eyes to discover Marcus's wife, Josie, standing there dressed for a ride. "I didn't want to wake up your household."

"It is not an issue now. Go inside and get some food. Mrs. Hughes will take you to your regular room to rest. Where is my husband?"

"He should be here later today. Have Phillip or Jared arrived yet?"

"Phillip arrived yesterday and only told us that the Black Diamond is no more."

Theo rose to his feet and brushed his clothing off.

"Jared?"

"Apparently went to London and may need to depart quickly for the Peninsula. We may not be seeing him again for some time."

Theo nodded. "Well, my lovely lady, I will do your bidding and get some food and rest. I will see you later."

"You'd better believe you will. We all want to know what happened."

"That would really not be my story to tell."

"We'll see about that." With that the lovely dark-haired woman strode off to her horse and the waiting groom.

Theo made his way inside to do exactly as she bid. He wondered if he could escape later before the interrogation began. At least Phillip was around to lend him aid should he need it.

~*~

Valeria didn't know whether to be furious or disappointed. Either way she wished for an opportunity to give Lord Harrow a piece of her mind. Riding off in the middle of the night? He was one of the few capable of defending them if they had any trouble. And even if he would not talk to her she still enjoyed looking at him.

Marcus would not tell her why Theo had departed. Or he didn't know the reason. She thought he had some idea but was too loyal to his friend to share. She appreciated that about him.

Michael was in more pain this morning and was sipping some brandy from a flask to help him endure the last leg of their journey.

"I am sorry you are still suffering." She patted Dartanian's hair as he napped on her lap while looking across the carriage to the man who was her brother-in-law. The kitten was curled up in Michael's lap getting equal attention.

"It was worth it to serve you, Valeria. I may not appreciate the agony at the moment, but I will get better. I am alive and will return to my wife and child. What more could I ask for?"

"You seem happy in your marriage." Valeria experienced a stab of jealousy.

Michael nodded and smiled. "I am indeed, but it was a rocky road to get there. I am grateful my wife did not give up on me. I doubt we would have made it through without knowing the Lord. Ask her yourself about the trouble it was getting me to be a husband. It's not a pretty tale and I don't make out well in it, but she has forgiven me, and God has granted me the life I never thought I would be able to have or deserved. I'm a blessed man and therein lies my contentment."

"I often believed I did not deserve that kind of happiness." Valeria looked away. Sometimes Michael's physical similarities to her husband unsettled her.

"I'm sorry my half-brother wasn't honorable. Having met my father, I'm glad I never met my brother. I almost wish I did not know who my father was. What have I gained from it? My wife was tortured and branded as a result of him. We all deserved better and someday, in heaven, we will have it. But I am certain God has some good yet in store for you here on this planet. Do you wish to remarry?"

"I thought I would never want to after what I had suffered."

"But now?"

Valeria bit her lip and glanced at Michael. "Now, if the right man proposed, I would gladly say yes."

"But he would need to be the right man?"

Valeria quirked one corner of her mouth and nodded.

"Have you found him?"

"I thought I had but I'm beginning to think I was mistaken."

"If you love him, do not give up. Sometimes we are a bit thick-skulled when it comes to women." Michael mimed knocking on his head with a closed fist.

Valeria laughed. "Women are not always very smart either."

"Don't give up, Val."

She smiled. No one had ever given her a nickname before.

~*~

Theo awoke and was grateful he always kept some of his clothing at Rose Hill since he spent more time at this estate than his own. He found his hostess and other guests in the drawing room enjoying their late afternoon tea.

"Good to see you, ol' man!" Phillip came forward to pat Theo on the back. He whispered, "Is everyone well?"

Theo nodded. "I left them all well."

"What has delayed the group from getting here sooner? I expected to meet you here when I returned from the coast." Phillip sat down.

Theo greeted the ladies and sat as well. Katrina, Josie, and Beth all waited for him to answer. He explained the fire and the influenza. He made Katrina aware of Michael's injuries, so she would not launch herself into her husband's arms at his return as was her wont.

"If everyone is well, why are you are here before them?" Katrina asked him.

Theo sipped his tea. What was he to say? While they were all believers would they understand how he needed to flee the temptation that Valeria was to his very soul? "I need to get home. I actually may depart within the hour."

"Wait a minute." Beth was speaking. "You went out of your way to help Lady St. John. You helped vanquish our darkest, most evil enemy. And now you want to go home? What are you running from, Theo?"

"Myself, mostly." Theo set his cup down and stood. "I have a confession to make." He walked toward the fireplace and stoked the flames as it was cool in the room. "I accepted Christ on this journey."

"That's wonderful news, Theo. We've all been praying for you." Phillip came and patted him on the back. "But what does this have to do with you running from yourself?"

"I made a vow to God and I am struggling to keep it. Marcus told me about how sometimes when faced with temptation we need to flee. Well, I'm fleeing."

The women frowned and looked at one another.

"Temptation? Theo, you never even flirted with temptation. If you have ever given into any kind of such you have been discreet about it." Phillip stood by Theo's side with his arms folded.

Theo felt surrounded. Lost. Alone. If he left he was leaving behind years of friendship with the only family he'd ever known. Cutting himself off from them to avoid Lady St. John was harsh and it grieved him.

"Theo? What is really wrong?" Josie's voice was soft. All of these women were like sisters he never had.

He could only shake his head. "Excuse me." He left the room, stopped in the study for brandy, ran to his room, locked the door and lost himself in the oblivion of the bottle.

The brandy burned down his throat. His clothes were loose on him. He had lost weight on this journey and with his illness. He'd pulled a Bible off the library shelf earlier and now read Paul's words about putting to death the old man, that all had become new. He definitely was grieving a death. Not that his previous life was all that spectacular and worthwhile. Sure he was a good landlord, but he was rarely home. His steward took care of things. He was a savvy investor having learned along with Marcus the best way to work the market. And he possessed wonderful friends.

Friends who all had wives and children.

Friends who would now embrace Valeria St. John.

The one woman he had fallen in love with.

The one woman he vowed to leave alone.

Theo groaned out loud.

She hadn't wanted him anyway. She'd made it clear she did not want to marry—ever.

He thought he could change her mind. But she'd planned to go to America. Now she was staying, and he didn't know which hurt more—the idea of her leaving or the idea of her staying when he couldn't have her for himself.

She offered him a physical relationship and there was certainly chemistry there, but he believed that offer was off the table. Why she sought to kiss him was beyond him. Maybe she hoped to comfort him? He shook his head.

He almost wished the thug had beaten him to death, so he wouldn't need to suffer anymore. But that was only minutes before he had submitted to Christ and he would have been lost in hell for eternity. He shivered at the thought as he stared into the blazing fire before him.

Instead he was in his own living hell. Eternally secure but determined he would live a life that would honor God. He didn't understand much about how to do that though except for the way his friends lived their lives.

He'd never been a man prone to impulsive decisions, but well and truly soused, he decided to head to the stables and take a ride. If the alcohol didn't help him escape his broken heart, maybe a ride would.

He stumbled in and managed to saddle one of Marcus's mares. He almost fell off when he tried to get up over the horse, but she was well-trained and didn't complain. He finally got on and although a bit dizzy he pulled the reins and headed out across one of the fields as the sun was setting. Maybe jumping a few hedges would help?

~*~

Valeria was welcomed warmly by Lady Remington, Lady Westcombe, and Mrs. Tidley.

Phillip, already reunited with his bride, escorted Dartanian up to the nursery.

"I feel a bit *de trop* with all of you lovebirds." Valeria tried to keep her voice light, teasing.

Katrina stopped her. "I hope you do not feel left out. We have missed our husbands so and worried and prayed for you all on your journey."

"I am grateful for your prayers and for allowing your men to come to my aid."

Katrina smiled. "Well, for one, we urged them to go. We have longed for an end to the Black Diamond's reign of terror over our lives. Although we had not been threatened for some time it was always there in the background, taunting us with the possibility that he could rise and strike again. And secondly, our husbands respect our wishes, but they will still do what they want."

Michael gave his wife a kiss and left her to care for Valeria. The Tidleys expected to leave for their estate in a day or two. Marcus greeted Josie warmly and the two went off to their quarters as well. Katrina walked Valeria to her suite.

Valeria and Katrina entered the suite to find her belongings had been brought from London.

Katrina broke the silence. "I thought that perhaps there were some sparks between you and Lord Harrow."

Valeria draped her cloak over a chair and walked to the window to look out into the darkness. The moon could not be seen and only a smattering of stars were visible through the clouds. "I thought so too."

"What happened?"

"I wish I knew. He practically proposed, and I rejected him, but he continued to pursue me. When I knew that my father-in-law was no longer a threat, I suddenly realized I did not want to spend the rest of my days without being able to see Theo's face. To feel his touch. To hear his soft voice..."

"You are enamored of him."

Valeria nodded. "But after we defeated Diamonte, it was as if he changed. He became distant. Not rude or angry, just closed off."

Katrina smiled. "Maybe you need to kiss him."

Valeria turned to her new friend. "I have, and it was wonderful. But the last time I tried he hopped a horse and headed for the hills. Rose Hill, to be exact."

"I see..."

"You do? Because I do not. The man is driving me crazy."

"Men have a tendency to do that, Valeria. At least the ones worth loving do." Katrina gave Valeria a hug.

"Now, let us get you ready for dinner. Perhaps we can help a bit where Lord Harrow is concerned." She wiggled her eyebrows and Valeria could not help but laugh.

13

"Buffleheaded idiot." Theo awoke face down on the edge of the river bank. His clothing was soaked through and he was shivering from the cold. Mud coated his face and hands and his head spun. Of his horse, there was no sign. He tried to rise but instead threw up. Forcing himself up, he staggered to the top of the rise and fell backwards on the grass. The world spun circles. His body was numb, and he remembered how quickly he'd finished off that bottle of brandy. Perhaps if he closed his eyes he would not feel quite so dizzy.

When he awoke later it was to rain softly falling on him. He sat up and struggled not to fall over. Even though he was not standing, he figured he could manage to fall over quite well. He laughed to himself. Since when had he ever gotten so drunk? His friends did not drink to excess and it was not something he'd ever had any inclination for.

Lights moved off in the distance. How odd. The lights danced back and forth and he was entranced by them as it was all he could see in the darkness. Then he heard his name.

Was this how one came to heaven? His clothes were soaked and covered with mud. His left arm and his leg ached. He tried to rise but intense pain forced him back down. He definitely was not ready to meet anyone in this condition. Perhaps if he were quiet they would pass him by.

He tried to move to his hands and knees and

crawl, but his left arm would not support any weight and his left knee and thigh hurt so bad he was laying back on his side in tears. He felt as if he was a child all over again. Humiliated. Alone. Beaten up.

How had he become injured? Where was he? He really could not think straight anymore and closed his eyes against the cold and pain.

~*~

Valeria paced back and forth in front of the fireplace.

When Theo missed dinner, Marcus went to check up on him, found the room empty, and a bottle of brandy laying on the floor. He soon discovered that Theo had taken a horse out hours ago and had not returned. The horse had.

It began to rain, and clouds obscured the moon. It was cold outside. Theo had only just recovered from influenza.

She paced and prayed as Josie, Beth, and Katrina kept vigil with her.

It was close to one in the morning when the men straggled in carrying an unconscious Theo.

The women jumped into action and proceeded to prepare a bath.

The men shoed them out so they could clean him up and get him to bed. A servant was awakened and Dr. Miller summoned.

"I will sit with Theo tonight," Valeria stated with her arms crossed.

Marcus argued with her about it. "You are our guest and you need your rest. It has been a long and tiring day."

"And you three men have not seen your wives for quite some time due to helping me out. My son is well cared for and I *want* to do this." Valeria stared down Marcus.

Marcus turned to the rest of the men. "I suggest we all get some rest. Lady St. John will appraise us of the doctor's orders when we rise in the morning." With that he escorted the men and their wives out of the room and left Valeria alone by Theo's bedside. The fire was blazing in the hearth and a lamp was lit by the bedside.

"Valeria?" Theo mumbled, and his head moved back and forth but his eyes remained closed.

"Yes, Theo. I am here. Rest now."

"My arm. My leg. Hurts."

"You are lucky you didn't break your neck."

"Buffleheaded idiot." The words were soft and slurred.

"What?"

"I'm a buffleheaded idiot." He said it a bit louder and laughed. A paroxysm of coughing followed.

Valeria lifted his head to help him drink some water.

"I love you," he said with a smile and began to snore.

Valeria finger-combed his hair, still slightly damp from the dunking the men had given him to get the mud off.

She leaned back and grinned. The buffleheaded idiot loved her, did he? Then why was he constantly running away?

The doctor came and examined Theo while she stepped out of the room. When he brought her back in his expression was grave.

"His lungs do not sound good. You said he recently recovered from influenza?"

Valeria nodded.

"I suspect he now has pneumonia, which can be quite deadly. He needs to rest with his head elevated. Lots of warm broth. I'll be back later today to check up on him."

"Laudanum?"

"Perhaps later today after the alcohol has worn off. He'll be fairly miserable with the head he'll have on top of the bruises and the pain in his chest. I don't want him so drugged up that he cannot breathe or drink."

"Understood."

"It was a pleasure to meet you, Lady St. John. Lord Harrow is fortunate in his friends." Dr. Miller put his hat on. "I'll see myself out."

The door closed behind her and she glanced back at the man in the bed. She sat next to him and held his right hand in hers. "Oh, Theo. What have you done?"

His eyes opened and were a bit glassy. "You're still here?"

She nodded.

"I didn't break my neck."

"No, you didn't."

"Only broke my heart."

She tipped her head. "What?"

"I love you but can't have you. Rather break my neck."

Valeria put a hand to his forehead. He was hot. Between the alcohol and the fever, she wondered if he realized what he was saying.

"Why can't you have me, Theo?"

"Made a bargain with God. He let you live and I

gave you up."

"Did God ask you to give me up?"

"No."

"Then how do you know He wants you to honor that vow?"

"Because I made it and He kept his end of the deal."

"God did not need your bargain to save me, Theo."

"He didn't? But I prayed."

"I'm glad you did. It shows me how much you love me."

"I love you, but you do not want to marry me."

"Why not, Theo? Why wouldn't I want to marry a gentle, caring, and very handsome man like you?"

Theo gave a silly grin. "You think I'm handsome?"

"I most certainly do."

"You kiss really good. I like kissing you."

Valeria smiled. "You are the only man I've ever enjoyed kissing."

Theo's eyes brightened. "Really?"

Valeria nodded. "Really."

"You smell good. Will you kiss me?"

"I do not think that would be a good idea. I will consider it when you are better."

"You are cruel." Theo pouted.

Valeria grinned and squeezed his hand. "Sleep now, Theo. I will be here when you wake up."

"You will stay with me?" His eyes were drooping.

"As long as you need."

Theo's eyes closed, and Valeria bent over to kiss his cheek. "I love you too, Theo," she whispered in his ear. She sat down and kept vigil for the rest of the night basking in the knowledge that Theo loved her.

~*~

Theo woke to intense pain and his tongue stuck to the roof of his mouth. 'Mwwr."

"What?" a soft, familiar female voice spoke.

Theo barely heard through the pounding in his head, the throbbing pain in his arm and leg, and the heaviness in his chest. "Mwwr?"

A strong and gentle hand came behind his head and lifted him up. His eyes felt as if they were glued shut. Water was brought to his lips and he eagerly drank even though he could tell he was making it difficult for the woman helping him. Water dribbled down his chin, but he didn't care. She pulled the glass away.

"More water."

"Just a moment."

The hand was behind his head again, the glass came to his lips, and he drank without dribbling this time. She gently placed his throbbing skull back on the mound of pillows. "Thank you," he mumbled. He felt so hot and weak.

The gentle hand came to his forehead and was replaced by a cool damp cloth. He fought to pry his eyes open.

"Angel."

"No angel, just a widow in love with a buffleheaded idiot."

"I don't know who you could be referring to." He grinned. She was here, caring for him. He had run from her, but God wouldn't let him. But he had not been Jonah running from God's call. Had he? No. God had not told him to pursue the beautiful widow. He only desired to.

And here she was. In his room. Watching over him. "Caring for a buffleheaded idiot is one of the qualifications for being an angel," he said.

"It is?" She smiled, and his heart flipped. He started to cough. She frowned as she lifted him up and rubbed his chest. It eased the pain. The coughing stopped, and she laid him back down.

"Would you like some broth?"

He shook his head. Sleep. All he wanted was sleep. And his angel.

The next time he woke his angel wasn't there.

"Welcome to the land of the living," a deep voice said.

"Marcus?"

"You gave us quite a scare. Your recklessness the other night took us all by surprise." Marcus was leaning back in his chair with his booted legs crossed and resting on the bed.

"I don't remember what happened."

Marcus nodded. "I'm not surprised. You normally do not drink much and yet you polished off a lot of brandy and took one of my horses out on a dark night, to jump hedges. Did you have a death wish?"

"Was the horse injured?"

"No, she's fine."

"I did want to die but I was not trying to kill myself."

"You've been acting strange lately."

"I am strange. Always have been. I really do not want to talk about this now." Theo groaned as pain radiated through his body and a herd of horses stampeded in his brain.

"Rest, Theo. But you had better get well."

"Or what, you'll kill me?" Someone was shutting his eyes and pulling him underwater. He coughed, tears came, and he blissfully sank into darkness.

~*~

"I am sorry my lady, but those are the terms of the will." The solicitor from London who represented Lord Diamonte's estate sat before her and Michael explaining the papers laid before him. Lord Wolton was the only trustee who had not been able to be contacted. The remaining two trustees had been found and insisted on enforcing the terms of the will.

"How much time does she have?" Michael asked.

"Lord Damon St. John died..."

"Ten months ago," Valeria answered in a flat voice. All the fire had gone out of her.

The solicitor looked up. "Yes, that would be correct. Which gives you less than two months to fulfill the terms of the will or lose the entire estate to a trust to be administered by those three men for whatever purposes they deem appropriate."

Valeria swallowed. Two months. Lord Wolton escaped and his whereabouts unknown. The other two lords were ones she did not have any acquaintance with.

Michael winked at her. "Thank you, Mr. Brownstone. We will be in touch with you when Lady St. John has wed."

The solicitor's eyebrows went up as he looked at her. "You have an appropriate suitor?"

Michael stood and assisted Valeria to her feet.

The solicitor rose as he placed the papers back in his bag.

"Lady St. John is a beautiful woman, Mr. Brownstone, the challenge for her will be selecting the man."

"Very well. Congratulations, then." The solicitor bobbed his head nervously and quickly departed the room.

"Michael! How could you?" She slapped him on the arm. As a brother-in-law, he was sometimes a pain. For all of that she was grateful for his support.

"How could I what?" Michael shrugged.

"I have no suitors and no time to find one." Valeria walked across the room and sat in a chair near the fire.

"I think you are misleading yourself. Where have you been this past week but in the room of a highly eligible bachelor, whom I believe is attracted to you."

"In his delirium."

"Well, let's pray he can be return to his normally sound mind and brought up to scratch."

"I really would not want to wed him or anyone only to keep my son's inheritance."

Michael nodded. "I realize that. But if you do not you will be destined for a life of servitude."

"Lord Harrow does not need the money."

"Of course not. He has wealth of his own. He would be a wonderful steward for the funds for your son, however, and when he comes of age, Theo would ensure Dartanian understood how to manage them wisely."

Valeria twisted her handkerchief in her hands only to stop and look at it. It was the one Theo gave her shortly after they'd met. She looked up to the ceiling as if the answer to her problem would be found there.

Lord, what am I to do?

~*~

The next time he awoke the room was dimly lit and when he moved his right hand it brushed up against something soft and silky. He adjusted his eyes to the darkness and saw a blonde head and part of a woman's body leaning on the bed with the rest of her still in a chair. Valeria.

Why was she here? He let his fingers play in her hair, but he erupted in a coughing fit that soon awoke her.

"Theo?"

He could not catch his breath. She helped him sit more upright and rearranged the mound of pillows before laying him back down. Orange blossoms. He could smell orange blossoms. Why did that scent always make him think of kissing her? She helped him drink some water and he kept his eyes focused on her. The water was cool and soothed his dry mouth and throat.

"Is that better?"

"Much." His voice sounded raspy and weak.

Her shoulders relaxed. "You had me worried."

"Really?" he croaked.

She smiled. "You do not understand how loved you are, do you? Everyone has been praying for you."

"How long..." he bit back another cough.

"A week."

"I need to leave." He struggled to try to rise but fell back in defeat.

"I think you need to rest and regain your strength."

"Why?"

"Because I need your help."

"I am unable to do much of anything at the present moment."

"Consciousness and being of sound mind would be the two qualifiers."

"Sound mind? Hasn't the information been passed along? I'm an idiot."

"But a gentle, lovable, and buffleheaded one." She smiled at him.

"What do you need me to do?" Theo was curious.

"I need you to marry me as soon as possible." Valeria held her hands in her lap and bit her lip.

"You what?" He started coughing again and when he was done he shook his head. "Now who is the foolish one?" He couldn't keep his eyes open any longer.

~*~

Valeria had shocked Theo and she felt bad unleashing that when he was still so sick. But she was nervous and afraid he would say no. Michael had suggested calling the banns right away so when Theo was better, they could be wed. She could not bring herself to agree to that plan unless Theo really understood why this was necessary.

It's not that she didn't want to marry him. She did. But she wanted to wed someone who wanted her for her, not her money. She also did not want to be married out of pity either. She knew Theo didn't care about the money, but he was a handsome man. She was sure he could have his pick of many women amongst the *beau monde* if he wanted. That puzzled her more than anything. Why would someone like him, so honorable and available, not be married already? Why would he have sought out her affections and even offer marriage before even being appraised about her noble lineage?

She was French. Wouldn't a good British lord desire an English rose for a bride? She didn't even physically fit the mold of an English aristocrat. She was taller than most women and her hair was quite blonde which was not the current fashion. She looked in the mirror and saw a square jaw and full lips and brown eyes with her sunshine hair. Nothing spectacular from what she could tell. So why had Theo pursued her and helped her? It didn't make sense. He and his friends saved hers and Dartanian's life.

To ask him to tie himself to her for the rest of their life did not seem like the best act of gratitude for all he had done.

She was grateful that she could care for him. With the influenza, he had moaned and slept, but with pneumonia he was actually at times entertaining. She was flattered even with some of his murmurings as he would talk in his sleep.

"Valeria?" His voice was raspy and soft, but he called for her often. Sometimes all he wanted was to feel her touch and he would calm again.

"I'm here, Theo," she whispered to him and clasped his good arm.

He visibly relaxed and smiled. "I really like you a lot."

"You do?"

"Um, hm. I'm glad those horses ran you over so I could meet you."

"You are happy I got hurt?" He had been horrified at her injuries, but she enjoyed teasing him.

"No. No. No." His voice was slow and slurred, almost as if he were drunk. "I do not want you to get hurt. Ever. I would take it for you."

"And you have. You are my hero." She squeezed his forearm for emphasis.

"I am?" He wore a silly grin.

"Yes, you are."

"Do I get a kiss then? Heroes ought to get kisses, I think."

"I think that would be a grand idea, Theo." She didn't move. He puckered up and she bit back a giggle.

"Valeria?"

"Hmmm?"

Now he was pouting. "Why won't you kiss me?"

"I want to kiss you very much, Theo, but you are sick and need to rest."

"Oh. I'm sick?"

"Very."

"Will I die?"

"I hope not."

"I get to go to heaven if I die so that's not too bad. But I would like to stay for more of your kisses. I really like kissing you."

Valeria smiled, leaned over, and kissed his forehead. Whispering in his ear she said, "There is no one I would rather kiss than you."

She sat back down, and Theo had a silly grin on his face.

"Maybe later?"

"Maybe. Rest now, *mon ami*."

~*~

Theo woke up to find the room brightly lit. For

once his head wasn't pounding and he was able to inhale deeply without coughing.

"You decided to rejoin the land of the living?" Marcus was sitting by his side.

"Was I that sick?" Theo felt groggy and his arm and leg still ached.

Marcus nodded. "Lady St. John has been particularly anxious for you to recover. I think the lady has a thing for you, Theo." Marcus was smiling.

"I remember a dream where she asked me to marry her. Can you imagine?" Theo shook his head.

"It wasn't a dream, Theo."

Theo looked at his friend. No smile. "Not a dream?"

Marcus shook his head.

"Why would she want to marry me?"

"Why wouldn't she? Don't sell yourself short, Theodore. You are a handsome, well-respected aristocrat who treats a lady well. You have repeatedly put yourself in harm's way for her."

"You think I'm handsome?" Theo grinned.

"I've heard the women talking."

"So now you have stooped to relaying gossip? My, how the mighty have fallen."

Marcus shook his head at his friend. "The fact is, Lady St. John is in a bit of a quandary and it appears that you would be the ideal person to once again rescue her."

"A knight in shining amour while laid up in bed?"

"Vows can be spoken anywhere."

"But why?"

Marcus frowned. "Hmm. Now if I told you that I might be gossiping. I guess you'll have to wait to hear it from the lady herself."

"When?"

"In a few hours after she's rested. In the meantime, I believe you will need some assistance to get bathed and some fresh clothes. I sent for Watkins to help tend to you. Your valet is vastly overpaid and needs to earn his keep more. You have been on this sickbed for too long. I don't know how Lady St. John has stood being in this room for any length of time."

Theodore inhaled. He definitely had been perspiring. "If I have to be ready to hear a marriage proposal than I should make myself smell better at least."

"At least." Marcus grinned and helped his friend rise from his sickbed.

Theo rubbed his stubbled chin. "A good shave would not go amiss either."

~*~

"Valeria?" The soft female voice penetrated the dark fog of sleep that had wrapped around her. Hadn't she just drifted off? Theo! She jerked awake with a start.

"Theo? Is he well?" Her hair was falling wildly about her and she was all twisted up in her clothes. She had fallen into bed still dressed.

Josie giggled. "He is well. And awake. You have been sleeping all day and I figured you may want to rise for dinner."

"All day?" Valeria rubbed her eyes. "I think I need a bath and a change of clothes."

Josie wrinkled her nose and nodded. "I think that would be wise. Now that Theo is on the mend you will want to look your best for him."

Valeria's heart beat faster. "Josie, what if?"

"What if, what? You need a husband and Theo has been drooling over you since he first ran you over. He speaks of you in his sleep. Are you worried he will deny your request?"

Valeria nodded. "He confuses me. Draws me near, and then is so distant."

Josie nodded. "Talk to Katrina about a man who is passionate and runs hot and cold. Before they finally resolved things, Michael had to be the most idiotic man around. I wanted to slap him silly for the way he treated her." Josie looked closely at Valeria and put her hands on her guest's shoulders. "Theo has to be one of the most faithful, stable men of my acquaintance. He has never fallen for a woman before. I've never seen it and neither have his friends. He's been waiting for you all his life. Don't be afraid. Have faith that God will work this all out."

Valeria nodded. "Thank you." She sniffed. Reassured but still scared. Since when did a woman propose to a man? How was she supposed to do this without sounding so needy? She prepared for a bath with the help of a maid assigned to her.

The fact was, without the will being held over her head, she still wanted Theo in her life. She mulled over how to get the man and his love without the will mucking it up. A slow smile spread across her face that had nothing to do with the warm scented bath she was slipping into. No. Maybe the will was a temporary aid to get her what she really wanted. Lord Theodore Harrow.

14

Lord Harrow was confined to his room for a few more days but Valeria was granted the opportunity to visit with him later in the evening. Theo sat in a chair by the fireplace. He had been permitted trousers and a shirt under his robe for the sake of decency. He thought it was a bit silly in a way since Lady St. John had been taking care of him for so long during his illness. But he acquiesced to the demands of his valet. Watkins could be quite stubborn, and Theo did not possess energy for a fight.

When Lady St. John entered the sitting room, he was struck again by her beauty. Her eyes looked tired and worried. Lines marred her forehead and her hair was pulled back in a tight bun. She was dressed in a lavender gown that hung on her. He may have lost weight during his illness, but it had taken a toll on her as well. And yet she still radiated that beauty. And the scent of orange blossoms came with her. When had anyone ever given so much of themselves on his behalf? His heart beat a little faster at the overwhelming emotions her presence fostered.

"Have a seat, Lady St. John. I understand we have something that must be discussed without delay."

She looked uncertainly at him and was holding something tightly in her hands. His eyes narrowed to see what it was. A handkerchief. He smiled. If the hint of embroidery he could see was what he thought it was, it was the one he had given her. She still had it. The thought humbled him.

She moved to sit across from him, her legs primly together, her feet flat on the floor and her back straight and not touching the chair. She appeared scared.

"Valeria? I'm a friend. I'm weak as a kitten and will not do anything to harm you or, I hope, distress you."

She nodded. "I am glad you are better."

Theo grinned. "I would not be so if it had not been for your kind ministrations."

Her smile was sad and she did not meet his eyes. "Has anyone told you what it is I needed to discuss with you?"

"I had a dream where you proposed marriage."

She blushed. She really was so pretty when she colored up like that.

"Marcus also mentioned something to that effect. I will admit I'm confused. You made it clear to me that you wished never to marry again. Given what was revealed when at the Diamonte estate, I could understand why. You were harshly used in your marriage."

She looked down at her hands. She would start to stay something and stop. She finally glanced up at him with tears in her eyes.

Theo's heart cracked.

"I never thought I would want to be in any way tied to a man again." She bit her lip. "But circumstances changed my perspective on that."

"Circumstances?" He was curious now.

"The will."

"The Duke's will? What has that to do with anything?"

She swallowed hard. "There is a stipulation in the will that if I have not remarried within a year of my husband's demise, then the estate falls into the hands of a trust and will be withheld from my son."

Theo's eyes narrowed. "Your son's inheritance is dependent upon your remarriage?"

Valeria nodded.

"If you do not marry within the allotted time period the estate reverts to the trust and other than a title, Dartanian is left with nothing."

She nodded and avoided his eyes.

"Valeria?"

She looked at him.

"How much time to do you have left?"

"One month."

"Not much time to plan a wedding."

"I have no need of a fancy wedding, my lord."

"Expedience overtakes luxury?"

She nodded.

"Is this to be a real marriage or one of convenience?"

Her eyes grew wide as she stared at him. "My lord?"

"You did not want to marry but you are now being forced into this. I need to understand if you desire a real marriage or one of convenience."

Valeria blushed. "I had not expected a *mariage de convenance*, but if that is what you would desire since you are being forced into this..."

"No one forces me, Lady St. John. If I agree to this marriage it is of my own free will. However, since you have in the past had so many choices withheld from you, I would be loath to be one more ogre on your list." *Lord, this is will kill me.* "If it is a *mariage de convenance* you desire, I would grant you that."

His gaze held hers. They were such a deep brown.

All he longed to do was drop to a knee and beg her to marry him because she loved him, not because she needed to. More than anything he would long to take his wife to bed and explore her every mystery. He was first and foremost a gentleman and if that was something she could not give him, he would take what he could have.

She was silent.

"Lady St. John, Valeria. Will you do me the honor of becoming my wife, the fifth Marchioness of Harrow?"

She solemnly nodded. "You do me a great honor in offering for me, Lord Harrow. I am pleased to accept."

"We have time to post the banns and marry in three weeks. Will that be enough time for you to prepare?"

She nodded.

"I will let you inform our friends of our happy news. I am finding that I am far more fatigued than I anticipated. If you would send Watkins to me, I would appreciate it."

Valeria stood and gave him a small curtsy.

Theo shook his head. "You are to be my bride, Valeria. There is no need for such formality between us."

She nodded and left the room, taking the smell of the orange blossoms with her.

Suddenly Theo felt cold and very alone.

A marriage of convenience? He never thought he would agree to such a thing. When Watkins came in and assisted him to bed he was finding himself quite frustrated. To be so near the woman he loved and not be able to touch her? To kiss and hold her? To explore the wonder of the marriage bed with her? This was not the way he'd envisioned his future. He wanted to cry at the injustice of it all. Yes he wanted to marry her and he was getting his wish. But he was not getting her heart and that grieved him to the depths of his soul. He prided himself as a man of honor and he would keep his word and his distance even though it killed him. Given the way he felt when he was in her presence he thought it very might well do that.

~*~

Valeria had mixed emotions as she prepared for her wedding day to Lord Harrow. Dartanian was excited that he was getting a new father and she truly believed Theo would be a wonderful role model for her son. They were frequently found together and Dartanian was already calling him *Père.*

Theo was regaining his strength. As his appetite returned he was starting to fill out and the gauntness in his face was gone. His eyes twinkled when he looked at her and she wished they were also promising her delights ahead. She had been shocked that he mentioned a *mariage de convenance.*

After the kisses they'd shared, why would he agree to a marriage where he would never bed her? She never thought that she would want to sleep with a man but something told her that with Lord Harrow in her bed, there would be no abuses, only gentle love and stoked passion. She pondered at night what it would be like to lay in his arms and awaken in the morning with him beside her. It felt like rejection that they would not share a bed or those intimacies. Would he be seeking that elsewhere? The very thought made her boil with jealousy, but she had no right to make demands when he was being so generous to her and her son.

Regardless of her concerns she tried to spend time with Theo every day, in the company of their friends. He treated her with courtesy and gave her warm smiles. Gone were the innuendos and flirtations that marked their trip north. He was all that was polite and kind. It made her want to cry.

~*~

The day was fast approaching, and they had not spent any time alone together. Theo seemed to take particular pains to ensure they had no private conversation. The three weeks passed quickly, and tomorrow was the day they would wed in the chapel on Rose Hill.

"Are you experiencing any bridal nerves?" Josie asked as they waited for the men to join them after their port.

"I've already been married. No jitters." Valeria played with her skirt. She'd changed her dresses to add colors more flattering to her. She had put off mourning. She wished to entice one man who seemed suddenly immune to her charms.

"You appear downpin. The past few days you have rarely smiled." Katrina reached out to touch Valeria's arm.

"This is not quite the marriage I envisioned," Valeria said.

"But I thought you loved Theo?" Beth asked.

Their conversation was interrupted by the men entering the room, led by Theo himself. He stopped and stared at her. His eyes looked like the softest grey. He didn't smile or wink as before. He gave her a nod, went to the sideboard, and poured a drink.

She wondered if he had heard her comment and wished she had kept her mouth shut. Their marriage was between the two of them. There was no need to bring his friends into it or on her side.

A megrim was beginning. Valeria begged to be excused and went to her suite. She barred the door and knelt before the heat of the fire to pour out her heart to God. What had she done?

~*~

"This is not quite the marriage I envisioned," she had said.

Theo had listened to the words and the weariness in her voice. He knew she didn't want to be married but he had thought he was making it as easy as possible for her to live with her decision. What more could he do?

What hurt more than anything was that she didn't love him. She only needed him to protect Dartanian's inheritance. She would have never considered marrying him otherwise. It did not bother him too much that he had no immediate heir to pass along his inheritance. A distant cousin living in America would inherit should anything happen to him and he'd already made generous provision for Valeria should he perish even now before the wedding. Perhaps he should offer her that?

No. That would not work because Dartanian deserved the estates and wealth that were part of his title. Without that he would not be respected in school.

The young man should not lose all that only to be supported by a family friend. Lady St. John would be maligned as well should the truth of her fortunes be made known. Even if his name were not attached they would assume she had been someone's fancy piece and she would be subject to further abuses. No, only marriage provided a safe place for her to raise her son. She may not want his heart or his body, but at least he could give her that.

The brandy burned down his throat. He almost wished he'd not survived that late night ride and tumble over the hedge. He wished he could turn his heart off or lock it away but only Valeria held the key and she didn't even want it.

What kind of man was he that a woman could not love or desire him? He did not want to marry for his title or wealth and yet, here he was on the eve of his wedding, sighing over the fact that this was exactly what he was doing. However, in any other marriage he would at least be compensated by some pleasures.

He saw the difference marriage had made in Marcus, Phillip, and Michael's lives. He knew it went beyond the bedroom, but he feared that he would never be able to enjoy the kind of intimacy he desired with his wife if that were not also part of the mix. He could not turn that part of his body off now that Lady St. John had lit the flame. He slammed his drink.

Marcus put a hand on his shoulder. "Come to my study, Theo."

Theo followed him to his inner sanctum.

Once the door closed Marcus motioned Theo to a set of chairs in front of the fire that was blazing cheerily in the grate. "You are getting married tomorrow and yet you do not seem happy about it. I thought you loved Lady St. John. This marriage was what you desired all along."

"Right. I'm not being married for the sake of my title and wealth. I'm not being married because of my rugged good looks."

Marcus laughed at that and so did Theo.

"I'm being married because I am tolerable, available, and I love her enough that I would do anything to make her happy."

"This marriage will not make you happy, Theo?"

"If anything, it will push me beyond the limits of my already strained self-control."

Marcus smiled. "Theo, that's the beauty of marriage. You do not need to keep those desires on a tight leash all the time anymore."

Theo stared at his friend. "Perhaps in a normal marriage. She didn't want to marry. She was horribly abused, Marcus, by her husband, and her father-in-law, and I suspect others like Lord Wolton, who is still at large. She is only seeking the sanctuary of a wedding certificate to protect herself and Dartanian."

"So, there is nothing in this for you?" Marcus frowned.

"I get a lovely hostess and a son. I will strive to be content with that. Since I've never had the 'experience' some men have had I do not know what I am missing. That should make it easier, right?"

"You will leave your bride untouched?"

Theo nodded. "Even if it kills me."

"If that doesn't, she might." Marcus grinned.

Theo frowned and raised an eyebrow. "You believe I'm in danger of being murdered?"

"Quite possibly. That woman looks at you like my wife looks at me when she wants more than to talk. I would assume that she wants a full marriage, Theo."

"She agreed to a *mariage de convenance*. I will not break that vow."

"Your vows tomorrow will include to worship her with your body."

Theo blushed. "I will fulfill that by restraining myself and honoring her wishes."

"What if her wishes change?"

"I doubt they would, given all she has been through."

"But what if you are the man God gave her to help her heal those wounds from the past?" Marcus rose and went to the door. "Think about it, Theo. I'll see you in the morning."

Theo sat in the study for a long time. Thinking brought no satisfactory conclusion so he rose and sought his bed. Tomorrow he was getting married. For better or for worse.

~*~

Valeria surveyed herself in the full mirror on a stand in the corner of her bedroom. Her hair was swept up with pink flowers and loose curls artistically put there by Josie's maid, Molly. Her dress was a deep blue with pink and white accents. The color and cut flattered her tall figure. She loved the fact that she did not tower over Theo. Would he think she was attractive?

She sighed. No magical wedding night for her but oh, how she wished she could get him to change his mind. Perhaps he really thought she was resistant to passion? She had turned him down often enough, even outright refusing his first marriage proposal.

He understood now the horrors she had been subjected to, or at least a hint of them. Maybe he found the thought of bedding her repulsive because of that? She had felt like damaged goods but until Theo had heard the truth from Lord Diamonte's lips, he had generally been affectionate, even passionate in his pursuit of her.

At first, she'd been offended. Until that first kiss. Then it all changed. She had never felt with her whole being as she did when his lips touched hers. No one had ever awakened passion in her. No one had ever treated her as precious and treasured.

When Theo heard the truth, he'd turned cold and distant. Yet he had saved her life. He had called out her name in his sleep and delirium and professed his love. But now, he was distant again.

She pinched her cheeks. It was her wedding day and not a time to dwell on something she could not change. She was marrying a good man. One she admired and loved. Even if he withheld himself from her, she could never be safer than under his protection. And Dartanian needed a father like Theo. She sucked in a deep breath, let it out, and put on her gloves.

A knock came to the door.

She opened it to find Michael standing there. He looked her over and whistled. "Wow, Val, you are stunning. If I weren't already married and a few inches taller..." He grinned and winked at her.

Valeria patted his cheek. "Thank you, Michael. Katrina is a fortunate woman to have you."

Michael whispered, "Has she told you that?"

She grinned as she placed her hand on his forearm. "No. She didn't need to. Her eyes say it all when she looks at you."

Michael stood up a little straighter. "Shall we take you to your groom?"

Valeria nodded, and they departed the mansion down the stone path towards the chapel.

The small entry to the chapel was dark, but when she entered the main room where their friends and Dartanian sat, she was enchanted by the stone and wood building and the high windows letting in the morning sun.

Theo stood at the front with the minister. The sun appeared to be focused directly on him making his sandy brown hair look almost golden. She caught his gaze and one corner of his mouth rose in half a smile. His gaze twinkled letting her know he admired her.

"Are you ready?" Michael asked as he stood beside her.

"As ready as I'll ever be."

They stepped down the aisle to a sweet violin melody played by Josie.

Valeria reached the front and stood side by side with Theo for the vows. Both said their words firmly and without hesitation. She wondered how he could promise to honor her with his body as he placed his signet ring on her finger. She trembled for wanting to be closer to him.

The minister announced their marriage and that they were man and wife.

She placed her hand on Theo's arm and his muscle tremored as he escorted her through their friends and back to the house for a celebratory luncheon. Toasts were made, and words of congratulations offered. Valeria did not have much of an appetite. Before she realized it she was back in her suite and changing into her traveling gown.

She looked forward to sharing a carriage with her husband. She might be able to coax a kiss out of him in the privacy of the enclosed coach.

She entered the coach with the well-wishes of their friends ringing in her ears but of Theo there was no sign.

The door opened again.

"Are you comfortable, my lady?" Theo asked, dressed in a greatcoat and less formal attire than previously

"I am well. Will you be joining me?"

"I will be driving the carriage. I hesitated to borrow any more of Marcus's staff than necessary. He has already done so much for us. If we are fortunate we'll be in Aylesbury tonight." With a nod, he set his hat on his head, closed the door, and through the window she saw his legs vanish as he ascended to the driver's seat. "Ha!"

The carriage jerked and moved forward.

Valeria sat alone with her longing.

~*~

It took great restraint to not ask for a groom to handle his carriage. He knew Marcus would have gladly lent one. He had even offered. Marcus had frowned when Theo had declined and insisted on driving his own carriage to Hartview.

A second carriage contained Dartanian, Watkins, and Mary, the young maid hired to care for the young lad.

Theo relished the strain and muscle required to manage the team and the jostling of the seat beneath him. He would arrive in Alyesbury too exhausted to even consider acting on any urges she unwittingly stirred in him.

He had almost stopped breathing when she entered the small chapel that morning. Her eyes were dark, her hair like honey, and the blue dress accentuated her every womanly curve.

They were only on the road for a few hours when they reached the King's Head in Alyesbury.

Theo assisted Valeria from the carriage. They entered the inn and he arranged for a private parlor for their meal, and rooms for the night. Dartanian joined them for dinner.

The little tyke was tired from the day. He still sat in Theo's lap to have a story told after their quiet meal. Valeria's eyes drooped, and they seemed a duller brown. She didn't smile and he he was probably the reason. But this was what she'd wanted. Dartanian's inheritance saved. He had accomplished that. As much as he wanted a real marriage, he would not take advantage of his position as her legal husband to claim rights he had promised her he would never pursue.

As he undressed for bed in his solitary room, he wondered if Valeria would ever change her mind. And if she did, would he be confident enough with this lack of experience to think he could please her? Sure, he had heard tales from other men on what women liked, but he hadn't personally navigated a woman's body to understand how to bring her pleasure which many had asserted was of utmost importance. Theo shook his head as he crawled under the cold blankets. Today he had become a married man and assumed responsibility for two human lives. Cold comfort as he shivered alone before drifting to sleep.

~*~

The next two days were filled with loneliness. Valeria watched the scenery go by. Occasionally Dartanian joined her in her carriage full of excitement over the adventure and his pleasure over having a new *papa*. But he didn't stay with her for long because he was afraid Mittens would be lonely in the other carriage.

Theo held her son at night and told him stories. Her heart weakened when Theo tucked Dartanian into bed and pray over him with his deep but gentle voice. She wanted those same strong arms to be holding her and that deep voice to be whispering in her ear.

She went to her lonely bed each night filled with longing and wondering how she could disabuse Theo of his understanding of what she really wanted in this marriage.

She was entranced as they drove into the gates of Hartview and she once again saw the palladium style place that she would now call home, at least until they went down to London for the season. She wished they would be able to stay here and enjoy some tranquility. Attending events in London as a Marchioness did not appeal to her, although being able to see the fury in Mr. Fishbottom's face when she would next encounter him might be worth it. That thought was not very Christian of her.

Had they not fired her she might have eventually found herself raped by the florid, short man and she would have missed getting better acquainted with Lord Harrow. She would still have been running and hiding from Lord Diamonte.

It was hard to realize that her son was now Lord

Diamonte. Such a heavy moniker for such a little boy. She worried about the satanic heritage that came with it. She was being dramatic in that.

Lord Diamonte and his cohort, Lord Wolton, worshipped the devil and acted like him on many occasions. At times, they had power that went beyond the natural realm of life and she found that terrifying. Even with Lord Diamonte banished to France, she wasn't totally at ease. After all, Lord Wolton was still at large.

She shivered, but not from the cold. She gazed out the window as the honey-hued building, basking in the sunset, welcomed her and gave her an illusory promise of safety.

Would she be safe? Would Dartanian? She trampled down the fears waging in her soul. Regardless of the misunderstanding that led to distance from her now-husband, Theodore would do everything in his power to keep them safe.

But would it be enough?

15

Theo pulled the carriage up to the front of his home and threw the reins down to a waiting stable hand. He jumped off his lofty perch and let down the stairs. He opened the carriage door and reached in to take the hand of his wife. Wife. In name only, but still his. She clasped his hand and a wave of warmth traveled through his gloves. She descended with graceful beauty and his heart slammed into his ribcage. She was his wife. *His wife.* He licked his lips and gave her a grin. "Welcome home, Lady Harrow."

The smile she gave him made him want to do whatever it took to make her smile like that again. He escorted her up the steps. She had been here before on their journey north, but now he would introduce her not as a guest—but as the lady of the manor.

As they entered, the staff assembled in the foyer and he introduced her to each servant. It was a bit of a stretch for him because he rarely spent time here in recent years. His housekeeper, Mrs. Brown, had to assist at times with the names of some of the lower maids and footmen.

After that business was done Theo escorted Valeria up to her suite of rooms which adjoined with his. He opened the door and motioned for her to enter but he stayed in the hallway.

"If you desire to change anything in your room or throughout the house, you have my permission to do so. Only my study would be off limits for your renovations."

She gave him a soft smile. "Thank you, Theo. You have been more than generous to us. I hope we can talk soon. I believe there is a misunderstanding…"

"I'm sure everything will be fine. Rest now. I asked for dinner to be held back to give you time to rest and refresh yourself." Theo gave a small nod, tuned to leave, and entered his own suite.

~*~

Theo fell on to his back on the bed. Watkins was quick to remove his boots for him and at his insistence, left him. Theo put his arms behind his head and stared up at the ceiling with its intricately carved wood border. He glanced over to the adjoining door to his wife's room and a wave of sorrow flowed over him that he would not ever be able to anticipate her coming through that door to seek comfort in his arms. In his bed. He groaned. Sure. He had never been tempted before and now that he had finally come to want to honor God, temptation would be a part of his daily life.

Unless he left her here and returned to London. Many marriages were like that. But he didn't want what some had—he wanted what his friends enjoyed. It felt patently unfair that after all he had been through that he would be denied his wife's body. But those were the terms, and with his lack of experience, it was better this way.

Dinner that evening was just the two of them.

"Have you found things to be to your satisfaction?" Theo asked as he cut his rabbit and tasted the tender meat.

"Your property and your staff have been wonderful, Theo." She sampled her food.

"I was wondering about Dartanian."

"What about?"

"I was an only child and found it quite lonely. I would hate to have that happen to him."

"And you have a solution?" Her face turned a delightful shade of pink.

"I thought we could consider adopting a child. Did you hope to have more children? Would that appeal to you?"

Valeria avoided his gaze and set down her fork and knife. "I have always loved being a mother. I would never want to deprive you of having the children you desire." She gazed at him with a boldness that intrigued and terrified him. What did she mean by that?

"Adoption would be something you would welcome?"

"There are other ways to expand a family." She picked up her fork and moved the meat around her plate.

Theo chewed. The only other way he knew was... Now heat rose in his own cheeks. Surely, she wasn't suggesting…? "As much as it would delight me to father my own children, I am a man of honor and would never go back on my agreement with regards to our marriage. I respect you too highly for that, Valeria."

"About that 'agreement' as you call it. We really did not discuss this at any length and I am unsure of why you assumed I wanted a *mariage de convenance*."

"This is neither the time nor the place to discuss such a subject." Theo set his napkin down and rose to his feet. "If you will excuse me." He left the room and headed to his study, closing the door. He poured himself a glass of brandy and sipped it. What was that about? He thought he would see if they could expand their family and now she questioned the very foundation their marriage was based on?

In the past she'd offered him the benefits of marriage without the legal ties and he'd refused. But that was before he understood how tragic her previous marriage had been. The fact that she would have even tempted him in that way shocked him. Certainly, she would not desire any intimacy with a man, much less one with as little experience as he had. He knew he would never compare well to anyone. The humiliation of his father and his first visit to a brothel washed all over him again.

But that prostitute had never made him feel the things he'd experienced when he held Valeria in his arms, inhaled her scent, and tasted her lips. He leaned back in his favorite chair and groaned. This marriage would be the death of him yet.

~*~

Enough was enough. Valeria pushed her meal aside and went in search of her elusive husband. She knocked on the door to his study.

"Who is it?"

"Your wife."

Silence.

"May I enter?"

The door opened.

Theo had untied his cravat and had a drink in his hand. His hair was mussed. If she hadn't known he was alone she would have suspected him of meeting a secret lover.

He looked at her with a raised eyebrow and a frown.

"We need to talk, Theo." Valeria pushed past him and entered the room. She had not been in his study before and loved the warmth of the burgundy leather chairs and the goldenrod colored wallpaper with soft white pattern. A large painting hung above the fireplace.

It contained a beautiful woman with lighter brown hair, hazel eyes and a sweet smile. Valeria walked over to the painting and observed it for a few moments.

The door close and Theo's footsteps padded on the rich rug.

"This must be your mother. You resemble her, Theo. She was lovely."

Theo was behind her. "She was lovely. She would have liked you." His voice was soft and filled with longing.

"You miss her."

"Every day."

"How long has she been gone?" She turned as he sat in an overstuffed leather chair.

"Six years. She was heartbroken when my father passed. He was a hard man, but she loved him completely."

"Do you share anything good of your father?"

Theo laughed. "His height and his ability to run an estate well. I'm a credible rider and skilled with a gun and sword, but I lack the hard edge he possessed. He always called me 'soft'."

Valeria came to sit down, lifted the glass out of his hands, and took a sip. She returned the glass to him. "The one thing I would never say about you, Theo, is that you are soft. Gentle, but strong. You are power held in control. Disciplined and respectful. I gather your father lacked those character traits."

"He was disciplined. As much as he loved my mother, he could not respect her enough to be faithful. Her heart was broken by him long before he died. I would never do that to my wife."

"Even if you have no other outlet for your needs?" Valeria asked with both eyebrows raised.

"Even if abstinence kills me, I would be faithful to you. I am a man of my word. When I spoke my vows, I meant them."

"You promised to worship me with your body yet you withhold it from me."

Theo stood up, his face turning red and his eyes a steely grey. "Confound it, woman! I do not need to be reminded of what I forfeited by our union. You wanted the protection of my name and you have it, but do not throw in my face what you made clear your boundaries are."

"*I* made it clear? What exactly did I say that leads you to believe I would not welcome your touch?"

"You did not desire marriage. Ever. I proposed to you before. I laid my heart at your feet and you kicked it out the carriage door. If that will had not forced your hand you would not have considered me. I was convenient, available, in love with you, and easy to persuade." He walked over the window and gazed out into the dark night.

"You love me? You hardly know me." Valeria came to stand behind and to the side of him. Both could view their reflections.

Their gazes met in the glass. "I loved you from the first moment I rolled you off that obnoxious Reginald Fishbottom. I didn't even know your name, but I loved you all the same."

"You are telling me you fell in love with an unconscious woman?"

"Ask Marcus, he will tell you he was in love with Josie before he ever knew her."

"That's ridiculous."

Theo's gaze fell. "My father would agree with your sentiment, I'm sure." He took a deep drink from his glass.

"Your father demeaned your masculinity, didn't he?"

Theo turned to her with his head tilted. "Why would you make that assumption?"

"Damon had the same problem. His father was bigger and stronger and put so much pressure on him. He was evil in his own right, but I wonder how much of that was a reaction to the abuses of his father?"

"You were abused as well. No man who does that can claim honor, regardless of his title or wealth."

"Honor is important to you, Theo, and I respect you for that. You are the kind of man I wish I'd met when I was younger and newly orphaned and searching for love and protection. I never experienced any of that until I met you." She placed a hand on his arm and tingles of heat radiated through her body. "You would have been the man I would have chosen then and you are the man I choose now. Rip up the will for all I care. Dartanian might do better without the legacy his grandfather left him—materially and spiritually."

She turned him to face her so they were looking at each other, eye to eye, nose to nose. She smiled and reached up to run her finger along the bridge of his nose. "You, Theodore, Marquess of Harrow, are who I have always wanted and dreamed of. You are a hero of my dreams. In your arms alone I have felt safe, protected, and cared for. In your presence, I found peace. You are the first man who has made me feel desirable as a woman. Theo. I do not want *mariage de convenance.* You somehow assumed I did, but it was never my desire." She ran her finger along the line of his jaw. "Your kisses are the first to ever stir a fire inside of me. A desire for you and no one else.

"You are right that I did not want to marry when I first met you. I was running in fear from my father-in-law. I did not want to bring his wrath on anyone. I could not risk being seen amongst the *beau monde.*" She ran her fingers through his hair. It was so soft. He smelled of horse, leather, and man. "I no longer have those fears. I am your wife and long to be so in every way." She touched her lips to his and closed her eyes. He responded to her kiss. Her arm came around his neck to draw him closer.

When she broke the kiss, she stepped back. "I will not force you, Theo. I want you however I can have you, but I would love for this to be a real marriage. To bear your children. To experience the pleasure of making them with you." She grabbed his glass again, sipped the brandy, and then handed it back. She leaned up to give him a kiss on the cheek. "The door between our rooms is unlocked on my side. It is up to you if you want to walk through it."

~*~

Theo watched her walk to the door. The sway of her hips, the straight line of her back, all drew him like a beacon. His lips still tingled from her touch and his body longed to go to her. His mind held him back. But why? She was all he ever longed for in a wife, but she was more than that as well. She was experienced. Was it that important to him that his wife be untouched? It hadn't mattered when he'd first learned she was a widow. It hadn't mattered at all.

Until he heard the ugliness of what she'd endured at the hands of the Black Diamond, and his son, Damon, her now deceased husband.

She was a treasure and for all she had been through she was soft and yielding and beckoned for him to join her.

So, what held him back?

Fear. Fear of having the same thing happen to him that happened that one time in the brothel that his father berated him for. As much as this woman made him react like no other ever had, would his fear keep him from being able to fully be the lover she longed for? Would he be humiliated once again?

He didn't know if he could bear it if she was in any way disappointed in that regard. Theo drank the rest of the brandy and headed up to bed. Alone.

Lying in bed he kept looking at the door. Frustrated desire warred with fear and punching his pillow, he rolled over to face away from the adjoining wall to try to find a reprieve in sleep.

The next morning dawned dark and grey with a fog hanging low over the valley.

Theo was restless and not eager to see the disappointment in Valeria's eyes over breakfast, so he sought refuge on the back of one his stallions. Zeus was bred for speed and endurance and his sable coat glistened in the early morning moisture as he pawed at the dirt while Theo tightened the girth on the saddle.

He mounted and took off down a path that ran along a creek bed. The horse was skittish at a canter so he let him have his head into a full-blown gallop that exhilarated and terrified him at the same time. When the horse finally slowed, they had come to the top of a rise where Theo could view all of his property around him. The neatly thatched huts. The nearby village of St. Neots in the distance. A low layer of haze obscured some of the lower pastures and their farms but above it all he saw a well-kept estate.

Theo dismounted and went to sit on a larger rock that was amongst many that someone had gone through the trouble to pile for some reason or another. Maybe an ancestor had planned to build a grotto up here at one time. As Theo took in the view he thought that perhaps that was something he could see done. It was a perfect spot.

Theo sat for a while. Alone. Always alone. But now he had a wife who'd expressed interest in a full marriage. It was what he'd always wanted. He was making himself dizzy by thinking about this. His bride did not seem to be the kind to humiliate one. He had no clue how to even begin once he walked through that door.

Maybe he needed to start with smaller steps. Touching. Kissing. Talking and getting to know one another better. Instead of forcing it, let it happen when it happened.

As the sun warmed the air, the haze that had hung over the valley dissipated. He had work to do and a wife to woo. He remounted and headed for home.

As he navigated Zeus down a rocky path, a shot rang out and the massive mount crumpled beneath him. Landing on his side the horse pinned Theo's left leg underneath him. Theo got the right one out of the stirrup and with much effort and intense pain freed his other leg, losing his boot in the process. He checked his mount. The horse was still alive. He crawled around to assess the injury. The stallion stared at him with a wild look, unable to move. Blood poured from his heart, and his eyes glassed over.

Theo pulled out his gun and shot the horse. Now Zeus lay dead on the path and he was at least a mile or more from home. He tried to rise, and his left leg crumpled beneath him. He scanned the area. Was he a sitting duck? Would the person who shot his horse be after him? He crawled, dragging his injured leg a few feet into the woods lining the path. He found a sturdy branch that had broken off. He removed his cravat and wove it around the space where branches had originally split. Using the makeshift crutch and another tree he dragged himself to his feet. Perspiration beaded on his forehead and down his back. With determination, he painfully set off at a slow measured pace toward home.

~*~

The night had been long and lonely. Valeria had thought he would come. Could she have made herself any clearer on the matter? Surely, he did not need her to approach him, did he? He was a man of the world. A man at his station in life had experiences and would not be shy in the bedroom but a gentle and sensitive lover.

Was she repulsive to him? She didn't think so with the way he'd responded to their kisses.

She left her room and spent time up in the nursery

with Dartanian, sharing breakfast and reading some of the books that had been there for a few decades since Theo had been a child. Eventually she descended to the lower regions of the house to meet with Mrs. Brown to see the household accounts and determine menus. This was not foreign territory to her as she had functionally been the housekeeper for Damon when he had been alive. He had often claimed he liked to sleep "with the help."

When all her tasks were done it was late morning. None of the staff had reported seeing Lord Harrow since he had ridden out earlier on Zeus. She made her way to the stables to investigate. "Hello?" she called out as she entered the shadowed building.

The smell of hay and horse permeated the air but the main corridor between rows of stalls was clean.

An older man came forward, doffed his hat, and bowed to her. "May I help you, my lady?"

"Murry?"

"Yes, Lady Harrow." The man was short and lean. He had probably been a jockey in his previous life.

"I'm searching for my husband. I heard he took a ride this morning."

"Yes, my lady, he rode out on Zeus nigh on two hours hence."

"Did he say where he was going?"

The man shook his head and frowned. "Not a word. He did not speak with me or my hands but saddled up the horse on his own and was out the door without a word t' anyone."

Valeria frowned. "He might be in trouble. Would you and your men be willing to go search for him to ease a wife's fears?"

The groom nodded his head. "Yes, m'lady." With

that he turned and yelled to the invisible stable hands. They saddled up various horses and took off in the direction Lord Harrow had last been seen.

Satisfied that she had done all she could do she went to the drawing room to sit by the window that looked out on the estate. The horses disappeared into the distance. She prayed that somehow her husband was well, so she could wring his neck and shake him silly, before kissing him again.

Not too much time had passed when the riders returned with an extra person mounted up behind Murry. Theo towered over the small man, even on horseback.

She hurried to the front door and was down the steps before they came to a full stop.

"My lady," Murry said as he held his horse steady. Two of the stable hands had dismounted and had rushed to Lord Harrow. "We found him walking with a crutch. His leg may be broken."

"Do not scare the woman, Murry," Theo barked.

"You have a wife now, Lord Harrow. Let her do her job and fuss over you." Murry winked at Valeria as the men kept Theo from crumpling to the ground.

"You are hurt, my lord." She turned to the head groom. "Would you ride for the doctor?"

Murry tipped his hat, nodded his head, and with a cheeky grin he was off. She thought she heard him say, "About time someone talked some sense around here."

Valeria took in the torn clothes, missing boot, and absent cravat. Theo's face was pale underneath the sun-kissed cheeks. "Take him to his room, men." She turned and led the way.

~*~

The pain in Theo's leg radiated through his entire body. Every inch of him ached from his tumble and all the steps he tried to take to make it home. It was humbling to be found sprawled in the grass, almost passed out from the heat and the pain when Murry and the stable hands came upon him. Trying to get up on to the back of a horse had been pure torture, as was holding on to the smaller man, and his faith.

Valeria took charge and he finally let himself escape the pain into blackness. She had cared for him with influenza and pneumonia. He could trust her even more so now that their present and future were permanently intertwined. When he awoke later his thigh had been splinted. He whimpered as he tried to move.

"Be still, Theo. You have bruises everywhere and your leg needs time to heal."

"Definitely broken then. I thought so."

"It was foolish to have tried to walk back home in your condition."

"I couldn't stay next to Zeus. I feared someone might use me for target practice."

Valeria frowned. "Murry told me he was a magnificent stallion and one you made good money off of for stud. I'm sorry he died, Theo."

Theo shook his head. "He was something to behold. Big. Strong. Wonderful temperament and so responsive. Fast. Many a thoroughbred came from him." Theo sighed. "Better him than me though. I have other horses—you only have one husband."

Her eyes were damp as they looked to him. "I'm glad you survived. So very glad. I've become quite fond of my husband."

He reached a hand out. She reached and he held her hand tight. "I'm fond of my wife too. Matter of fact, I have it on good authority that her kisses are a restorative."

Valeria's eyebrows went up. "Really? And just who may this authority be?"

"Why, Dartanian, of course. He has told me how you have kissed his scratches and bruises and how much better he felt and how fast he healed."

She eyed him suspiciously as she nodded. "That may be due to a mother's kisses being potent for children and you, my lord, are most definitely not *mon enfant*."

Theo pouted. "I thought that since you were a wife that made them especially potent."

Valeria grinned. "Perhaps they do. Maybe that is something we should test. All for the benefit of science, of course."

"Well, of course, my lady. And the sake of medicine as well. We would not want to inhibit progress there."

"Entirely altruistic, of course." She grinned as she stood.

"Where are you going?" Theo asked as her hand slipped out of his.

"I'm sending Watkins to assist in caring for your more personal needs."

"What about testing our hypothesis?"

Valeria winked at him. "Perhaps later, if you deem you are truly in need of that kind of pain relief."

With that, Theo watched her hips sway as she walked to the door and closed it behind her. He closed his eyes. What was he doing flirting with his wife? Now? At a time when he was totally unable to pursue the marriage bed? He grinned to himself. Maybe this would give him the time to court his wife properly and get comfortable and less afraid of exposing his inexperience to her when the time finally came? He certainly hoped so.

16

After Watkins departed, Theo was left trying to remember what happened to bring him to this impasse. Could Lord Wolton or one of his minions be seeking to eliminate him to gain Valeria? He drew comfort from the fact that he had made his will clear in what would be provided to his widow and to her son.

Should anything happen to him, and regardless of what happened to Dartanian's estate, the young Lord Diamonte would have the resources to live life as a titled man should, even if he lost the property. There were always more coming on the market from destitute personages. Dartanian also had his own property that had been burnt and could always be rebuilt. He would need to discuss that with Valeria soon.

Valeria returned after dinner and he patted the mattress next to him to invite her to sit there.

"I do not want to add to your pain," she protested.

"It will hurt me more to have you distant from me, my lady." He grinned as he grabbed her hand and tugged until she was sitting next to him.

"Are you well, Theo? You appear flushed. Did you get too much sun this morning?" Her free hand gently caressed his forehead and a finger trailed down his nose. When it came to his lips he kissed it.

She pulled her finger away.

"Alas, my dear wife, I am unwell and in need of some medicine only you can administer." He was being dramatic.

Valeria had a serious look on her face. "Well, the doctor did say laudanum would be acceptable if brandy was not sufficient to numb your pain. Which shall it be?"

"I would prefer the brandy to the opiate and I would rather your kisses to either."

"The doctor did not order kisses as a part of your rehabilitation." Valeria frowned.

"Ah, but remember, my dear, we are conducting research on the theory that kisses have a restorative and healing effect on an injured person." Theo winked at her.

She sighed and shook her head. "Well, I suppose if it is for the purposes of science we could give it a try." She leaned forward, and like a feather, her lips brushed his. She leaned back. "There. Did that help?"

Theo scowled. "Most certainly not a sufficient dose given the gravity of my injuries."

She raised her eyebrows. "Really? Well, I must try harder." This time she leaned forward and placed her hands on his chest to keep her from falling on him. Her lips met in a firm and demanding way and instantly Theo's entire body was aflame. He returned the kisses and when she finally withdrew he was short of breath.

She was breathing heavy as well. "Restored yet, my lord?" Her voice came out breathy and low.

Theo was experiencing a dream. "Several hours of that kind of medicine and I will be well in no time, I assure you." He grinned at her, brought one hand off his chest, and placed a kiss in the palm. Closing her fingers around it he placed it in her lap. "Stay with me tonight."

Her eyes grew wide and the other hand went to cover her heart. "Is this part of the experiment?"

"No, Lady Harrow. This is part of marriage." He grabbed the elbow closest to him and pulled her to him. With both hands, he cupped her cheeks and brought her down for another sizzling kiss. When he broke it off, she was nose to nose with him.

"Yes, Theo. I will stay the night." She gave him a small smile, and then rose.

Theo chilled as she walked away from him. The fire was burning merrily in the hearth and the windows were closed, even though it was a relatively warm evening. He drew the blankets up higher over his chest and tried to get warm, but it wasn't until a short while later when his wife, *his wife,* entered the room dressed in a gown that highlighted her curves and hinted at the wonders beneath. The warmth returned when she slipped under the covers. He drew her close and allowed his fingers the freedom to trail through the creamy silk of her long hair. He pulled her close and fell asleep quite content, all pain forgotten.

~*~

Valeria awoke the next morning disoriented. She was holding a large, warm body. Her eyes opened, and she gazed up into Theo's resting face. He snored softly. She kissed his cheek and his arm tightened around her, pulling her closer. Her hand rested on his chest and his heart pounded, steady and strong, beating just a bit faster. She smiled to herself.

"I could get used to this," a low voice whispered.

"Used to a broken leg?" She stifled a giggle.

He chuckled deep in his chest. "No, sweetheart, having you snuggled against me every night."

"Oh?"

"That's all you have to say? Oh?"

"Well, I personally would like to do more than snuggle."

"You would? And what activity do you propose? Before you answer, realize I have a strong dislike for bread crumbs in my bed."

"Well, that takes away my first option. I am quite hungry." She grinned as she tucked her head in close to his chest and inhaled his scent.

"Do you have an appetite for anything in particular?" Theo said sleepily.

"Most definitely."

"And what would that be? Would you care to share?"

"I have an appetite for you, Theodore, Marquess of Harrow. I am loathe to share you with anyone."

His hand came under her chin and lifted her face until she could see his own. She grinned at him and his hazel eyes were the green of a storm-tossed sea. She drowned in their depths. "I refuse to share you with anyone either, my lady." His lips met hers in a tantalizingly light kiss. He released her head and let his sink into his pillow.

"Theo?"

"Hmmmm?" His eyes closed.

"I'm still hungry." She pouted.

"Help yourself to all you want," were the teasing words whispered huskily.

"I think I shall." She pulled herself up to be able to look down on his face, a face that became dearer to her with each passing day. She leaned in and kissed him deeply and he responded with passion. Her hair flowed down around their faces.

Theo reached up to pet it and also massage her

back with one of his hands.

The more she tasted of him, the more she wanted.

"Ahem." The male voice broke into the haze of passion she was experiencing in Theo's arms. She pulled away and glanced into Theo's eyes.

His lips quirked in amusement. "Watkins, my wife tells me she is hungry. Please have breakfast brought up here for us this morning."

"As you wish, my lord." The door closed behind the valet.

Valeria bit back her own grin. She was grateful that her hair precluded the valet from seeing how warm her face had become. She was especially grateful that she had donned her modest nightgown rather than the more seductive one that had been given to her as a wedding gift from Elizabeth.

With Theo's injury, acting on any urges regarding consummation would be painful at present. Maybe the snuggling and kissing would open the door for further intimacies as he recovered.

Theo put a hand behind her head and pulled her back down. "Now, where were we?"

~*~

After breakfast in bed, where Valeria accommodated him by licking any errant crumbs off his face, she left to dress and prepare for the day.

Theo's leg throbbed painfully now that he was not distracted by his lovely wife.

He tolerated the ministrations of his valet as he was shaved and clothed so as not to spend the entire day in his bed. A sturdier crutch was unearthed in the attics from some previous injury of someone at some time in the ancient past. The crutch was too short for him—but it at least allowed him some stability.

Theo managed to make it to his study and sit at his desk to write some letters to his friends, relating to them the recent attack and asking for help in tracking down Lord Wolton. He suspected that evil man to be a potential threat to his newly married life and did not want to jeopardize Valeria or Dartanian in any way possible.

A week passed where they fell into a relatively peaceful routine. Theo worked in his office and consulted with his steward.

Valeria took inventory in the house and spent time with Dartanian.

Evenings were spent with Valeria in his arms and a deep sense of contentment he never thought would be possible.

A knock on the door went unanswered one day so Theo hobbled to the entryway to greet whoever deigned to visit them. He opened the door to find a travel-weary Sir Michael Tidley. "Come in, Michael. I'm not sure where Wiggins is at the moment."

"Theo, I wish I could say married life suits you but if she's beating you this badly," Michael pointed to his crutch and splinted leg, "I'm glad I got here in time." The grin gave way the humor.

Theo reached out to give his friend a fist to the shoulder. The movement knocked him off balance and he almost fell to the floor, rescued by Michael.

"Come, let us talk before I head up to a room to wash my dirt off and greet your lovely bride."

With Michael's help, they managed to go back to the study and the door shut behind them.

"Would you like something to drink?" Theo

offered.

"I will help myself. You. Sit." He pointed to a leather chair. "Can I get you anything?"

"Not at the moment. Thank you." Theo lowered himself to the chair and leaned back, biting back a groan at the throbbing pain his movements caused. "Are you here with regards to the letter I sent?"

"Letter? No. The wives were filled with foreboding shortly after you left. Beth was especially anxious knowing that Lord Wolton was still at large. Phillip is bringing Beth and Katrina and the kids with them here, and Marcus and Josie have gone to London to enlist help there in tracking Wolton." Michael came to sit down across from Theo and pointed to the leg. "Is that courtesy of our missing nemesis or the product of abject clumsiness?"

Theo grinned. He was overcome with gratitude at the care his friends had for him and Valeria. "A week ago, I went for a ride, and no, I was not drunk this time. On my return home Zeus got shot out from under me. I broke my leg when he fell."

"He was a beautiful stallion. I'm sorry, Theo. Did you need to finish him off?"

Theo nodded. "I couldn't hide behind him and protect myself while he was in pain. Even if it made me a target, I couldn't let him suffer."

"So, the leg broke but there have been no more incidents? Could it have been a poacher?"

"We've never had problems with poachers on the land. We've allowed tenants the opportunity to hunt when they need to. You've seen Zeus. There was no way he would have been mistaken for wildlife." Theo steepled his hands in front of his face, tapping his nose with his fingers. "The day after it happened I sent letters out to you and the rest asking for your assistance. I need to make sure Valeria and Dartanian stay safe, but I'm hindered in my ability to do that. As a precaution, they have been kept inside, but I'm not fooling myself that the next attack could come from within these walls."

Michael smiled. "God knew you were going to need help and sent us before you could even ask."

"He can do that?" Theo hadn't thought of God in those terms before.

"He had me marry Katrina when I didn't even realize that was what I had been wanting all along."

"Well…"

"Yeah, I know. I didn't want her. Then I did. Then I didn't. Then I couldn't remember and married her. Then I remembered and was angry and God brought me back to what I had really wanted all along—Katrina. I was such an idiot."

"Buffleheaded idiot," Theo whispered to himself as he closed his eyes and groaned.

"What did you say?" Michael's voice held a tinge of a threat to it.

"Only talking to myself. You were not an idiot, by the way. You were definitely put in some difficult challenges with the Black Diamond."

"Hard to believe he's been banished from Britain."

"Do you think he will stay away, if he has even survived? Will this be the last we hear of him?"

Michael shrugged. "I would hope so, but he was determined. I wouldn't put it past him to return again on our shores." He took a sip of his amber drink. "I refuse to lose sleep over it. God has been with us so far. I believe we can trust him for the future as well."

"Is that not a bit foolish, Michael?"

"What are you afraid of, Theo?" Michael arched an eyebrow and nailed him with his unwavering gaze.

Theo wished he could get up and pace. He massaged his injured thigh instead, finding some twisted comfort in the pain. "It hit me after I got home that Valeria could have been made a widow."

"You provided for her and Dartanian and any unborn children in your will?"

"There are no unborn children to worry about yet."

"It would be too soon to know, of course."

"There's no chance of her being *enceinte,* Michael. Immaculate conception has only ever occurred once in history."

"You wanted her so badly and you still haven't…?"

Theo frowned and waved a hand at Michael. He didn't want to talk about this.

Then why did you bring it up?

Because I'm scared and need assurance I'll be fine.

And you think Michael is the man to give that to you?

I don't know!

"So, you have provided for her and Dartanian, what is the problem?"

"I cannot protect them from Lord Wolton or the Black Diamond's minions if I am dead."

Michael didn't respond to that. He looked off in the distance then turned his gaze to his drink. "In some ways, Theo, that would be my deepest fear. I would hate not being there for my family when they would need me the most. I'm a man. It's my job. It's why I gave up working for the government. I couldn't take those kinds of risks anymore. I remind myself that God loves my family more than I do and that He would somehow work things out. Maybe not the same as if I were here, and they would be grief-stricken but well. Remember, you have friends, Theo. Should anything happen to you we would do everything in our power to help Valeria and Dartanian, if she would let us."

"That eases my mind."

"I think I'll go wash the dirt off. I'll see you and your lovely bride for dinner." Michael rose and left his glass on the drink table. He walked to the door, and then stopped and looked at Theo. "Do you need help getting up to your rooms?"

Theo sighed. "Yes. I can manage on my own, but having you around guarantees I would stumble and prove myself incapable. If we can skip that humiliation I would be grateful."

Michael laughed and came over to help Theo up the stairs.

Once the bedroom door was closed, Theo took the last steps to his bed and threw himself upon it.

Watkins awakened him. "My lord. You have company and it is almost time for dinner."

"What?" Theo's brain was encased in cotton and he was tempted to stay and sleep. Why was he so tired? His leg throbbed with intensity. With great effort, he worked with Watkins to repair his appearance and to descend the stairs using his crutch.

~*~

Valeria entered the drawing room before dinner expecting Theo to be there before her. Instead she was caught off guard by the appearance of her brother-in-law. "Michael! I hadn't been informed you arrived. What a delightful surprise."

Michael appraised her with sharp eyes.

She was sure she paled as she often did when seeing him without anticipating it. The physical resemblance to Damon was strong.

"I would have thought Theo would have informed you to lessen the shock of my presence. I pray that someday you will not have to remind yourself that I am not my brother."

Valeria came over to him and gave him a kiss on the cheek. With most men she was at eye level or looked up to—but Michael, like Damon, she actually had to bend over slightly to do such a thing. It made her self-conscious of her height. "You are always welcome here, Michael, whether I expect you or not."

Michael grinned and lifted her hand up to his mouth for a kiss. "You are good for Theo. I'm grateful that he has you."

"You are too kind. Any woman would have been fortunate to be married to Lord Harrow, Michael. I still cannot believe the way God has blessed me after all we've been through."

Thunk. Thunk. Thunk. Thunk.

Theodore entered on his crutch.

Valeria rushed over to help him.

Theo grinned. "See what happened to me? I marry and am already being treated as if I am in my dotage."

"Do not expect me to be waiting on you when you are better," Valeria replied. She helped Theo sit and no sooner had she done so than Wiggins came to alert them that dinner was served.

Both Michael and Valeria assisted Theo to the dining room where a merry meal was had.

Valeria lay in Theo's arms that night, more content than she ever remembered being. "I do love you,

Theodore," she whispered in his ear.

"Hmmm?" He'd been drifting to sleep but turned his head to kiss her.

"I'm glad your friends will help us."

"Me, too," he mumbled.

"I would hate it if anything happened to you. I would hate to be a widow twice."

"Hmmm."

"The only way that would be acceptable is if I killed you myself."

"What?"

Theo's body shook as he tried to wake up enough to make out what she was saying. She bit back a grin. "Well, if you die, I would rather it be for something important. Like not buying me a certain piece of jewelry I liked or not giving me enough pin money. Or perhaps neglecting to take me to the opera."

"Hmmm."

"The only question is just how I would go about doing the deed. A gun is too quick, but poison has its merits."

"Valeria?"

"What?"

"Kiss me and stop talking. If anything will kill me right now, that will."

"The kissing or the talking?"

She never did hear his response as their lips met, but she wasn't complaining.

The next day, Valeria chafed at the imprisonment of being in the house. She understood Theo's concerns since the shooting, but she was being controlled much like she had been during her previous marriage. She understood Theo meant well, but it was lonely being here with no other women to talk to. Michael was entertaining company, but he preferred to spend time with Theo.

She doubted Lord Wolton would attack close to the house, so she slipped out the side door to the garden while Theo and Michael visited in his study.

The day promised to be warm and the sun was already drying up the dew on the grass and leaves. The spring garden was in full bloom and she meandered through the paths filled with flowers and shrubs of many varieties.

The garden had the same softness she saw in her husband. Not a tightly confined and precise garden such as she would expect from someone like Phillip—but this one reflected its owner. Knowing he'd not spent much time here, the attention to this aspect of the property surprised her.

She finally reached a gazebo she had spied from the nursery window and sat in its shade to take in the beauty of all that was around her.

How had she come all the way from war in France and being orphaned, to being a tortured bride, a widow in hiding, and to this life she now led? How did she go from having such a dark marriage to this one filled with gentleness and light?

They had been spending time each evening reading Scripture to each other and discussing what they read. Both were so new in their faith they were eager to grow and understand who this knowable God was. He was so much bigger and powerful than she had ever grasped. She smiled as she realized that the gods that Lord Diamonte served, as powerful as they were, were never more powerful than Jesus Christ. While she still feared the evil that surrounded the Black Diamond and Lord Wolton, she remembered that her God was ultimately the victor. She still struggled to trust Him, but primarily because she didn't know Him well enough yet.

But they both would. Just the thought of those precious times with her husband made her smile.

Blessed. She was truly blessed.

She glanced back at the house that rose up so beautifully from the earth. She was taken aback to see smoke rising from the third floor. She watched as it thickened, and then panic rose up within her.

The nursery was on fire!

She ran to the house screaming.

Michael ran out of the study. "What is wrong?"

"The nursery is on fire. Dartanian! We must get Dartanian out!" She took to the stairs.

Michael held her back. "I will go. Please, rouse the rest of the staff and start a water brigade. And find Theo."

Valeria fought back the tears. "Please hurry!"

Michael ran up the stairs two at a time and Valeria ran to the kitchens, calling for staff along the way.

Fire. Again. A fire. It must be Wolton.

The water started to be pumped and buckets handed over and carried up the stairs by servants.

Valeria helped in the relay when it dawned on her. *Theo!* Where was he? He couldn't move very fast with his leg. She broke rank to run back into the house.

Theo came down the stairs with Dartanian and the kitten snuggled against his chest. No crutch, but pain was etched clearly on his face. He was covered in smoke and his clothes were singed.

She took Dartanian from him. "Theo. Come with me." She tried to help him further down the stairs.

"No. I am needed to fight the fire. I must join

Michael who is at the head of the bucket brigade. It's my home. My responsibility."

"Theo," she pleaded.

He moved up the stairs and her heart went with him. Knowing it was useless to argue, she took Dartanian from the house and went away to a spot where she could view the progress from a point of safety.

Dartanian coughed but he seemed unharmed.

"Père?" he asked.

"He went back to fight the fire, Dartanian. Let us pray he stays safe."

"*Oui, Maman.*" Together they bent their heads and prayed.

With the noise from the fire licking the outside of the third floor and the smoke billowing out from a window that had exploded, she failed to hear horses coming into the yard.

"Lady Harrow!" Phillip rode up. "What happened?"

"A fire in the nursery. Michael and Theo are there. Theo has a broken leg. He is not in a position to be helping."

"Katrina and Beth are close behind me." He dismounted and ran into the front doors that she had left wide open. Smoke had started to come through there as well.

The carriage pulled up. Valeria was embraced by the two women as their nurse took charge of the children and Dartanian.

The smoke slowed and while the stone on the outside of the house was singed, the fire was contained to the nursery alone.

Michael escorted Valeria to her husband who had

been taken to his room. "There's your hero."

"Thank you, Michael. I believe your wife is waiting for you."

He bowed and closed the door as he departed.

Valeria rushed to be by her husband's side. He lay so still on the bed. "Theo?"

He opened his eyes and looked at her. Tears came down. "Dartanian?"

"He is fine. He told me how he was trapped within the flames and how you came through to get him out. How you did that without him being singed…"

"Kiss me."

"What?"

"I love you. Kiss me. Please."

Valeria sat down on the bed next to him. He smelled of smoke. She leaned over and kissed him. Long. Lingering. Lovely. She broke it off and the tears finally came. "I could not have born losing you."

"It would not give you a good reputation."

"What?"

"Well, if your husbands keep dying, no one will want to marry you."

"Really?"

"Guess I'll be forced to stay alive to keep you from that fate."

Valeria grinned and kissed him again.

His valet interrupted them with the news that the bath for Lord Harrow was ready for him.

Valeria smiled at her husband. "Thank you, Watkins. I will tend to his lordship. Please have food brought up in an hour."

Theo's brows rose when she mentioned bathing him, but he grinned.

Their guests did not see them for the rest of the day.

17

"The nursery will need to be gutted and redone," Theo told his friends the next day as he sat with his leg propped up on an ottoman.

"Your home is large enough that it will not inconvenience you too badly. But I'm sorry you lost all those childhood memories." Phillip stood, looking out the window at the rain as it fell.

"Dartanian deserves his own memories. I have the fortune to spend on him. I'm grateful no one was hurt." Theo frowned. "I wish I knew how it started though. Was it an accident or was it intentional? With everything that has happened I am becoming paranoid about every disaster that befalls us."

"You have every justification for paranoia, Theo." Michael sat across from him with his legs outstretched, twiddling his thumbs.

"I realize you all just arrived, but I'm tempted to take Valeria and Dartanian to London," Theo said.

"You cannot dance attendance on her there with that leg. I think you should wait a few weeks until you are more healed up."

Theo growled. "I feel as if we are sitting ducks here."

"The enemy would have an easier time getting to you or Valeria or Dartanian if you were in London. It will be far easier to post guards here and keep you all safe." Phillip sat across from him. "We'll be here to keep you company and provide extra protection."

"I'm grateful." Theo leaned his head back as a

fresh wave of pain from his leg flowed over him.

"Still hurts?" Michael asked.

"Even worse after yesterday." Theo rubbed it, wincing as he touched his thigh.

"Perhaps you should be resting in bed?" Phillip suggested.

"I cannot do that."

"Why?" Michael asked. "We can fend for ourselves. You do not need to entertain us."

"I would go crazy up in that room alone."

"We could send your wife to be with you. Then we would always know where the two of you are—together and safe." Michael winked at Phillip who grinned.

Theo's face grew warm.

~*~

Valeria visited with Katrina and Beth out in the gazebo.

"This is where you first spotted the fire?" Katrina asked as they all looked at the back of the house and the burned marks on the stone around the third-floor nursery windows.

Valeria nodded. "I'm so grateful that both Dartanian and Theo survived."

"I'm amazed that Theo not only rescued Dartanian with a broken leg but then proceeded to fight the fire. He never spent much time here. I didn't realize how attached he was to this place. I wouldn't have thought he would care." Katrina spoke softly as she gazed at the estate.

"Perhaps now that he has a family to share it with it has more value?" Beth smiled at Valeria. "How has it been to be married to Theo? Is it everything you would have hoped for?"

Valeria stood but did not say anything. What could she say? She had been married only a few weeks but had still not consummated the marriage. With Theo's injury, she suspected it would be a few more weeks before he might make an attempt.

"Valeria?" Beth asked. "Is everything well between you and Theo?"

Valeria turned at the concern and love she heard in her friend's voice. "He is gentle and kind, and I am content in our marriage."

"That doesn't sound honeymoonish to me." Katrina teased.

Valeria sighed. "Maybe we haven't had our honeymoon yet."

"I would have thought, with the way he looked at you, that you would have been fortunate to have made it to the first inn." Beth giggled.

"He drove the carriage. I rode inside. Not physically possible." Valeria folded her arms as she looked to the wooded area in the distance. Something shimmered in the sunlight. "Duck!"

The report of a gun was heard, but the women had already hit the floor of the gazebo as a bullet whizzed past and embedded itself in the post opposite where Valeria had been standing.

The three women crept low out of the gazebo, quickly maneuvered to the protection of some bushes, and ran to the house. They rushed down the hallway and stopped outside Theo's study.

The three women were breathing heavily and still holding hands. Valeria let go of Beth's hand and knocked on the door.

"Enter," came Theo's voice.

She opened the door.

Each woman made a beeline for their husbands. Beth went to Phillip who was standing and wrapped her arms around him. Katrina launched herself in to Michael's lap, sitting sideways, throwing her arms around his neck and burying her head in his shoulder. Valeria looked at Theo and he held out his hand to her. She came and sat down on the loveseat next to him and gave him a kiss.

Valeria took a deep breath. "We were out in the gazebo, visiting."

"Valeria was shot at," Katrina said softly.

Michael sat up straight almost knocking his wife off his lap.

Phillip hugged Beth closer and placed a kiss on her forehead.

Theo placed a hand on Valeria's jaw. "Were you injured?" He was furious. His muscles had tightened along his entire body. His mouth was set in a firm line and his eyes were a steely grey.

"I spied something shiny and saw a flash. We ducked before the report and the bullet reached us."

"You will need to stay in the house until we have this resolved," Theo said.

Valeria pouted.

"I think he's being wise, Val," Michael said. "All of you need to stay put."

Valeria nodded.

Theo drew her close and gave her a kiss.

She melted into his embrace, planting a hand on his chest, forgetting about the company in the room.

A throat cleared breaking through her haze. For a moment, she had forgotten about the bullet and their guests.

Theo broke the kiss and gave her a broad grin.

Phillip was the first to excuse himself and Beth. They left the room, soon followed by Michael and Katrina.

Valeria laid her head on Theo's shoulder and his arm wrapped around her.

"I am thankful God spared you, sweetheart." He kissed her forehead.

"Me, too. My eternal home is with Him, but I would like to live in this one for a few years with you first."

Theo gave her a lingering kiss. He broke it off and grinned. "Do you think you could help a poor, crippled man to his room?"

"Will you also need some help when you get there?" Valeria stood and pulled him up.

He reached for his crutch. "I most certainly will need some help when I get there." He gave her a grin and a quick kiss.

Together they managed to get up the stairs to their suite.

~*~

Theo lay in bed with Valeria tucked up beside him, asleep. He gently caressed her shoulder. His leg throbbed, and his heart ached at the idea of losing her. *Lord, help me find Wolton so we can live free of this fear.* He was tortured by thoughts of losing his wife and frustrated that they had become so comfortable together. Due to his leg he had not felt comfortable pursuing her physically beyond the kisses and a few caresses. She had not complained, but she was frustrated. He could see, hear, and feel the desire in her. He fought against those emotions himself.

Finally, he was willing to pursue this and his body was unable to accommodate him. The splint was too high up and the pain far more severe since the fire. That one event set his healing back and it frustrated him. He was grateful for one result of his broken leg though, and that was the comfort he found every night having his beautiful wife by his side.

~*~

The next week passed quickly, with the women spending time together and with the children, and Michael and Phillip scouting the area and asking questions of the villagers. No strangers had been seen in the neighborhood. A letter finally arrived from Marcus, along with a few men.

Dear Theodore,

I'm sending several Bow Street Runners to help provide protection for you and help you find Wolton. There has been no sign of him in London, but that is not unusual as this is not a frequent haunt of his. We are praying for your safety and hope to join you there soon.

Stay safe, my friend,

Remy

The Runners were set up around the property wearing Harrow livery and one was in the house specifically to protect Dartanian.

Theo should be more at ease, but as time went on, he lived in a state of agitation, waiting for the next catastrophe to hit but not knowing where it would come from.

Marcus and Josie arrived within the week and the house was filled with laughter and chaos of old friends and new, along with many young children, of which Dartanian was the oldest. Help had been hired from the village to work on restoring the nursery.

Theo sat in his study with his friends while their wives had tea in the drawing room. "I'm chafing at the wait," Theo said to no one in particular.

Michael sipped his tea and sighed. "If I didn't remember that God knows the end I would be anxious myself."

"Is that why I'm out of sorts? Because I'm not in control of events?"

Marcus let out a grunt of laughter. "Take it from me, that's always been my challenge, to relax and let God be in control."

"Relax. That's about all I can do with this bum leg right now. I'm afraid I'll become one of those doddering old fools able to tell the weather by the ache in my thigh."

"I doubt you will ever be doddering, Theo. You are too good a man for that and I don't think Valeria will allow it."

Theo grinned at the mention of his wife. They had come to such a nice balance of routine, even with guests in the house, and she had proven herself to be an able hostess and the perfect Marchioness. He longed for the day, hopefully soon, when he could bring her to London and introduce her to the *ton*.

She would shine like a brilliant star on his arm at any event they would attend. Who would have thought that Theo would gain such a lovely bride? Yes, with his title and wealth he could have bought beauty, but not someone he could respect and love.

"So, what is the plan now? Do we even have one beyond waiting?" Phillip popped a small cake in his mouth and gave a satisfied grin as he chewed.

"What can we do but wait? We don't know where the attack will come or in what form. We just need to be ready." Marcus set his cup down and leaned back, lacing his hands over his abdomen.

"Maybe we should all go to London," Theo offered.

"I think there would be more danger there. Are you chafing at being home? This has to be the longest you have stayed here since your mother died."

Theo nodded. "I'm not complaining about being here. Having you all around has been a blessing. Maybe I'm finally being domesticated?" He chuckled.

"Right, if anyone was more suited to married life and fatherhood, it would be you, Theo." Michael set his cup and saucer down on the tea tray.

"It seems fitting that you got an instant family with Dartanian. He's fortunate to have you for a step-father." Phillip set his cup down.

Heat rose in Theo's cheeks. "I've never been around children and was an only child, so what makes you think I will be any good at this?"

"Maybe because you are older than us you have functioned more in a father-like role for us time and again." Marcus's brown eyes met Theo's and he could read the love there in their dark depths.

"Now you are making me seem ancient. Maybe I am closer to doddering than I thought?" Theo joked. He really wasn't used to compliments. He never had them from his own father.

"Far from it, Theo. You've held your own in every battle we have undertaken. I've always been glad to have you on our side when things got tough." Michael leaned forward as he spoke with his hands clasped together, elbows resting on his knees. "You are a rare prince of a man. I'm glad you found a woman worthy of you."

Theo squirmed in his chair and grew frustrated at his lame leg that kept him from moving easily or even suggesting a horse race to take the edge off the anxiety he had been feeling with the wait. And now with these unasked-for comments. They warmed his heart though. He treasured these men, his friends, and would do anything for any of them. And they had returned the favor in his time of need. Who could ask for more?

He could. He could ask that God would end this stand-off with Wolton, so he could move on with his life and his family.

Mittens, resting on the back of his chair, stood up, stretched, stepped down onto Theo's shoulder, and into his lap.

Theo absentmindedly started petting him.

"I never pegged you as a cat man," Michael joked.

"It is a bit more normal than a ferret," Theo quipped.

Michael frowned and shrugged. "Fidget died a while ago."

"I'm sorry, Michael. I know you were fond of that skinny rat." Theo scratched the cat behind the ears and it purred loudly.

"I have kids now and don't need Fidget to do my work anymore. As patient as Katrina was with him, she was never fond of his scent."

Phillip chuckled. "I wish I could have been there when Fidget sprayed all over the Black Diamond. That had to be a sight to behold."

"More like an odor to make you vomit. I'm amazed Katrina married me after that fiasco. But compared to the evil my father had in store for her I think she found it more palatable to cope with the ferret stench."

"At least Mittens doesn't have that problem." Theo smiled down at the cat. "And he definitely helped us in rescuing Dartanian and Valeria. Who knew that cat allergies could be so debilitating?"

The men all chuckled.

"Well, Mittens, do not get too comfortable yet. We may need your help to defeat Wolton."

"That's a lot of pressure to put on a kitten." Phillip grinned.

"It's a lot of pressure to put on any of us." Theo frowned. Picking the cat up, he deposited him on the floor and struggled to rise to his feet. "I'm heading up to prepare for dinner. I will see you men later."

~*~

Valeria heard her husband thump into the adjoining room and murmur to his valet. She was enjoying her visit with her new friends but was becoming increasingly frustrated at how her relationship with Theo stalled.

It seemed he was content to treat her like a stuffed animal a child would take to bed and hold tight through the night. There were never more than a few kisses. He acted too much like the gentleman. Sure, his leg was broken but there were things they could still do. So, why didn't he?

He kept talking about the possibility of removing

to London and when she'd tried to dissuade him, she got a pat on the back of her hand as though she was a child who didn't know better.

How could she tell him she had no knowledge of the *beau monde?* She was French, and would be ostracized for that or suspected of being a spy. To marry into the peerage, twice? She would be considered a social climber at the very least.

There were the ongoing restrictions on her movements as they waited for the next attack by Lord Wolton. If only they could get past that she could possibly relax and enjoy her new life more.

Dartanian was tense as well. Things were still unsettled after the fire and she spent hours with him daily, reassuring him, playing with him, reading to him, and teaching him how to read from one of the few primers that survived the fire. His English was improving. He was also enjoying time playing with Mittens and sitting with Theo to learn how to play checkers and the rudiments of chess. She could not have picked a better man to be a father to her son.

She sat on the side of the bed as she awaited her maid, her hand slowly tracing the stitching on the duvet. She had not really slept in this bed. Every night was spent in the master bedroom and yet the marriage was not consummated. Was it her? Was there something lacking in her appearance that Theo was repulsed by? It seemed she had gone from being an object to be fought over and used for men's baser desires to being rejected for those same qualities. She couldn't understand it. How could she get Theo to move beyond a few kisses and a hug?

She wanted so much more from their marriage than comfortable friendship. She wanted the passion she'd experienced in those early days before they'd confronted the Duke.

Before Theo knew the depravity she had been sujected to. Not that she had approved or had a choice. She hadn't. She despised everything about the Duke and his son. She was grateful for the freedom from that kind of abuse of power. But to go from power to passive? What about passion? What happened?

Shame washed over her, and she rose to go to the table near the fireplace where her Bible lay. She had just read something that morning in Romans. She flipped through the pages and found it. No condemnation. She was free from the shame of her past. It did not need to hover like a cloud over her. And yet it seemed as if it did with the way Theo treated her.

Her new abigail, Daisy, came in to help her dress for dinner and put fresh order to her hair. She set her Bible aside and quietly prayed in her heart. *Lord, please help me know what to do about Theo and Lord Wolton. Guide us so we can be free from the past once and for all. I am so glad I am Yours, Jesus.*

Valeria was surprised at how much she enjoyed having Theo's friends and their wives all together at mealtime. She had grown up as an only child and once orphaned had been isolated by the Duke and his son. She only ever entertained their friends and oftentimes those meals were followed by drunken debauchery that meant she lost more and more of herself in the process.

If Dartanian had not been born she might have resorted to suicide. She had thought about it often enough. She had prayed frequently for God to let her die. But He never had.

But she had not grown up with the kind of abuse Beth experienced. She hadn't been tortured like Katrina. Josie seemed the only one who had gotten away lightly with her brush with the Black Diamond.

But all that had changed for them. Now they enjoyed a camaraderie that was rare for the unique background they shared. And they all loved Christ, but some were newer to the faith, as she and Theo were.

The love and grace she found amongst these women was hard to accept as real. The respect she received from the men and saw extended to their wives was heart-warming. Marcus had a secret smile only for Josie which she returned. Katrina and Michael flirted playfully. Phillip gave steamy looks to Beth which she returned with a wink and a nod before they would disappear.

And then there was Theo. He treated her with all courtesy and respect and only kissed her or touched her while in the bedroom, alone. No secret hidden messages or warmth when in public. She should not complain. She was treated well. She was provided and cared for. But she wanted so much more. She wanted that passion and adoration she saw between the other couples. But how could that come about when he shut down every attempt of hers to discuss it and was never alone with her outside of his bed?

She climbed into bed next to Theo but did not get close to him. Laying on her side she looked at him lying on his back. Strong and soft. Forceful and gentle. He was such an odd combination of a man. She was safe with him.

His head turned to her. "Will you give me a good-night kiss?"

Valeria frowned. "I don't think so. Not tonight."

Theo's brows drew together as his eyes searched her face. "Have I transgressed somehow?"

Valeria blinked back a threatening tear. "Not intentionally. You didn't do anything. And that is the problem."

"A sin of omission?"

"An appropriate term, I suppose." She rolled on to her back and stared up at the ceiling.

"So, what didn't I do?"

"Theo. We are married and there are a lot of things we do not do as a married couple."

"This was supposed to be a *mariage de convenance*," he protested.

"And that was not what I agreed to. You assumed that, but it was never my desire. I thought I had made that clear." She was gritting her teeth together.

"I broke my leg."

"Running from your wife."

"That's not true."

"Isn't it?" She turned her head to him, but he wouldn't meet her gaze. "I thought so." She pulled back the blankets.

A strong hand clasped her arm before she could swing her feet over the edge of the mattress.

"Where are you going?"

"To sleep in my own bed, where a woman who is not desired by her husband should sleep." She yanked her arm free and he let it drop. She put her feet on the cold floor and wrapped her robe around herself. She tied the sash and pulled the blankets back. "Goodnight, Theo."

She left the room and could feel his gaze following her. When she got to the other side she turned the key in the lock. Valeria crawled into bed and cried herself to sleep.

~*~

She had walked out on him. The one thing he looked forward to all day, holding his wife as she slept, she took away. The key turned in the lock and his heart sank.

She was right. He had run away. But she was wrong about him not desiring her. How would he convince her and woo her back to his bed? What else had he failed to do?

The next two days, Valeria acted the same as usual around him. She respected his distance and acted more like a hostess than wife, tending to everyone's needs and making sure he had what he needed.

He was ashamed to ask his friends for help with his marriage but decided to watch them instead. He envied what they had and didn't understand how three independent men had come to be so completely happy with their wives. And they were cheerful about it.

Josie, Beth, and Katrina were never unreasonable in their requests either. There seemed to be such a mutual understanding of the needs of the other. Not that there were not occasional spats but it seemed that each couple, when it happened, was eager to resolve the issue and would disappear for some time. He had assumed it was to talk it through.

Now as he watched closer he saw the winks, smiles, and little touches as well as the kind words of affection that each couple shared discreetly. How had he missed what was going on right in front of his face? It was almost as if whatever went on the bedroom spilled over into the rest of their lives. Or was it the other way around?

His heart cracked knowing that he had wronged Valeria by treating her more as a servant during the day than a beloved wife. How could she be happy when she saw what he was just now beginning to understand? No wonder she had abandoned his bed. He had abandoned her. Hadn't she had enough of that in her life?

The larger question now was what would he do about it? How did a man go about courting his own wife?

18

Theo prayed about it. He decided to start as unobtrusively as possible. He didn't want to scare her off or make her skeptical of him if he came on too hard and fast with his attentions. So, he started by joining the ladies for tea.

"Theo? What brings you here?" Valeria rose to help him get seated.

"The men are playing at billiards and I am unable to participate. I decided I would prefer to spend time with my lovely bride and three other delightful women." He accepted the teacup from Valeria with a smile.

She sat down next to him but kept a space between their bodies.

Theo could feel her heat and smell orange blossoms. The past few nights he had been sleeping on her pillow just to feel her near because it smelled of her.

"Theo, we are glad you have joined us. Valeria tells us that Dartanian's birthday is coming up soon and we need to plan a special party for him."

"When is it?" Theo asked, surprised and a bit saddened that she had not shared that with him. But then when would she have? The only time they had ever talked was in bed at night. He had a dawning awareness of how gravely he had erred.

Valeria named a day a few days hence.

Theo made suggestions for them all to enjoy the property. To go fishing and boating in the pond as well as a picnic out on the lawn were all discussed.

The twinkle in Valeria's eyes brightened as she planned for Dartanian's seventh birthday party.

He needed to rise.

Valeria helped him to the door.

"Sweetheart, I would like to purchase something from my neighbor to the south. He is a horse breeder and if he has a pony I would love to get that for Dartanian for his birthday. He is old enough to learn to ride. Would that be acceptable to you?"

Valeria looked at him with her mouth open. "A pony? Oh, Theo, Dartanian would be delighted. Thank you for being so generous with my son."

Theo gave her a half grin. "You mean our son. I love him too, Valeria." He raised her hand to his lips, kissed the back, and massaged the space with his thumb before releasing it and leaving the room.

Later that afternoon, Theo came into Valeria's room as Daisy was finishing up her hair. Her look of surprise at his presence made him grin. Under his arm was a box.

Valeria dismissed Daisy.

Theo set the box on the top of her dresser.

"I have been remiss in providing you with the jewels that rightfully belong to the Marchioness of Harrow." He opened it and pointed to some of the rings neatly displayed within. "One of these should be your wedding ring. I apologize for not thinking of it sooner. I have dishonored you by not following through on this."

She scanned the items and drew out a sapphire and diamond ring. She held it up.

He took it from her and slid it on her ring finger. "With this ring, I thee wed." He bent down and gave her a feather-light kiss. He backed up a step and pointed to the rest of the jewelry. "This is all yours whenever you want it. I keep it in a safe in my room. Let me know whenever you desire something from the collection. It is yours, Lady Harrow."

"Theo..." Valeria looked through the pieces, gently picking them up and testing their weight. She finally picked out a small cross on a chain. "May I?" she asked.

Theo swallowed and nodded. "It was my mother's. She wore it all the time. I would be honored if you chose to have it grace your neck as well." He took the necklace from her and clasped it .

She looked in the mirror and finger the dainty gold cross. How did he ever manage to find a bride so lovely and pure? Sure, she had a dark past, but her heart was one he could trust and longed to know better. Her beauty shone through her eyes. "You look lovely, my dear." He held out his arm. "Shall we?"

Her gratitude shown in her brown eyes. She reached to put the lid down on the box of jewelry.

He locked it and turned to her. "I will replace it in the vault later." With that he took her hand and escorted her to the drawing room.

Theo did not leave her side once they entered the room. They stood talking to Marcus and Josie when the rest came in. Soon they were at dinner and he seated her. Before leaving to take his own seat, he bent to place a kiss on the top of her head.

Without another word, he left to tend the guests. The dinner was enjoyable with these men who were more family to him than his own had been. These men had eased his lonely existence and gave him a feeling of worth and belonging. A band of brothers, as it were.

The wives had become as dear to him as he imagined sisters ever would be. And there at the other end of the table was Valeria. She took his breath away. Her golden hair swept up off her face with a few tendrils framing it.

She tipped her head in question at his gaze. Theo raised his glass to her and nodded his head slightly with a gentle smile before taking a sip, never breaking eye contact until he set his glass back down. As he tended to the conversation with Katrina on his left he glanced at his bride and found her slightly flushed. He stifled a grin. Perhaps this wooing business wasn't so hard after all.

After the women left the men to their port, Michael cleared his throat. "I do not mean to complain, but the wait for Wolton is getting dashed long."

"Would you like me to extend him an invitation to attack so we can get it over with? If so, give me his address," Theo said. He enjoyed tweaking Michael who gave as good as he got.

"Buffleheaded definitely does suit you at times, Theo." Michael grinned as he sipped dark liquid. "I was thinking we might want to draw him out of hiding. Provide him with the opportunity he has been waiting for."

"You want to use bait?" Phillip asked.

Michael nodded.

"I do not want to put Valeria at risk."

"She is already at risk, Theo. As are you and Dartanian." Michael defended his idea and his lips were set in a firm line. There was no humor behind his suggestion.

Marcus frowned as well. "What you are suggesting has some value, Michael." He paused to look at Theo. "Hear me out. First, I would be loath to put my own wife in such a situation, so I understand your fears there. I can safely speak for all of us that we would hesitate to take a step like this. Second. If we did set a trap with you and Valeria as bait, we could control the situation better because we would be prepared for it. We can plot and plan and defeat him before any harm is done to either of you."

Theo leaned back in his chair and his shoulders sagged. He, too, was tired of the wait. What Marcus said made sense. He glanced to the door his wife had recently walked through. When this was over they would be able to have a regular marriage without the threat of danger hanging over them. They could go to London and he could indulge Valeria's every whim. Buy her new dresses and waltz with her at every ball and find comfort in her arms at night without the fear of anything coming to part them.

It hit like a knife to his heart. Even with Wolton out of the way, there were no guarantees. His father died tragically and quick and his mother grieved horribly for him. As much as he loathed his father, seeing his mother suffer had been heart wrenching. He swallowed. Anything could happen to him—or to her—and there was no way to prepare for it.

"Theo?" Phillip's voice was soft and laced with concern as his eyes searched and met his.

"Hmmmm?"

"You grew pale all of a sudden. Are you unwell?" Phillip leaned forward scrutinizing Theo's face and the other two men now did the same.

"I'm fine. I appreciate your concern. I wasn't pleased with where my thoughts had led me." Theo sipped more of his wine, savoring the heavy fruity flavor. "I hate to say I agree with you, but I think you have hit on a solution to our waiting. How do you think we should proceed?"

The men leaned together to conspire and opted to keep the women out of the planning, so they would be less likely to interfere and possibly be harmed. They decided they would plan for the day after Dartanian's party.

That suited Theo fine as it gave him a few more days to woo his wife. He wanted her to remember him fondly should anything go wrong with all they had planned.

Theo walked Valeria to her door later that evening and lifted her hand up. He kissed her palm and curled her fingers over it. He opened her door and she stepped inside, brows furrowed. She frowned as if she wanted to speak but said nothing.

"Good night, Lady Harrow. Sweet dreams." With that he limped to his own room and entered. He stared at that large bed and dreaded laying down in it alone again. *But it won't be for too much longer, old man. Soon you will have her in your arms again. Patience. Have patience. Lord, help me trust You in the waiting.*

~*~

Valeria was puzzled. Who was this man? She slowly removed the cross and placed it back in the jewelry box. She glanced down at the ring on her left hand. It was stunning, and the women had commented on it after dinner. They were not jealous as they all had their own treasured gifts from their husbands. But that he had even thought of it shocked her. She wanted to hope he was understanding what her complaint was, but she still wasn't sure.

Yet every time he had touched her or looked at her, even across the room, she saw heat in his eyes. They would turn a deep green and his smile promised hidden secrets only for her.

Could she trust that he was really seeking to court her? Was she wrong that he did not want her? Perhaps he did. He had been acting as if he was afraid. A man of the world like him? Afraid of what? She was the tainted one.

She closed the jewelry box and prepared for bed. Even with a fire and the warmer spring evening, she became chilled as she crawled into her bed alone. She missed the scent of Theo that was uniquely his. Horse and man and something else she couldn't quite place but one that had a comforting effect on her. She tossed to her other side and her fist hit her pillow. She should not be sleeping alone. But she was the one who had walked out and locked the door. Maybe it would not be for too much longer. She could only pray that would be so.

~*~

The day of Dartanian's birthday party Valeria rose from her bed and stretched. She was tired of being alone. She looked forward to the day and seeing how Dartanian liked the mount Theo had chosen for him, a sweet and docile grey pony named Silver. Theo had shown her the horse the day before and she saw the excitement in his eyes at giving her son this gift.

Their son. He had corrected her every time she'd said 'mine.' She longed for the day when the two could freely go about the estate without fear.

Today they would be outdoors for their celebration. While she longed for the sunshine and freedom to roam the property, the idea of being in sight of Lord Wolton or his minions was terrifying. She had tried to voice her concerns, but Theo said that it would be safe and protection was in place. Nothing should mar Dartanian's birthday.

In spite of all that she could not repress the shiver that traveled up her spine. She had been living on the edge for too long and Wolton would be deriving great pleasure from that. *Lord, please keep Dartanian safe from harm today.*

After Daisy left her, she sat at her mirror and put the golden cross around her neck. She reached into a drawer and pulled out a small knife and sheath and placed that deep into a side pocket. One just never knew...

After breakfast, the younger children were assigned to the makeshift nursery while Dartanian came out with the adults for the first of his birthday presents.

Theo held Dartanian's hand for the walk to the stables.

Dartanian quickly spotted the new pony in the pen outside scampering playfully. "*Papa!* That horse is new." Dartanian's voice was filled with breathless wonder.

"He sure is. He came to live here because he has a new master."

"He does? That would be you, *Papa*?"

"No, son, that new owner would be you." Theo lifted the boy to the bottom rung of the wood fence enclosing the pen. He placed a sugar cube in the boy's hand. "Hold it out. His name is Silver."

Dartanian held out the sugar on a flat palm. "Silver. I have a treat for you."

The horse willingly trotted over to the young boy.

Valeria could not help but smile as the lips of the horse tickled her son's hand. She delighted in hearing him laugh. He reached up to pet the horse.

"Dartanian, Silver is your horse. I want to teach you to ride him and care for him so you can be a good Duke when you grow up, knowing how to care for the animals that will serve you."

The little boy's brows knit together. "Serve me?"

Theo nodded. "We care for them, but they are here to serve us. They pull our carriages and give us rides and take us places. That's their job. If we want them to do it well and for a long time we need to take good care of them. This horse is for you to learn on and grow with. He will serve you for many years if you care for him well."

"He won't get shot like Zeus, will he?" The little boy stopped petting the horse to look up at Theo.

Theo frowned. They tried to avoid telling Dartanian about that incident, but someone must have let it slip. "I hope not, son. I cannot guarantee that nothing bad will ever happen to you or your horse, but we can trust God for the future. We do not need to worry about it. We have today and as it's your birthday, we will focus on what is good. Can you do that, Dartanian?"

Valeria's heart warmed as her little boy smiled up at the man next to him and nodded.

"Shall we put a saddle on him and take a ride around the ring here?"

"May I, *Maman?*"

Valeria smiled. "You may. It is your birthday. We

will try to make wishes come true as much as we are able."

Dartanian looked thoughtful. "I can have what I wish on my birthday?"

Valeria had misspoken, and he had caught it. He was so literal at this age. "We cannot give you everything, but we will try to make you happy. Is there something you particularly wished for?" She held her breath, almost afraid of what he might request.

"I want a brother." He jumped off his wooden perch and grabbed Theo's hand heading to the door of the stable. "Come, *Papa!* I want to ride Silver."

The color drained out of Theo's face as Dartanian took him away.

Valeria averted her gaze. She deeply longed for another child, but if things did not change with Theo, it would never come to pass. But how did one explain that to a seven-year-old?

She leaned against the fence and waited for them to emerge in the paddock. Soon Dartanian was up on the horse and her heart warmed as he learned the rudimentaries of holding the reins and how to stay in the saddle.

The man struggling to walk alongside Dartanian was tall and strong, good looking in a boyish kind of way as his hair fell onto his forehead and the sun shining on his head made him appear blonder. Theo was wearing more casual trousers and his boots. If it weren't for his posture he would probably pass for a commoner with his easy smile and his laughter. His hazel eyes looked gray in the bright light but up close she had seen streaks of green in them. The way they changed color with his moods fascinated her.

Her hand slid to her waist. A baby. What would it

be like to have a baby with Theo? He was already a wonderful father to Dartanian. He would do anything to protect either of them if it were called for. Remembering that brought back fears raised by Dartanian's comment. She hoped that they really were protected and safe today.

Lunch was a joyful affair and afterwards the women either went to tend the younger children or nap while the men took Dartanian out to the pond to fish. Theo had talked about taking a small boat out as well.

Michael laughed. "Dartanian, you need to understand that this introduction to fishing will not entail catching fish. It is the wrong time of day for that."

Dartanian looked up at him with squinting eyes. "But you told us how Lord Remington, Lord Westbrooke, and Papa would go fishing as little boys while you kept Mrs. Tidley from getting into trouble in the afternoon."

Phillip patted the young man on the back. "Very true. That is what we did. They sat under a tree and talked about life and women and periodically threw out lures and found it a great way to hide from the tutor who wanted to make us conjugate our Latin verbs even on a holiday. Fish were never required."

Dartanian frowned. "So, I won't catch any fish, but I will hear about life and girls? I really don't want to know about girls. *Maman* is OK, but I don't want any more girls. I told Papa that I want a brother."

Valeria bit back a chuckle at Phillip's expression and how his face turned red. Phillip glanced over at her and she covered her mouth to hide her grin.

Michael patted Dartanian on the head. "I never

had any brothers or sisters so I understand how you don't want to be the only child. But your parents cannot control whether they have a boy or a girl."

"But *Maman* said I could have what I wished. I wish for a brother." With that Dartanian shook his head at Michael and walked out to the garden where Theo had gone ahead with the supplies.

Valeria burst out laughing after her son left.

Michael gave his trademark grin. "Sounds as though you and Theo had better get busy with the baby making, Val." With that he left her alone.

She sat down feeling as if the wind had been knocked out from her. How many times today was she to be taunted with what she could not have?

~*~

Theo enjoyed himself. To be limping alongside his son, *their* son, on a pony for the first time. He had missed first words and steps with Dartanian but there were so many other firsts he longed to be a part of. He was determined he would not be the one cutting down this little man when he failed to reach perfection. Who could? This little boy was already perfect in his eyes.

That comment though about wanting a brother unsettled him. Where had he gotten an idea like that? Theo set out the rods and tied on the hooks. He had no idea how to address the topic and Valeria had been silent, but he had witnessed the pain in her eyes that Dartanian had missed. He spied her hand go to her waist. She wanted another child.

And if he were honest, he did too.

Dartanian came running down the hill and plopped his bottom next to Theo.

The other men were following along at a more leisurely pace. There were armed guards hiding around the pond, the estate, and even in the house making sure they were safe. He wanted nothing to interfere with Dartanian's birthday.

"Papa?"

"Yes, Dartanian?"

"Lord Westbrooke said that we would talk about life and women. I don't want to do that. Can we talk about something else while we wait for no fish?" The little boy picked up a pole and bobbed it up and down.

Phillip tilted his head with a grin. "What would you like to talk about?"

The lad leaned back against the tree and stared up into its branches as if that would give an answer. After a long pause, he finally spoke. "I want to learn how to fight, shoot, and fence."

"At some point those are good things to learn," said Michael as he picked up a pole and cast out into the peaceful lake breaking the smooth surface with ripples.

"Why, Dartanian?" Theo asked.

"So, I can protect *Maman* in case *Grand-père* or Lord Wolton ever try to come back for her."

Theo saw the fire in the little boy's eyes and the clenched fists. "You want to protect your *Maman*? That is a noble thing for a son to want to do."

The boy's eyes brightened and he smiled. "You will teach me?"

Marcus laughed and bent down to ruffle the little boy's hair. "Protecting your *Maman* is now Theo's job."

"But what if something happens to him and *Maman* and I are alone again?"

Theo swallowed. That had been one of his own

fears. "If something happens to me, Uncle Michael or Phillip or Marcus will help care for you and your *Maman*. I pray it will not come to that. I will do everything I can to keep you both safe."

"So, you won't teach me?" Dartanian looked as if he would cry.

"I will teach you and be glad to do so. I need a sparring partner when my friends return to their own homes."

Dartanian's face lit up and his eyes were bright. "Thank you, Papa!" He stood up and threw his arms around Theo's neck.

Theo dropped the hook he had been holding and hesitantly wrapped his own arms around the child. His heart barely fit in his chest it had grown so large.

The fishing trip ended up being a success in more ways than one. Dartanian had an opportunity to hang out with the men and they all delighted in telling him tales of their own childhood mischief.

Theo wondered at the wisdom of that, fearing that he would have a little terror on his hands as his son thought up his own means of getting into trouble.

The other success of the afternoon was that Dartanian was the only one to catch anything. The young man proudly walked back to the house with three little fish dangling from his line to proudly present to cook to prepare as part of the evening meal.

Theo walked the young man to his nanny to prepare for dinner with the adults, a rare treat for the little boy.

Dartanian wrapped his arms around the top of Theo's legs. "Today was smashing! Thank you for the bestest birthday ever, Papa!"

The pain was worth it to Theo. He patted his son

on the back. "It has been my pleasure, Dartanian." Theo loosened the little arms and bent over so he could see the boy eye to eye. "I'm glad God let me be your new Papa. I love you, son."

Dartanian's eyes welled with tears and his lips trembled. "My old Papa never told me that. I love you too." The arms wrapped around Theo's neck and Theo held the boy tight as he cried out his loss and love, soaking Theo's jacket. Theo fought back a few tears of his own. Had his own father ever said those words to him? If so, he couldn't remember. He vowed in his heart that he would make sure this little boy heard those words and accompanying actions, often.

Later that evening, Theo walked Valeria to her door. She turned and placed a hand on his chest. "Thank you for making Dartanian's day wonderful, Theo."

Theo risked gazing into her dark brown eyes reflecting a golden warmth from the lit candles in the hallway. "I love you and Dartanian. I could do no less." He took hold of the hand on his chest, removing the warmth penetrating his waistcoat and shirt. He pulled the hand to his lips and placed a kiss there. Letting it go, he said softly, "Sweet dreams, Lady Harrow." With that he turned to go to his room and his own empty, cold bed.

19

The day after the party, Theo awoke early and went to the kitchen to have Cook prepare a special picnic basket. It was time to get on to the business of seriously wooing his bride.

He sat in the breakfast parlor and sipped his coffee, awaiting Valeria's appearance. He grinned in anticipation of spending uninterrupted time alone with her.

When she appeared, wearing a mauve gown, he marveled again at the blessing in finding a woman whom he could see eye to eye with and as lovely she was.

She sat to his right with her plate and the footman poured her hot chocolate.

He dismissed the servant and as the doors to the room closed, he cleared his throat. "Would you go riding with me this morning? I realize you are tired of being cooped up in the house. I would like to show you more of the estate."

Valeria peered up at him with a smile slowly spreading over her face. "I would like that above all things. I am an indifferent rider at best, so you would need to be patient with me."

"I will help you get better. I have a perfect mount for you and delight in teaching people how to ride." He winked at her .

She blushed. "Will it be safe?" She set her cup down in the saucer, every move graceful.

"I will be armed. We have guards around the

estate. We are as safe as we could be."

Her smile got brighter. "How soon do you wish to depart?"

"Finish your breakfast and go change into your riding habit. We will leave when you are ready."

The door opened, and they were joined by Marcus and Josie. The conversation flowed to the general niceties of how well yesterday's party went.

Valeria rose and trailed her finger along Theo's back as she walked out of the room to go change.

Theo pretended he didn't notice but could not keep himself from a little grin in response which she saw. She responded with a wink and was gone.

Theo experienced the thrum of anticipation as he excused himself from the table. He limped to the kitchen to grab the basket that Cook had prepared. He headed to the stable into the damp morning air. He could smell the hay and manure mixed in with the scent of fresh cut grass. He inhaled deeply and grinned.

A young stable-hand, Joe, brought him the two horses he had requested. A gentle brown mare, named Coco for Valeria, and a more spirited white with grey markings, named Penelope. Theo checked the girths and attached his parcel to the back of his. He led the two out into the yard.

Valeria came down the stairs in a stylish riding habit in a blue that made her hair shimmer in contrast. Her hat was set at a jaunty angle and the smile she gave him took his breath away.

"This is Coco, she has a sweet temper. I think you will like her."

Valeria came up to the horse and petted its nose. "Good morning, Coco. I think you and I will be good friends." She opened up her hand and revealed a sugar cube that the horse pulled into her mouth. Valeria giggled.

Theo walked her around to the side and gave her a leg up to the side-saddle. He waited until she was settled and adjusted her stirrup. He moved around to his own horse and pulled up to the saddle. He winced as his thigh tried to rest along the curve of the horse's body.

"Are you OK, Theo?"

He shook his head. "Guess my leg is not as healed as I had hoped."

"We can postpone this until you are better." Her horse skittered to the side, but she patted the mare's neck and it calmed down.

"No, I want to spend time with you and the only way to do that right now is to escape the house. I promise I will try not to push too hard." The pain was easing so he clicked his tongue to the mare and the two horses took off down a side lane into the woods.

"Are you sure we are safe?"

Theo shrugged. "As safe as we ever were. We cannot continue to live our lives in fear."

They rode side by side down the wide track of beaten down grass under the shade of the trees in full leaf above. The birds sang and flitted around.

"It is peaceful out here." Her voice was soft.

Theo sighed. "It is. One of my favorite things to do when I need to clear my mind, here or in the city, is to escape it all with a horse and the beauty of this world God created."

"But you only recently came to believe in God."

"True. That doesn't mean I didn't appreciate His creation before that or recognize that all of this was here by His hands."

She didn't respond.

They entered a meadow.

"Are you up for a gallop?" Theo grinned in anticipation.

Valeria nodded and was off in a flash, her sweet-tempered mare eager to please.

Reaching the edge of the meadow neck and neck, Theo enjoyed seeing his wife's face flushed and her hair falling out of its coiffeur.

She slowed her horse and turned toward him as they both came to a stop. "That was wonderful!" She smiled at him and Theo became lost in the beauty of her face and form and the endless depths of her brown eyes alight with pure joy.

He positioned his horse close to hers and leaned over for a light kiss. Pulling back, he nodded. "I agree, that was wonderful."

As he pulled away, one gloved hand moved to touch her lips.

"Let us ride on. There is so much more to show you."

Theo took her up and down hills and around to some of the tenant farms. He introduced her to them, but they did not stay to visit. Theo came to a lake further away from the house and moved to get off his horse. He nearly fell as the muscles in his leg complained about the abuse it had endured. He clutched his thigh as he held on to his horse for balance. *Blast it. Now is not the time to appear weak. You want to woo your wife not make her play nursemaid.*

"Theo?"

Concern laced her voice. She was on the other side of the horse so could not really see him in his agony.

He struggled to stand up straight and hoped he could hide his pain. "I will get you down." He tied off the reins to a low hanging branch, limped over to Valeria, and bracing himself carefully, he helped her dismount.

After she had her feet on the ground, she stood with her body flushed to his and he leaned in again for a longer kiss. *I could really get used to doing this for the rest of my life.* Her arms reached up around his neck and he let his wander up her back. Soon he had her hat on the ground and the few remaining pins out of her hair. When they came up for air he stepped back and gazed into her eyes. Both were breathing heavily. Theo momentarily forgot the pain in his leg.

She licked her swollen lips.

Theo was tempted to resume the activity. His stomach rumbled.

She giggled.

"I guess that's my cue for us to eat lunch." He turned to get the basket and his leg gave up supporting him. He would have hit the ground if Valeria had not been quick to keep him from falling.

"Your leg?"

He nodded and bit his lip to keep from crying out due to the sharp pain that radiated through his entire body.

"We should go back to the house."

"I don't think I can get back on my horse right now." Theo leaned on Valeria as they made it to a spot under the tree.

She left him standing with his back against the tree, then went to his horse to get a blanket and the basket containing their picnic lunch. Valeria spread the blanket out, helped ease Theo down onto it, and sat next to him.

Her eyes flashed and narrowed. "You are most definitely a buffleheaded idiot. You are not healed enough but insist on coming out here to spend time away from the house."

"With you."

"What?"

"I wanted to be alone with my wife." Theo was gritting his teeth as he talked, as much from anger as pain. He reached into the basket and pulled out a bottle of wine. Popping the cork, he drank from the bottle and handed it to Valeria.

"It would serve you well for me to leave you and send your friends for you." She set the wine aside, pulled out the food, and arranged it in front of them.

"If I am not better by the time we are done here, you may leave me and go for help." Theo leaned his head against the tree and took a bite of some cold chicken.

"Why can't you take better care of yourself? Don't you realize Dartanian and I need you?" Tears trailed down her face.

"Sweetheart, I know you need me. You were right. I was an idiot. But not having you in my bed every night has been driving me crazy. I could not wait any longer to try to find a way to let you know how much I love and admire you and long to be a real husband to you." Theo put his arm around her shoulder and drew her to his chest. She melted into him and he kissed the top her head.

Valeria looked up at him.

He could not resist any more. He tipped his head and kissed her.

When they finally came up for air Theo leaned his head back again to savor the moment. The bees buzzed nearby and the birds sang in the trees. The soft wind rustling the leaves above and the bright sun winking at them through the branches created a perfect setting for their courtship.

"I'm still angry with you," Valeria whispered as she snuggled close. She handed him the bottle of wine and he drank deeply. He offered it to her and she took a sip.

"I'm sorry I have not been the husband you needed me to be. I'm new at this and to be honest, I'm scared."

She pulled back and sat up, looking at him. "I scare you?"

"Being a husband scares me."

Valeria's head tipped to the side and her hand came up to caress his cheek. It sent waves of desire through him. "Why would being a husband scare you? You are a wonderful provider and protector. Dartanian adores you. I adore you."

"But I have not loved you the way a man should love his wife." Heat rushed to Theo's face.

Valeria frowned. "I'm not happy about that, but in your defense, you had a broken leg. I think it is rather foolish for you to abandon your splint so early. You limped a lot yesterday and were in pain last night. I'm not sure you've yet fully recovered from your injury."

"So, what excuse do you give me for the days, and nights, before that?" Theo's gaze challenged her.

"I thought perhaps you regretted marrying me because you needed to. I wouldn't have blamed you."

"I would have wed you because I wanted to. I didn't need that silly will to force my hand. Perhaps you forgot that I proposed to you before that?"

She smiled but wouldn't meet his gaze. Her finger

traced a design on the blanket. "How could I forget? You were like an eager puppy salivating after a bone."

"What an attractive image."

"Well, you are cuddly." She grinned.

Theo sighed. "I don't understand why you would even want me. I have no experience."

"Experience? What are you talking about?" Valeria asked

"You thought I had abstained from brothels?"

"No. Of course not. I understand men partake of that before marriage, but I expect you to be faithful now."

"I was faithful to you before I ever met you," Theo asserted.

Her head tilted as she looked at him, her eyes searching his face. "How could you…"

Theo knew the moment she understood. He looked away out to the lake where a family of ducks was swimming near the shore. He sighed.

"Theo?" A finger touched his chin and brought his face back towards her. "You've never…?"

"Never." Shame infused him.

Valeria smiled and leaned in for a kiss. When she pulled away he longed to follow her, for more. He thought of the image of an eager puppy and leaned back. When would he learn?

"I think that's wonderful."

His gaze snapped to hers. "You do?"

She grinned. "I do. You don't need to be afraid. I can teach you." She leaned in for another kiss. He tipped over and she rolled with him. His thigh protested but was soon forgotten.

A click brought him to awareness that they were not alone. They both looked up at the barrel of a gun pointed at where their heads had been joined.

Lord Wolton gave an evil grin.

~*~

"What do we have here? The lovebirds have flown the nest and right into my hands. How convenient." He took a step back and motioned them to stand. "Get up."

Valeria fought against the fear that exploded in her heart. She stood first and helped Theo up.

He leaned heavily against her.

Wolton grinned. "That leg still bothering you, Lord Harrow?" He laughed. "It won't be bothering you much longer." He motioned in front of them. "Move."

"Where are we going?" Valeria asked.

"You want some privacy? I'll give you some privacy."

They stumbled a bit down the hill toward the lake and a small dock with a wooden rowboat.

Lord Wolton motioned them to the dock. He pulled out some rope and grabbed Theo's hands. "No funny business or I'll shoot her dead before you can blink." Wolton pulled Theo's hands behind his back and tied them tight. Then he did the same for Valeria. "Get in the boat."

"We can't get in without someone to assist us." Valeria stood tall, trying to hide her shaking.

"I'll help you." Wolton shoved her off the dock.

She landed on her hip and one of the arms tied behind her, hitting the inside of the boat hard. She yelped in pain.

Theo spoke. "I will get in without your

assistance." In spite of his bold words he struggled to lower his leg into the boat. It collapsed beneath him dragging the other one off the doc and almost tipping him over the side.

Wolton quickly untied the boat and pushed it hard towards the middle of the lake. The momentum took them a distance from the shore.

"What do you think he's planning, Theo?" Valeria asked.

Theo whispered, "I don't know but sound carries over the water—shhhh. When we get far enough out we will tip the boat over."

She couldn't believe it. How much wine did he drink? "I can't swim, Theo, and my arms are tied behind my back."

"Wolton doesn't know this lake. I do. It will only come to about your shoulders. If we tip the boat upside down, we can hide under it. He will think we've drowned, but we can stay safe."

Wolton paced along the shore. His holding his rifle. "How far can he shoot us with that?"

Theo looked over his shoulder. "Quite far. But those bullets will not get far through the wood of this boat if we tip it. Keep an eye on him. Do you have any weapons on you?"

"Weapons. Why would I bring a weapon with me when you assured me it would be safe and we were going on a picnic?"

Theo looked at her. "Do you?"

Valeria blushed.

Theo smiled. "That's my girl. What and where?"

"I have a knife strapped to my right thigh. I cannot reach it with my hands tied."

"But when we are under the boat, out of his sight,

I can get it and try to cut your ropes."

Valeria's eyes were wide. She was filled with fear. "I don't think I can do this."

"You can, and you will." Theo looked her in the eyes. "I love you. Trust me."

She glanced to him, and then back to the shore. "I love you too, Theo. He's raising the gun."

"Then now is the time to act. To the right, and try to grab the boat to take it with us."

"I don't know..."

A shot rang out singing past Theo's ear.

"Now!" he hissed.

The boat jerked and together they went over the side. The small wooden craft turned over in the water.

Valeria sank under the water, confused. She struggled with her skirts floating up around her. Theo came to her under the water as she was losing air. He pushed her body up. They broke the surface but were not under the boat.

"Quick. Duck under here."

She obeyed him and soon they were in the darkness of the boat, not able to fully stand upright. She shivered from the cold and terror.

"I'll try to get that knife."

Theo took a breath and sank under the water. With hands tied behind his back he awkwardly moved her skirts out of the way. Touching her thigh, he soon found the strap, and then the knife. He slid it out carefully, and then came back up gasping for air.

"You got it!" Relief washed over her.

"I did. Turn. I'll try to cut your rope. Tell me if I get close to your hands or wrist. I don't want to slip and cut you."

"Can you do this under water?"

This seemed futile.

"Not easily. Just pray I don't slip and drop it." They both turned around until their backs were to each other.

She could feel the pressure against her wrists as the ropes were stretched. She could feel him sawing, slowed by the water that sloshed around them.

The boat moved banging them in the head.

Lord, please help us!

Gun shots were heard. A few hit the boat.

Valeria gasped. "Theo?"

"Hold steady. We are safer here than anywhere else for the moment."

The cords loosened, and she was able to break free. "You did it!" She turned around, carefully took the knife, and began sawing through the wet rope around his wrists. It took forever, and her fingers were numb from the cold water. She shivered uncontrollably.

"You are doing great, Valeria," Theo whispered.

She could feel tremors going through his body. "How is your leg?" she asked softly.

"It is easier to stand in the water than on land. But I banged it getting in the boat. If we have to run, I'll not be able to."

"Will we be alive long enough?"

"I pray he gives up and assumes we're dead, or that our friends find him first."

"They don't even know where we are."

Theo was quiet. Too quiet.

"Theo?" Valeria had a sneaking suspicion he knew something she didn't. "Do your friends know where we are?"

"They do."

"Did they follow us?"

"If all went according to plan they should be here."

"This was a set up? You used us as bait to draw out Wolton?"

Silence.

"Theo?"

"Yes."

"So, this was not about wooing your wife or enjoying a little time alone?"

"I meant everything I said to you."

Silence.

"Valeria?"

"What?" She couldn't hide the irritation in her voice. The knife had stilled but he was not free yet.

"I'm sorry. Please don't leave my hands tied. They are getting numb."

"You deserve to be left tied up."

"You can do that later when we are safe in our bed. You can tie me up as much as you want then."

"I'm not like that, Theo."

Silence.

"Do you think Wolton is gone?"

She could feel his arms move as if he had shrugged his shoulders. "I hope so."

Splash! Splash!

"Someone is swimming toward us."

Could it be Wolton? She knew the man despised water. Even taking a bath was something he had an aversion to and she would know. "Wolton hates water."

"Friend or foe?"

"I don't know, Theo. I'm scared." She resumed sawing. The bonds loosened, and she slid the knife back into its sheath.

Someone swam up under the boat and popped up between them.

"I figured this would be where you were. Idiot Wolton didn't know that this lake isn't deep enough to drown you guys in." Michael sounded cheerful.

"Is he gone?" Theo asked.

"We got him. He's dead. So how about we get out of this dark hole and get you two lovebirds back home and dry?"

"Sounds good to me," Theo said.

Michael sank down and stepped out from under the boat.

Theo reached for her. "Before we go." His lips pressed against hers for the briefest moment. "I'm sorry I put you through this. Will you forgive me?"

Valeria sighed. "I love you, Theo. But I'm not sure how I'll feel about this when I finally recover."

She could hear the sorrow in his voice. "I understand. I accept the consequences. I'm glad you and Dartanian are alive and well and no longer threatened by Wolton." With that he pushed her head under the water and brought her back up into the sunshine.

She sputtered as she caught the fresh air and blinked at the brightness of the light. She glanced over at her husband.

He was frowning, his jaw was clenched, and there were lines on his forehead. He grabbed her hand and started walking towards the shore. She could hear him gasp at times when his leg struggled as his boots would sink into the soft bottom of the lake and stick. Her shoes had been lost once they had fallen out of the boat.

Michael was pulling the boat to the dock after he had righted it. He was close behind her. The other two men stood waiting for them. A blanket covered a lump on the dock and she turned her gaze away.

Phillip pulled her up on the shore and wrapped the picnic blanket around her.

Marcus helped Theo out of the water.

Theo collapsed to the ground. His wrists were raw. With Marcus's help he got his boots off and slowly stumbled to his horse. Marcus assisted him in getting in the saddle.

Phillip assisted her, and the two men mounted and led them back to the house.

Valeria was led ahead of her husband and she shivered, only glancing back to see how he fared. Had she hurt him by her unwillingness to forgive? She was angry that he had put them both in such a situation. He had told her they would be safe. And look what happened!

You didn't drown. Your wrists are barely even bruised. You are cold and wet but otherwise unharmed. Had you been alone, you would not have fared so well. The Holy Spirit chastised her for her uncharitable attitude toward her husband.

I repent, Lord. Help me make it up to him. The men thought to end this and free me from my prison of fear and they succeeded. Theo took all the harm upon himself. I should be grateful instead of angry.

They arrived home and Marcus helped her dismount and escorted her to the house, shouting for a bath to be brought up to her and Daisy to tend to her needs. As he left her in the care of her servant, she heard him also call down to the butler to get a doctor.

She didn't need one, but she'd agree if it made

Michael feel better.

She luxuriated in the warm bath and getting the smell of the lake out of her hair. After she had dried off and dressed in her warmest nightgown, in spite of the warmer weather, she sat as close to the fire as she could, sipping beef broth provided by Cook. She was hungry, but dinner was not for another hour. She was to be served in her room and not leave until morning.

She went over the events of the afternoon like a bad dream. Only slight bruising on her body from when she fell into the boat indicated that it all really happened.

Someone knocked on the door.

"Come in."

Josie entered, closed the door and came to sit across from her. "How are you, Valeria?"

"I'm well. A bit bruised but otherwise hale and whole."

Josie smiled. "Sometimes a man has to do drastic things to help someone they love. I almost hit Marcus when he told me what happened and how they'd planned for you and Theo to be bait to draw out Wolton."

"You do not need to chastise me, Josie." Valeria's heart warmed at Josie's belligerent tone of voice.

"I'm not. I am concerned though. Sometimes it can be hard to understand how deeply our husbands love us and that their actions are well-intended. Marcus acted once in my best interest, but I was furious because he couldn't share why he had done it. I refused to have anything to do with him. It was not until almost a year later, after we had wed, that I realized the depth of pain I caused him because I doubted his love and integrity." Josie looked down at her hands sitting still in her lap. "I needed to share that so that you don't suffer as I did."

"I realize Theo's intentions were good. And I was spared any serious harm. I have forgiven him."

"Does he know?" Josie's brown eyes watered. "I need to know because Theo is the best of men. He would never intentionally hurt you. I believe he loves you."

Valeria frowned. "I haven't talked to him since everything happened. Is he well?"

Josie's eyebrows rose. "You weren't aware? The doctor is with him now. He was grazed by that bullet and his leg is not faring well. The doctor thinks the damage may result in a permanent limp and possibly permanent discomfort. He is in considerable pain at the moment."

"I should go to him."

"He has requested that he be left alone. Watkins is the only one allowed in to his room." Josie reached out and grabbed Valeria's hand. "You rest tonight, and tomorrow things will look much better for everyone. Your enemy is dead, and you can finally live your lives the way you want to."

"If I only understood what that looked like," Valeria said almost to herself.

~*~

Theo tried not to cry. The pain in his leg left him weak. The empty bed taunted him in his ability to be a husband the way he longed to. If he hadn't reinjured his leg he could be sleeping with his wife right now and possibly doing more than 'sleep'. He groaned as much from frustration as pain.

"My lord, would you like the laudanum now?" Watkins had sneaked in on him.

Theo sighed. "Might as well. It's a lot faster than trying to drink enough brandy to erase the results of today's events." He swallowed the bitter liquid and followed that with some broth Cook had sent for him. He rolled on to his good side and glanced at his bandaged wrists. *Lord, please heal my marriage. Thank You for protecting Valeria today. I could not have made it through without You*. He fell into a dreamless sleep.

20

Theo spent two days in bed. He dreaded seeing Valeria again, knowing how disappointed she had to be in him. All his hopes of making their marriage move forward had probably drowned in that lake.

After the laudanum wore off, the doctor told him he was fighting infection in the sores on his wrists. Something about dirty water. Watkins guarded him like a hawk, refusing any visitors, but Theo didn't mind. He had no energy, physically or emotionally, to talk to anyone. Marcus would deal with the local magistrate. He didn't know what story he would weave but they were blameless. Wolton sealed his own fate when he'd stepped on to Theo's land and threatened his family.

He swallowed bile as he thought of his family. He had a wife and a child and had somehow broken faith with both of them. Was there any other action he could have taken? He wracked his brain to think of it and couldn't. Wolton would have struck when they least expected and that lack of warning would have limited his ability to protect them.

All I wanted was a wife to love. Was that too much to ask? I didn't want drama and I did not want more rejection. He was never good enough for his father. Other than his close friends, he never fit in at school. And now the only woman he had loved since his mother passed away would turn her back on him as well. Why was he so unworthy of anything but a mother's love? Sure his friends loved him, but his bed was still empty and so was his heart. He spent time praying and reading Scripture which felt doubly sad since he wasn't doing it with his wife as he was used to before she'd abandoned his bed.

Why are you downcast, oh my soul? Trust in the Lord.

He leaned back as those words returned to him from the Psalms. *OK, Lord. I will trust in You. I'm not sure how to do that but I have nothing left to give.* He rolled over and fell back to sleep.

~*~

Valeria was going crazy. Watkins denied her access to her husband's room. But he was her husband! Enough was enough. She took her key and unlocked the adjoining door. Theo had never locked his. She slipped into the room quietly and shut the door behind her. She crossed to the hallway door and turned the key in the lock. She did not want to be disturbed.

She walked toward the bed in her stocking feet.

Theo lay there against the pillows, his face flushed from fever and his hair falling onto his forehead. His lips were moving but there was no sound.

The doctor had resplinted his thigh. His arms were laying on top of the covers and some of the liniment had soaked through and was tinged with red. Some plaster was stuck to the side of his head where the bullet had grazed him. It was almost identical in location to the one on the other side that he had received when they had been traveling north.

Her dearest Theo. He was more of a man than she could have ever dreamed of. He loved the Lord, he was selfless, faithful, gentle, and more handsome than any man she knew. Maybe love biased one that way?

She didn't care. All she knew was she wanted to spend the rest of her life with this man, laughing, loving, and raising a family. She wanted to be the one who massaged his aching thigh when he was old. He was the one she wanted to flirt with as they cuddled in bed.

"Valeria," Theo murmured.

"Yes, Theo? I'm here."

His eyes were closed. He reached for her. "I need you."

That was all the invitation she needed. She kicked off her slippers and crawled into bed next to him, fully clothed, and snuggled up to his side, feeling at home with his arm around her.

"I forgive you, Theo," she whispered in his ear.

"You do? That's good." Soft snores were soon heard.

She grinned and closed her eyes.

~*~

Theo heard a pounding on the door. The valet was anxiously calling to him. "I'm fine, Watkins. I will ring for you when I need you."

He snuggled his face in the silky yellow hair that flowed over his chest and pillow. Orange blossoms. How he loved that scent. His wife stirred.

"Good morning, sweetheart."

"Good morning, handsome."

"Handsome? I thought I was a buffleheaded idiot."

"You are, but an extremely good looking one. I don't think I could love an ugly buffleheaded idiot." She grinned at him and kissed his cheek.

He turned his face and brought a hand up under

her chin. "You will not lie in my bed and get away with a kiss like that."

"I won't?"

"Most definitely not." Their lips met, and he savored the moment. Time stopped just for them.

"I love you, Lady Harrow."

"I love you too, Lord Harrow."

"You forgive me?"

Valeria nodded and smiled, and he felt as if his heart could fly.

"Will you forgive me?" Her smile was gone.

"What do I need to forgive you for?" Theo asked.

"For not trusting you. You never gave me any reason to doubt your word or your love and yet I made assumptions and drew conclusions that were wrong and treated you accordingly. You did not deserve that."

"What kind of assumptions?" His interest was piqued.

"I assumed you were a man of the world and yet when you found out about what happened in my marriage you had a disgust of me. I thought you could never love me."

Theo laughed. "And here I thought that as a woman of the world you would find my 'experience' so totally lacking that you would want to have nothing to do with me."

Valeria giggled. "Maybe we can start over?"

Theo grinned and pulled her close. "I'm ready and willing if you are."

Valeria's kiss gave him no reason to doubt she was ready as well.

Epilogue

Christmas was a festive time and they were all together at Rose Hill.

Theo glanced across the room to his lovely bride, her stomach protruding noticeably even with the empire style dress she wore. The new year would bring an addition to their family and Theo could not be more thrilled. Dartanian was praying for a brother, but Theo did not care either way. A child to love filled his heart with hope and joy.

Marcus and Josie were celebrating another anniversary and Josie was also with child again.

Michael and Katrina were there with their newborn son, Adam.

Beth had only just discovered that they too were expecting, but she wasn't showing yet.

"I got a letter from Jared," Marcus said.

"How is he?" Theo asked.

"He's leaving Wellesley's service. He has one more mission to complete, and then he plans to head home and settle down. He said he envies the love we have all found and wants a bit of the action for himself."

"Action?" Theo laughed. "I've had enough action for a while."

"Don't get too comfortable. You'll find a child turns your life upside down in the most delightful ways." Michael laughed. "Just wait."

Phillip raised his glass. "How about a toast to faith, love, and Jared's homecoming? May he find the love he longs for and safely arrive back in England, hale and whole."

"Here! Here!" All the glasses raised, and sips were taken as they all celebrated the birth of the Savior they had all come to love.

Don't miss the rest of the
Black Diamond Christian Gothic Regency
Suspense Series

Here's a peek at
The Lord Phillip's Folly

Prologue

London

Across the misty sky flew a dark figure with wings flapping silently amidst the noise of the city of London where the elite of the *ton* prepared for this night's entertainments. As the black bird swooped and dipped amongst the chimneys, he found what he searched for. Make that "whom" he searched for. He spied her on the balcony gazing up at the sky awaiting him. He dove from his height only spreading his wings within a few feet to slow descent and land lightly on her outstretched arm.

"Duke," the young woman whispered. "You're back. I've been waiting for you."

His head bobbed but he refrained from speaking. His mistress frowned. He longed to see her smile. He tilted his head to the right, straightened it, and reached his neck forward to put his long dark beak to her cheek and rub gently.

Tears dangled at the edge of her eyelashes. "Tonight is the night, Duke. I cannot go through with what Papa plans. I must escape. All these years… I cannot endure any longer."

Duke was silent, listening. He bobbed his head.

She continued. "Lord Wolton has to be sixty, if not older and has the most nauseating odor. He is creepy and I'm certain he has some evil hold over Papa. But I cannot. I will not allow myself to pay the price for Papa's salvation. He's acted foolishly, and I love him, but I won't..." She glanced up at the sky. "Why would God allow this to happen?" She shivered, although the mid-April evening was warm. "Why couldn't I simply be loved for who I am? Why all this unrelenting…evil?"

Duke ruffled his feathers and shook them, once again rubbing his beak against her cheek.

"Watch over me tonight. I've no clue how I'll escape, but I don't want to lose you when I do. Wait outside in the garden and follow wherever I go. Can you do that, sweetheart?" Her intense golden-green eyes gazed into his.

"I love you," Duke squawked, nodding and making a kissing sound. He'd do anything for her.

"I love you too, Duke. What would I have done this past year without you?"

Movement from the dressing room alerted him to danger. Duke flapped his wings and took off, circling twice above her before settling on a nearby tree. She blew him a kiss.

He bobbed his head in acknowledgment as she turned to step back off the narrow balcony and close the doors to the bedroom behind her.

He would protect his mistress.

1

Spring 1810
Manchester

Despicable town. Infuriating family. Frustrating obligations. In spite of all that Lord Phillip Westcombe had returned to London. He enjoyed hibernating in the North Country the past few months. Peace and solitude had become a comfortable companion since his friend, Lord Marcus Remington, married Miss Josephine Storm at Christmas. Their happiness was something he did not begrudge them, but he found it difficult to be around. It pointed to a gaping hole in his own heart.

Instead, he spent the time studiously applying himself to his estate, and enjoyed managing the property. He was happy for Marcus and Josie, but the process of falling in love tended to be messy and complicated if their path to the altar was any indication. He did not want that in his life.

Yet here he was, back in London for the season.

If it hadn't been for his mother's pleas, his father's command, and his little sister's enthusiastic encouragement, he would still be at Stanton Hall. Avoiding the matchmaking mammas and the cloying attempts of young debutantes trying to trap him into the parson's mousetrap was one of his least favorite pastimes. At five and twenty he had spent the last few years gaining some town polish along with experience in how to avoid the snares of the marriage mart.

It was primarily his adoration for his sister, Penelope, that brought him here. He hoped she would find a man worthy of her hand. As one of her family, he owed her the courtesy of squiring her through the season, keeping a careful watch on the court of admirers she was sure to develop.

As Fenway, his valet, stepped away from tying his cravat into a spectacular waterfall, Phillip looked in the mirror. His blond hair carefully combed off of his face—every hair in its place. His ice-blue eyes scanned the image before him as he attached a ruby pin into the folds of the linen and smiled. Perfect white teeth set in a long face with a strong jaw and aristocratic nose and full lips. His new black coat fit like a glove. Perfection was an art. With the help of his tailor and valet, he was a master.

It was time to do his duty to his sister, please his parents, and dance with the wallflowers. With a final tug to his jacket, he nodded to Fenway. "Don't bother waiting up for me." He left his chambers determined to make the best of the evening.

~*~

The Earl of Manchester and his wife of thirty-two years stood ahead of him in the receiving line. They had asked only that Phillip, their second son, remain by the side of his sister Penelope for her come-out ball. He was the last person to greet people before they entered the ballroom.

Faces swam past him in a blur of color and stench. Why some in the upper ten-thousand refused to bathe perplexed him. He greeted each gentleman with a bow of his head and every woman with a lift of their gloved hands within an inch of his lips. His sister simpered next to him, giddy that this evening was in her honor and likely to be a 'crush,' to propel his mother into rapturous delight.

Waiting for an escape, he discovered an unknown face presented to him.

"I'm Lord Follett." The older man gave him a bow. Phillip could see the balding head, and the odor of alcohol on his breath warned him the man was already in his cups. "This is my daughter, the Honorable Elizabeth Follett."

Phillip sucked in a breath at the vision before him. Her soft red hair was pulled up and held in place by small white flowers. Her dress did not do her coloring justice. But it was the eyes, those green eyes that drew him. They spoke a message to him he couldn't quite decipher. It wasn't one of desire or seduction as he so often saw. More of abject terror.

Because of him?

He held her hand. "Welcome to Manchester Hall, Miss Follett." He allowed his lips to touch the glove and a shock traveled through him as she gasped. He straightened as one corner of his lips rose. *Ah, she'd felt it too.* Instead of terror, there was curiosity, and, as those lashes lowered, he sensed a mystery.

"You are too kind, my lord." Her husky voice whispered as the crowd pushed her forward toward the ballroom. He watched her go, the sway of her hips barely discernable beneath her gown.

"Phillip?" His sister nudged him.

"Yes, Penny?"

"Will you escort me in? Father said he would lead me out for the first dance. Anthony is to dance with me next and then you. You won't forget, will you?" Her brown eyes held an eagerness he knew would someday turn to *ennui* as the years marched on and she was subjected to these now exciting activities over and over again.

"How could I ever forget? You are by far the most beautiful woman in the room and I would be honored to dance with you."

She slapped him with her fan and giggled. "I'm glad you came home, Phillip. I've missed you."

He tapped a finger on her nose and lifted his elbow. She placed her hand on his forearm and he escorted her into the ballroom. Handing her off to his father he skirted the room, periodically shaking hands with people he knew but not stopping to chat. He wasn't in the mood for talk. His eyes scanned the mass of bodies. The Earl of Manchester determined it was late enough to begin the ball.

Phillip hated these events. When he was younger, he didn't mind attending and flirting with the available misses, but now it wore thin. Was he getting old or growing up? Managing the estate left to him by his maternal aunt, Martha, upon her removal to the hereafter two years hence had been a better use of his time and energy. He'd encountered success in turning a modest inheritance into profitable investments after Lord Remington took him aside and encouraged him that even as a second son, he could be prosperous and productive.

Phillip failed in his attempt to share his successes with his family. They persisted in the belief he was a ne'er-do-well, frolicking around aimlessly, gambling, and wenching his way through his monthly allowance and inheritance. As if he were still a callow youth fresh on the town.

Before Lord Remington's warnings and direction, that might have been true.

Yet his family considered him to be a wastrel, doomed to destruction if he didn't settle down with a wife soon. His father even suspected he was hiding in the north with a mistress. As if he'd waste money on such as that? He was long over his dalliances with ladies of the night. It irked him that his father would hold such a low opinion of him.

Phillip was fully cognizant that although his family loved him, he was far from the perfection of his older brother. He glanced around the ballroom and spied Anthony, only two years older than himself. Anthony tended towards portliness and while he pretended adoration toward his wife, Phillip knew that Anthony's excesses far surpassed his own when he was younger. He feared his father was misled in the belief that his heir was honorable and trustworthy to inherit the earldom someday. Phillip shrugged. Since Anthony's wife had presented him with two sons already, the title would never pass to Phillip. He found contentment in establishing his own path, and a wife was not integral to his success.

If his mother and sisters were any indication, women usually spent money, which did not help much in increasing wealth. Marcus's bride might be the exception, but it was really too early to tell on that account as they were fairly new to marriage. They had come in earlier and were on the dance floor, besotted with one another.

The orchestra finished playing the first dance. Phillip sought out his mother to lead her into the next one.

~*~

The Honorable Elizabeth Follett escaped the first dance with an excuse to check her hem but now she couldn't avoid the inevitable as she was led to the floor by Lord Wolton.

His face quickly grew red. He started wheezing with the execution of the steps of the dance. At over three times her own age, he was a prosperous landowner and neighbor. He possessed small dark eyes, bushy eyebrows, and very little hair on top of his head, which perspired terribly. His long sideburns only served to emphasize his jowls. His hands were plump and clammy to the touch.

A shiver of distaste overtook Lizzy every time his reached for hers as required by the movements of the dance, and even more at the lascivious look in his eyes as he would scan her body. His smile, crooked with a few darker teeth accompanied by his foul breath, made her fight against the bile threatening to rise inside when they drew close.

The only highlight of the exercise was the sight of the golden god dancing two couples down. Occasionally his eyes met hers in the course of the dance and she only hoped he could read her desperation. Ah, but beautiful sons of earls were not known to rescue the daughters of barons were they?

Led back to her father after the dance, she nodded her head and murmured a soft thanks to Lord Wolton.

Lord Follett had no real repute in the *ton* and felt his position keenly. He nudged his daughter and urged her, "Smile, Lizzy, for heaven's sake. Lord Wolton desires your hand, the least you could do is encourage him a little."

Lizzy once again tried to suppress a cold shiver at the very thought of any more interaction with Lord Wolton. Her father blustered and yelled when she stated her objection to the match. There would be no rescue for her from that quarter. She closed her eyes and took a deep breath, clenching her hands tightly together silently praying to a God she wasn't quite sure even existed, for a way out of the hell destined for her.

Opening her eyes, she glanced across the room to observe Lord Phillip Westcombe leading his sister out in the country dance. She could not take her gaze off of him. His kindly manner as he interacted with his sister was charming. And that smile. Would she even be able to breathe if he ever smiled at her like that? He was the stuff dreams were made of. She felt hope surge through her. Maybe, just maybe...

~*~

The evening dragged on with one dance after another. After supper, Phillip returned his young partner to her chaperone with an elegant bow. He found his attention captivated by the young woman who'd haunted him since her introduction earlier. She was difficult to miss with her red hair, although red was a bit strong to describe its softer hue. Hair that once curled around her face hung straight. She was pale, standing alone near a potted plant by the doors leading to the gardens below, as though she were hiding. She glanced his way and their gaze held. He read a silent plea and began to move in her direction.

He wove through the crowd surrounding the ballroom, stopping for brief handshakes and pats on the back as he maneuvered to that side of the room. He kept an eye on the young woman. She tracked his progress at times furtively searching the crowd. His curiosity was aroused.

"Miss Follett." Lord Phillip bowed over her hand and spoke softly so as not to be overheard in the noise of the ballroom. "May I be of assistance?"

"Lord Westcombe..." Elizabeth sighed. "Yes…I wonder…" Her eyes once again held a silent entreaty.

"Would you perhaps like to stroll in the garden?" Phillip extended his arm, and nodding, she wound her hand around it and walked outside into the fresh, cool evening air. Heat radiated up his arm at her touch. With every step, he was more aware of the woman by his side than any he'd ever known. It puzzled him. They stepped down into the garden lit with lanterns. Her lack of chatter perplexed him. Most women he met attempted to talk their way into a proposal. Few couples were in the gardens this early in the evening although lamps had been lit. He knew all the best places to engage in less than gentlemanly behavior due to his wayward youth. He led her down a path to an area by a small pond. Open and exposed. He would not compromise this young woman.

Phillip assisted Miss Follett to the bench, leaned against the tree next to it, and waited. She clenched her hands in her lap, took a deep breath, and began. "I need to escape. My father is forcing me into a marriage I do not want." Cautiously, she raised her eyes to meet his and he noted the tears at the edges.

He reached for his handkerchief and extended it to her as he came to sit beside her. "Is there no other way out of this marriage? Surely, they cannot force you to the altar. We do live in a civilized society."

"Civilized?" A short bark of laughter escaped the young woman. "My life has never been civilized. You'd be truly horrified if I told you the things I've endured." She turned slightly to look him in the eye and reached forward to put her hand on his arm. "Truly, if I do not escape tonight I have no other hope except—"

Phillip's eyes narrowed as she considered her words. Was she being overly dramatic? Was this a manipulation? Miss Follett wasn't trying to trap him into marriage herself, was she? From what he understood, she came with a healthy dowry, something he certainly didn't need. She was far from unattractive and given time during the season her own court of admirers would vie for her favors. Yet he sensed truth in what she claimed and that before him sat a desperate woman. The knight-errant in him fought its way to the surface disturbing the peaceful waters he tried hard to maintain. "What is it you require?"

"To disappear. Somewhere, anywhere they cannot find me."

"And then what? You re-appear elsewhere? How would that be explained? The scandal-mongers would have a feast that could destroy any hope you would have of making a respectable match. What about your future? Where might you live and how would you marry if you are cut off from your father and your inheritance?"

"You fully understand the complexities of my circumstances, Lord Westcombe. To me this matter is of life and death. My life. My certain death. If I am forced to marry, I guarantee I will be dead within the year. So, my only hope is to escape. Will you assist me?"

Phillip stared at her, considering, as the silence stretched taut between them. He tended to be a good judge of people and this woman told the truth. Finally, he came to a decision and nodded to her. "Can you remain here for a few minutes? Will you be all right?"

"You won't fetch my father?"

"No, merely a discreet friend who might assist. Trust me. I am a man of my word."

"I'll be fine. I'm not alone." Her face relaxed as she looked up past the tree to the stars twinkling in the sky.

Phillip wondered at her odd statement. There were other couples in the garden, but none near here. Giving her a short bow he surreptitiously returned to the ballroom. Once he entered he searched until he spied Lord Marcus Remington finishing up a dance with his bride. Phillip wove his way through the crowd to Marcus's side and whispered in his ear, "I require your assistance."

Marcus raised one eyebrow, nodded, and together all three made their way to the hallway and a private room. Phillip shut the door behind them.

"Well, Phillip, what is it?" Marcus relaxed one hand on his wife's waist as he stood beside her.

"I need shelter for a young woman in desperate need." *Now* who sounded melodramatic?

Marcus and Josie exchanged looks before staring at him.

"Phillip? Why does this woman need immediate shelter?" asked Lady Remington.

"I've done nothing wrong or to be ashamed of. She came to me for help."

"What do you want?" asked Marcus.

His wife nodded her head in agreement.

"I must spirit her away immediately. Could you depart and have your carriage go down to the corner alley? I'll bring her there unnoticed. After we arrive at your home, you can hear her story for yourselves."

Marcus nodded and escorted Josie out of the room.

"Dearest, I'm feeling tired and would like to go home now," Josie simpered as she fanned herself.

"Certainly dear. You look fatigued." Marcus's strong deep voice would suggest they were leaving for that reason alone.

Phillip slipped out the door of the library and wandered back to the garden, avoiding the few partygoers there. He accidentally came upon a few couples engaged in flirtation before he found his way back to Miss Elizabeth Follett. "Come," he whispered as he gave her his hand to help her stand.

"Where…?"

"You ask for my help yet now you resist? Trust me. I shan't harm you."

"I never doubted that for a minute." She rushed alongside him as they slipped through a spot in the hedge and made their way down the alley. Staying in the shadows they waited silently for the Remington coach to pull up. The rise and fall of her chest as she caught her breath was distracting.

He forced himself to focus elsewhere.

The carriage arrived and Lord Phillip assisted Elizabeth inside, entering behind her and closing the door. Marcus tapped on the roof to signal for them to start and they headed for the Remington home.

"Lord and Lady Remington, may I present the Honorable Elizabeth Follett to you?" Lord Westcombe intoned.

"Miss Follett, it is our honor to meet and assist you this evening." Josie reached across the carriage to squeeze the newcomer's hand. "You shall be safe with us."

"Thank you," Miss Follett whispered.

Phillip leaned back against the squabs and willed his pulse to slow. What had he done? He had acted on her behalf but belatedly wondered how this would reflect on him. Where was his neat, orderly life now?

2

Lizzy leaned forward to look out the window as they pulled up to the Remington house. Her awareness of the man sitting next to her caused her stomach to flutter. *Silly girl!* He was a kind soul helping a damsel in distress. Nothing more. Lord Phillip assisted her from the carriage and they followed Marcus and Josie to the entrance of the building. Leading her to the drawing room, Josie requested tea be brought. As Lizzy paced in front of the unlit hearth, Lord Remington moved past her to put the kindling in and strike the match to get a fire started. Phillip had gone to the sideboard for a glass of brandy and brought one for his friend.

Silence hung in the air until the tea tray arrived and the servants departed, closing the door behind them.

"I cannot stay long, my parents will miss me if I am not back before the end of the ball," said Phillip.

Lizzy stopped pacing as her heart raced. "What?"

Lord Remington went to her side to escort her to the settee next to his wife who handed her a cup of tea after quietly inquiring how she preferred hers.

"Phillip, you cannot rescue her and then abandon her here," Lady Remington protested.

"I will return once the ball is finished."

"But what is to become of me?" Lizzy whispered.

Phillip looked at Marcus. "Her father is forcing her to marry Lord Wolton against her will."

Lord Remington's eyebrows rose. He nodded. "You were kind to help her escape such a fate. But why would your father do that?"

A shudder shook Lizzy and she placed her cup and saucer on the table lest she spill it. "Wolton has some kind of hold over my father." She pulled off her gloves revealing red wrists with the marks of fingers on her pale skin.

Phillip growled. "Your father did this to you?"

Lizzy nodded.

Josie reached over to touch her arm gently above the injured area. "I'm eager to hear your story, but in due time. You may spend the night here until we can figure out how to best assist you." She glanced over at her husband who nodded in agreement.

"Phillip, I hope you realize what you're doing. We don't want to be caught interfering between a young woman and her legal guardian."

Lizzy piped up, "I am of age. I possess my own inheritance."

Phillip looked surprised. "Given that, how can your father force you to marry someone you dislike?"

Elizabeth wouldn't meet his gaze, looking down into her teacup as tears started to flow. "Trust me, he will."

Josie looked at Phillip with pleading eyes. "We shall figure this out in due time."

Lizzy pulled his handkerchief out of her reticule and used it to dab her eyes.

Lord Westcombe moved over to stand in front of her and she looked up at him. "I'm sorry I must leave. I promise you, I will return in a few hours. I could leave you in no better hands than Lord and Lady Remington's. You'll be safe here." He bowed to her and with a brief good night, he left the room to return to the Manchester ball.

~*~

Twice in one evening he had abandoned Miss Follett. It went against the grain of gentlemanly behavior. Being seen at the dance, however, would absolve him of any participation in the matter. In the end, it could possibly save her reputation and keep him from the parson's mousetrap.

The dancing was winding down and he took to the floor with another debutante. After the dance concluded he returned her to her chaperone's side and sought out his mother. Lady Manchester was short but retained her youthful figure. In spite of a few grey streaks in her light brown hair, she was still considered a beauty. Phillip tended to take after his father in looks and temperament.

"Oh, Phillip, there you are. I wondered where you had disappeared to." She tapped his arm with her fan. "Found someone you simply couldn't resist, did you? I heard the gardens were busy this evening." She giggled.

Phillip grew warm at the suggestion he'd been carrying on with a guest on his parents' property. It saddened him that she would believe something like that of him. Sometimes a past was a hard thing to live down. "You were searching for me, Mother? What can I do for you?"

"Lord Wolton was agitated earlier as the young woman he was pledged to dance with disappeared. Lord Follett, the young lady's father, was unable to locate her. We had the withdrawing room checked and surreptitiously asked around but nobody remembers seeing her. It's as if she has vanished into thin air. I do not need to tell you that this is not the kind of notoriety we want associated with your sister's come out." She gave him a coy wink. His mother enjoyed the fact that along with being a squeeze her ball would be remembered for the disappearance of the Follett woman.

"What do you think has happened to her?" he asked, schooling his features to impassiveness.

She leaned toward him and was forced to look up as she whispered. "She is worth a fortune and has sole control of the money as of yesterday when she turned one and twenty. Rumor has it that Lord Wolton intended to marry her by Special License tomorrow." She paused and gave a shiver of disgust. "Personally, Phillip, I think the girl ran away and I couldn't blame her. I'd do the same if Wolton were my intended groom."

"If they were eager for her to wed him, why wait until she gained her majority? She no longer needs his permission for her marriage. I'm praying she is safe from that sorry end. But where would she go? Does she have relatives in town who might shelter and protect her?"

"None that I'm aware of. It troubles me. A young woman alone in this town is destined for only one thing and already her reputation is ruined by this event." Lady Remington shook her head sadly. "It's too bad, really, as she seemed to be a sweet girl and was passably pretty." Of course, she probably thought no one could ever be as beautiful as her own daughter.

Phillip listened to his mother and remained silent as he scanned the room for Lord Follett or Lord

Wolton. He failed to locate them. "Where is her father and the potential bridegroom now?"

"I believe they left for the evening in an attempt to keep things quiet so when they find her they can whisk her away to the church and prevent a scandal."

"What if they fail to locate her?"

"I pray for that, Phillip, and I hope she is safe. At some point, however, she will need to access her fortune which will expose her to discovery."

"You are far too wise, Mother. Is there anything you need from me for the rest of this evening? I wouldn't mind calling it a night myself."

"Really? Phillip, you seriously cannot be thinking of going to your club or any of those other places tonight."

"No. However, I do plan to meet a friend."

"Fine. You may leave, Phillip, but remember, I expect you to accompany us to some of the balls this season to help keep an eye on a potential suitor for your sister's hand. I am counting on your support. I will send a list of entertainments I expect you to attend."

"I'll do my best, Mother." Phillip bent and gave her a kiss on the cheek. "Good night." He strode out the door and took a brisk walk to the Remington house. He wondered if Miss Follett was yet awake. He wouldn't mind seeing her again.

~*~

"Come, Elsa will help you change. You are a little taller than me but I'm sure I have a gown that will suit you for sleeping," Josie urged.

Elizabeth sank into the chair by the cheerful

fireplace. "It's hopeless. There is no way out of this."

"Miss Follett…"

"Elizabeth please, or Lizzy."

"Elizabeth it is, then. A name that speaks of dignity, determination, and grace."

Lizzy looked up at that, startled. "Thank you."

"You may call me Josie. Now, what is concerning you?"

Elsa began pulling the pins out of Lizzy's hair and letting the heavy locks fall down around her shoulders. "My father has evil friends. He told me I needed to marry Wolton. I had no choice. But I'm tired of being a victim of men's schemes and debauchery."

"What *are* you talking about?"

Lizzy rose as the abigail put the pins on the dressing table and left to get a nightgown. She turned to Josie. "Maybe I can show you. Would you undo my dress?" Elizabeth turned around.

Josie rose to undo the fasteners going down the back of Elizabeth's gown. Letting it fall to the floor she pulled up the back of her chemise to reveal her back.

Josie's gasp echoed around the room.

Elizabeth walked behind a screen and finished dressing. She suspected her face was now the color of her hair.

Josie sat, mouth agape. "I'm so sorry, Elizabeth. I suspect there is much more you are not telling me."

"Yes, m'lady." Lizzy sat across from her with her head bent, awaiting condemnation from the Viscountess.

"Elizabeth, what you have endured was not your fault. It is a crime this can be done to a young woman with no one to protect her. God loves you, and Lord Remington and myself will do all in our power to protect you from further harm."

"You won't force me to leave? I am unworthy of your kindness."

"You are more than worthy. You are a precious young woman who has suffered evil. I suspect your battle will not be only one with your father and disappointed groom, but that a spiritual dimension underlies this."

"I don't understand." Lizzy folded and unfolded the handkerchief she still held, her thumb unconsciously tracing the initials embroidered in the corner.

"You've been subjected to great evil. More I'm sure than you've shared thus far. These things are not normal or in any way condoned by God. Like you, I don't understand what hold Lord Wolton has over your father that would force him to sell you in this manner. If your suspicions are correct you are destined for more of the same. I will need to share some of this with my husband, and possibly Lord Westcombe, so they can make discreet inquiries."

Lizzy panicked. "Must you?"

"I believe it is necessary if we are to protect you and give you freedom from the terror you've experienced." Josie leaned forward, put her arm on Elizabeth's, and looked her in the eye. "I want you to be free of the prison you find yourself in. Free to select a husband of your choice. Free to be all God has created you to be as a woman, a wife, and a mother someday."

"I never dared to dream that far." She hugged herself.

"I understand," said Josie kindly. "I believe it would be good for you to get some rest now. We will talk more in the morning when we can consider this with a fresh perspective as to what's to be done. By then Phillip might be able to give us information on what happened at the ball when they discovered you missing. I'm sure there was an uproar over that and his mother is relishing the notoriety it is giving her daughter's come out."

"Oh, I've ruined it for them, haven't I?"

"No. She will be in alt. Never fear. Phillip won't fail in keeping your secret. He has too much to lose by confessing anything."

"What do you mean?"

"A marriageable man kidnapping a young woman from his parents' ball? The only way he'd ever live that down would be to marry you himself."

Lizzy's heart sank. "I could never dream so high as to seek someone as fine as him for a husband."

"He is quite a figure of manhood is he not? A man of honor, as well. You can trust him. Now get some rest."

"May I keep the fire burning?"

"That's fine. I'll instruct Elsa." She rang the bell and the maid appeared.

"You've been all kindness, m'lady."

"Josie."

"Thank you, Josie."

"It is our pleasure. Sleep well and have pleasant dreams." Josie departed after giving discreet instructions to the maid.

Lizzy blew out the candles and strode to the window. She lifted the pane. Duke came to sit on the sill. "I'm well, Duke. Thank you. I'll see you on the morrow."

Duke nodded and flew off.

The windows were closed and the drapes were drawn. She settled into a chair by the fire, the vision of blue eyes and a strong chin were better dreamt of awake. *I'm in a safe place, I'll be fine.* She'd abandoned everything for safety. But in doing so she courted scandal. There was no way to save face after this. Even under the auspices of the Viscount and his wife, there was little cachet to be had as a runaway daughter of a baron. Even if she could gain her fortune, she'd expose her location. How would she live? Where would she go? Wearily she sought her bed and drifted into an uneasy sleep.

She ran away from one nightmare straight into unknown darkness with few options.

~*~

Duke flew to the top of the tree and settled in to sleep. The noise of the city made that hard. The gas lamps encroached on the darkness he was accustomed to in the country. His mistress was well. He spied the man who brought his mistress here, return. Duke bobbed his head. He'd do. Lizzy went with him willingly. She was safe and the terror he'd seen in her the past few days was momentarily gone. He could rest and wait to find out what would happen next. She wasn't clear of all danger yet. Evil lurked in the darkness and he would do anything to protect her.

Download the rest of Lord Phillip's Folly from your favourite online retailer.

ACKNOWLEDGEMENTS

It would be impossible to thank everyone who has helped me on my journey, so I apologize in advance for those I will miss. It doesn't mean you are any less valuable and thankfully God keeps better track of those things than I do and His "well done, good and faithful servant" has more merit than any thanks written here.

So here it goes. Special thanks to:

Susan Karsten – for being a beta reader for his story and giving me valuable feedback.

Faye Daniels – for being a beta-reader and helping me with the French required for this story.

Doris Pollard Wichern – another early reader and one of my most faithful cheerleaders in this writing adventure. I rest in knowing you were proud of all my work even though you didn't live to see this series reach publication.

Lisa Lickel – thanks for being such a wonderful mentor, friend, and shoulder to cry on when the publishing process throws me those curve balls. I don't think I would have ever taken that first step in this journey to publication without your gentle push.

David Mundt – for your support and believing in me and the calling God has on my life.

Sally Shupe – my faithful editor. Thank you for finding all those silly errors!

Nicola Martinez – my friend, boss, and publisher. Thanks for believing in this series and in my writing and continuing to give me a platform to serve God in this way.

ABOUT THE AUTHOR

Susan M. Baganz chases after three Hobbits, and is a native of Wisconsin. She is an Editor with Pelican Book Group specializing in bringing great romance to publication. Susan writes adventurous historical and contemporary romances with a biblical world-view.

This book is the fourth full-length novel in the Black Diamond Regency series. *The Baron's Blunder,* Henrietta's story, is a novella and prequel. Prior stories include: *The Virtuous Viscount, Lord Phillip's Folly, Sir Michael's Mayhem,* and the final book is *The Captain's Conquest.* A Christmas Regency, *Gabriel's Gift* released last year but is not part of the series. She is also the author of contemporary romances in the Orchard Hill Romance Series, *Pesto & Potholes, Salsa & Speed Bumps, Feta & Freeways, Root Beer & Roadblocks, Bratwurst & Bridges,* and *Donuts & Detours* with *Truffles & Traffic* due out soon.

Susan speaks, teaches, and encourages others to follow God in being all He has created them to be. With her seminary degree in counseling psychology, a background in the field of mental health, and years serving in church ministry, she understands the complexities and pain of life as well as its craziness. She serves behind-the-scenes in various capacities at her church and is a member of American Christian Fiction Writers (ACFW), and serves on the board of the southeast chapter. Her favorite pastimes are snuggling with her dog while reading a good book or sitting with a friend chatting over a cup of spiced chai latte. Learn more by following her blog, www.susanbaganz.com, her Twitter feed @susanbaganz or her fan page: facebook.com/susanmbaganz

Thank you

We appreciate you reading this Prism title. For other Christian fiction and clean-and-wholesome stories, please visit our on-line bookstore at www.prismbookgroup.com.

For questions or more information, contact us at customer@pelicanbookgroup.com.

Prism is an imprint of
Pelican Book Group
www.PelicanBookGroup.com

Connect with Us
www.facebook.com/Pelicanbookgroup
www.twitter.com/pelicanbookgrp

To receive news and specials, subscribe to our bulletin
http://pelink.us/bulletin

May God's glory shine through
this inspirational work of fiction.

AMDG

You Can Help!

At Pelican Book Group it is our mission to entertain readers with fiction that uplifts the Gospel. It is our privilege to spend time with you awhile as you read our stories.

We believe you can help us to bring Christ into the lives of people across the globe. And you don't have to open your wallet or even leave your house!

Here are 3 simple things you can do to help us bring illuminating fiction™ to people everywhere.

1) If you enjoyed this book, write a positive review. Post it at online retailers and websites where readers gather. And share your review with us at reviews@pelicanbookgroup.com (this does give us permission to reprint your review in whole or in part.)

2) If you enjoyed this book, recommend it to a friend in person, at a book club or on social media.

3) If you have suggestions on how we can improve or expand our selection, let us know. We value your opinion. Use the contact form on our web site or e-mail us at customer@pelicanbookgroup.com

God Can Help!

Are you in need? The Almighty can do great things for you. Holy is His Name! He has mercy in every generation. He can lift up the lowly and accomplish all things. Reach out today.

Do not fear: I am with you; do not be anxious: I am your God. I will strengthen you, I will help you, I will uphold you with my victorious right hand.

~Isaiah 41:10 (NAB)

We pray daily, and we especially pray for everyone connected to Pelican Book Group—that includes you! If you have a specific need, we welcome the opportunity to pray for you. Share your needs or praise reports at http://pelink.us/pray4us

Free Book Offer

We're looking for booklovers like you to partner with us! Join our team of influencers today and periodically receive free eBooks and exclusive offers.

For more information
Visit http://pelicanbookgroup.com/booklovers

www.ingramcontent.com/pod-product-compliance
Lightning Source LLC
Chambersburg PA
CBHW020931260626
47169CB00006B/1669